I've travelled the world twice over,
Met the famous: saints and sinners,
Poets and artists, kings and queens,
Old stars and hopeful beginners,
I've been where no-one's been before,
Learned secrets from writers and cooks
All with one library ticket
To the wonderful world of books.

© JANICE JAMES.

VOYAGE BEYOND BELIEF

What happens when men of different ages and backgrounds find themselves in a situation for which nothing could have prepared them? During the Second World War an antiquated Japanese freighter, the DAI NICHI MARU, carried Allied prisoners on a nightmare voyage that lasted four weeks. Two prisoners, a mature Naval Officer and a disadvantaged youngster, share the same narrow groundsheet. Slowly, they build an interdependence which will reshape their future lives.

Books by Terence Kelly
in the Ulverscroft Large Print Series:

LONG LIVE THE SPY
THE SPY IS DEAD

TERENCE KELLY

VOYAGE
BEYOND
BELIEF

Complete and Unabridged

ULVERSCROFT
Leicester

First published in Great Britain in 1985

This book was originally entitled
'FEPOW'
The story of a Voyage Beyond Belief

First Large Print Edition
published April 1993

British Library CIP Data

Kelly, Terence
  Voyage beyond belief.—Large print ed.—
Ulverscroft large print series: adventure & suspense
I. Title
823.914 [F]

ISBN 0–7089–2844–7

Published by
F. A. Thorpe (Publishing) Ltd.
Anstey, Leicestershire
Set by Words & Graphics Ltd.
Anstey, Leicestershire
Printed and bound in Great Britain by
T. J. Press (Padstow) Ltd., Padstow, Cornwall

Dedication

To all Far East Prisoners of the Japanese and especially to those who were transported in any of the many freighters from one camp to another, this book is dedicated, with my thanks to all of you — too numerous to list — who have written to me from all over the world or otherwise supplied me with information and refreshed my memory.

Terence ('Flash') Kelly

Frieth, England, 1985

Preface

Dr Marcel Junod, head of the International Committee of the Red Cross Delegation in Japan in 1945, in his book, *Warrior Without Weapons*, published by the MacMillan Co in 1945, wrote:

'Out of 300,000 prisoners captured by the Japanese in the first months of the war in the Pacific, 100,000 were already dead when the day of liberation dawned. The 200,000 survivors staggered emaciated and exhausted from unknown villages and prison camps scattered over the islands or in the interior of the Asiatic mainland from the rocky shores of the Banda Sea to the Burma jungle.'

These prisoners included Americans, Australians, British, Canadians, Dutch, Filipinos, Indians, New Zealanders, Rhodesians, South Africans and others from elsewhere and each of these countries has, since the war, been inclined to visualise the lot of the Japanese P.O.W. from a particular standpoint. To Americans and Filipinos the hardships were perhaps best exemplified by the 'March of Death' from Bataan; to the British, Australians and others by the 'Railway'; to the Dutch by the horror of Sumatra.

★ ★ ★

There was, however, a different kind of hardship which scores of thousands of Japanese prisoners had to endure which seems to be less well known and about which surprisingly little seems to have been written in depth, this being the hardship of being crammed into prison ships transporting them to innumerable destinations ranging from tiny Indonesian islands to the mainland of Japan. Mostly old and antiquated, these freighters crawled their way across the seas, many to be sunk by Allied aircraft and submarines, often with total loss of life to the battened down prisoners lying in the filth and squalor of their unlit holds, while even in those cases where the vessel escaped attention and reached its

VOYAGES OF YOSEDA MARU ———————
AND DAI NICHI MARU
(October 22nd. to November 26th.)

Yoseda Maru:
Left Tandjeonpriok October 22nd.
Arrived Singapore October 26th.
−transferred to−

Dai Nichi Maru:
Left Singapore October 28th.
Arrived Saigon November 4th.
Left Saigon November 4th.
Arrived Takao November 11th.
Left Takao November 14th.
Arrived Shimonoseki November 23rd.

Disembarked November 26th.

destination unscathed the death toll was normally horrendous.

★ ★ ★

This novel is set in just such a ship — the *Dai Nichi Maru*, a freighter of about four thousand tons built, we understood, on the Clyde at the turn of the century. On October 28th, 1942, the *Dai Nichi* sailed from Singapore to Japan carrying two thousand two hundred men of whom slightly more than half were Japanese and the balance Allied prisoners of war. After many incidents, which included encountering a typhoon *en route*, the prisoners were disembarked at Moji, Japan, on November 26th — had the voyage lasted for a few more days it is doubtful if more than a small proportion of the prisoners would have survived. Some weeks earlier another prison ship, the *Lisbon Maru*, was torpedoed off Shanghai and, of the two thousand prisoners aboard her, twelve hundred perished for exactly the reasons I have woven into the novel.

★ ★ ★

I do not suggest that the conditions which I have used as the background to this novel were the worst experienced on Japanese prison ships; probably they were about par for the course. What may, possibly, distinguish this particular voyage from the majority is its duration and the fact that it was transporting men equipped only for the tropics, from the Equator to the winter of Japan.

★ ★ ★

FEPOW is the generic term used nowadays to describe a common experience by those who were Far East Prisoners of War and it is to them this book is dedicated. So far as the subtitle is concerned I wish to assure the reader there is no exaggeration — many of the most unlikely incidents within the novel are strictly based on fact.

★ ★ ★

I have been assisted by scores of letters written by men who shared this voyage with me; but forty years is a long time and memories fade or become confused so that in minor matters many of these letters contradict each other. Whilst I managed to retain notes made at the time, these were far from complete for it did not occur to me I should one day use the experience as the basis of a novel. Also it is necessary in the construction of a novel to bend truth now and then to make the novel work. Therefore I ask those with me in No 2 Hold of the *Dai Nichi Maru* who find points of disagreement to bear in mind that although based on fact this is a work of fiction and also that a writer whose memory is shaky in a particular direction, and who has been unable to find anyone who can fill that gap, has to do the best he can. My own experience was limited to No 2 Hold. I know that in other holds some prisoners were housed in different ways and in some cases (although more cramped) had the type of accommodation given to the Japanese. I cannot bring such conditions into the book because (except briefly on the *Yoseda Maru* on the short trip from Java to Singapore) I did not experience them.

The question of characters creates more difficulties. All my characters are fictional yet I am sure that some will find similarities between them and men they remember. In one or two cases it would be right to do so for there were men in that hold whose behaviour was so superb that it should not be ignored. In other cases they would be in error. To give a few examples: I have used the fact that a bridge four used a corpse as a card table but I have not drawn my bridge players from those men; there *was* a certain high-ranking officer who conceived the somewhat bizarre notion of taking the ship over from the Japanese but he was not my Brimmacombe; we *did* have a Lieutenant Commander but he was neither our Commanding Officer nor my Jim Moore. Where fact is used for fictional purposes it is natural for someone who remembers the fact to relate it to a remembered individual — but I give my assurance that, excepting as stated above, all of my characters are fictional and any likeness ascribed to someone dimly remembered after forty years is not intended by me and any such likeness must be purely coincidental.

Terence Kelly, Frieth, 1985

1

THE hold, one of four on the ship, measured sixty feet by eighty feet and was lit by an open hatch about fifteen feet square. The bed of the hold was a mound of bauxite ore, glistening wet, roughly levelled under the hatch and then sloping down steeply in all directions until it met the ship's sides or bulkheads. The ore was alive with bugs and crawling insects of many types and rather soft to the feet like shingle on a beach. A single bulb suspended on a long flex provided the sole illumination and, not quite reaching into the hold, cast a shadow like the hood over a fire built in the middle of a room — but the flex was old and mended so that the bulb hung on a cant and the shadow was distorted. Beyond the shadow, in those areas where the light failed to reach, was blackness into which the rats retreated as the men began to occupy the hold.

The men formed a seemingly endless

and barely moving line very much like that formed by ants foraging from one large colony to a source of food, a line which to the eye showed movement yet never seemed to change. The beginning of this line was a phalanx on the dockside, the end the bowels of the ship. Between, the line stretched unbroken along the quay, up the gangplank, across the deck and down a vertical iron ladder. Its speed of change was dictated by the speed with which a man could lower himself hand over hand thirty feet down this ladder until his feet met ore. The guttural curses of the captors, their threats, their banging of rifle butts, their poking of bayonets, made little difference: there could only be the one speed of descent. There was an alternative route which was by way of the ship's internal stairways down to the lower deck from which the hold could be reached via the last ten rungs or so of the ladder but the Japanese restricted the stairways for their own use.

In this particular hold there were to be two hundred and sixty-eight men with the vast majority twenty one years of age or less. They were dressed, for

2

the most part, in khaki shirts and shorts — although to say this is to convey the impression of an orderly looking group which they certainly were not for their shirts and shorts were of varying types and styles, some fairly new, some faded, some patched, some torn, some clean, some stained and oily. Again there were those who were wearing slacks and others shorts of different and curious kinds, some vivid green, some barely longer than trunks, ragged at the edges. A few had stout boots, even puttees, but mostly their footgear ranged from boots with weeping welts, through sandals and plimsolls down to handmade clogs with fraying straps of materials of bewildering variety held in place by rusty tacks and nails. Many were bareheaded, others wore solar topees or forage caps of R.A.F. blue or army brown, one or two officers wore peaked caps, some sported greasy trilbies or wide-brimmed straw, Australian and even boy scout hats.

Their gear was also weirdly assorted. Hung about many of them were metal items such as billy-cans, battered kettles, chipped enamelled mugs, water bottles and tin plates which jingled one against the other and against the gangrails as they edged along. The gangplank was steep and some, with difficulty, carried kitbags on their shoulders while others clutched rolls of bedding, rattan or leather attache cases, blankets knotted to make sacks, cardboard boxes, parcels, string bags, gas capes, even groundsheets threaded through the eyelets with drawstrings. Once on the deck, under instructions, they pitched off these belongings into a massive heap. This they did unwillingly, pausing to cast a reluctant backward glance as if doubting they would ever regain their few and miserable possessions and only moving on again under the encouragement of a yell or prodding rifle butt.

This, the last of four groups to come aboard, comprised men from a prison camp in Java. The forward hold and the two rear holds were already filled with men from Singapore and the Japanese troops (who slightly outnumbered their prisoners) were already slotted into place in four horizontal layers in the 'tween and main decks. These layers were formed out of timber structures, like scaffolding, in Us around the hold, and floored with boarding. The space between each layer was just sufficient for a soldier to sit and just deep enough to lie full length but so crammed were the spaces that the small groups who were jabbering and playing *Go* had to sit cross-legged with their backs jammed hard against their sweating neighbours. Lowering themselves downwards the prisoners bore the catcalls and jeers of these their shipmates as they passed by them with a stunned and sullen acceptance born of many months of captivity and, having been brought up to Singapore from Java in another ship in similar openfronted chests of drawers, were only faintly surprised to observe a victorious army being transported homewards in such discomfort.

As for the ship herself, she was named *Dai Nichi Maru* which, roughly translated, means 'Great Day'. She had been built at the turn of the century on the Clyde and her weight was perhaps four thousand tons. She was old, rusted, unpainted, inefficient. If a torpedo struck her she would disintegrate without a struggle. She was about to begin a voyage from the tropics to an unnamed destination which was, in fact, the winter of Japan. She carried rather more than two thousand men of whom one half, the prisoners, were already in doubtful condition. They faced a daunting prospect — a voyage of unknown duration, dressed in their shirts and shorts, lying on a bed of soaking wet bauxite ore which, except where it was roughly levelled under the open hatch, sloped in the most inconvenient manner. There was no way of levelling it. There was, except for those with groundsheets, no way of preventing its oozing reddish moisture from permeating all belongings. There was little air and little light. There was for the men, disbelievingly marking out their locations, nothing to guide them to a good selection. The only choice was near the hatch towards the future rain or snow or away from the hatch towards the darkness and the rats. Each chose his space — a space of about graveyard size — and sat there as on a sodden, muddy bank, his hands clasped round his knees, waiting. But what he waited for he did not know.

2

THERE were only five officers in the hold: two, Captain Brimmacombe and Lieutenant Anderson, were Army, two, Flight Lieutenant Dixon and Flying Officer Stacey, were R.A.F. and the fifth was a Lieutenant Commander, James Moore, who had commanded a destroyer which had been sunk by the Japanese in the Banka Straits. Moore, nearing forty, was the oldest, a man of almost six feet with the decided features and firm eyes of one who has wielded authority for far longer than mere wartime command — it was not only because he wore shorts and shirts (which were still comparatively white and therefore dazzling in the gloom of the hold) that the eyes of most of the other ranks were focused upon him as he stood with the other four on the levelled area under the open hatch.

"Well, I'm sorry that while the only naval type aboard I happen to have rank seniority," he was saying, "but there it is. I'm placing myself in command of this hold. Any objections?"

"Well, I don't know," said Brimmacombe. "I mean — theoretically . . . well, yes. Why not? But practically. I mean . . . " The idea of a naval officer being in overall and final command of his men was anathema to Freddie Brimmacombe.

"I don't," said Moore pointedly, "need your permission, Brimmacombe." He glanced round the groups of aimless, grumbling, unhappy men crammed in the hold and he was very conscious of the row upon row of Japanese watching his performance from their tiers above. "The sooner," he said, "we get some order into this the better."

"I disagree," said Stacey.

"Oh?"

"Making order out of this is tantamount to accepting these conditions. I think we should object. Get something done."

"Off you go then."

"As you are senior officer, Commander Moore, that surely is your responsibility."

Moore knew Flying Officer Stacey's

story. The whole camp had known his story.

"I don't speak Japanese and I don't speak Malay," he replied. "Why don't you try being a hero again?" He spoke to the other three, Brimmacombe, Second Lieutenant Anderson and Flight Lieutenant Dixon. "The men must be divided into sections. Brimmacombe, I suggest you muster half your army people and put them in the forward section and that you, Anderson, look after the other half in the stern. Dixon, will you take port side with R.A.F. men and you, Stacey, starboard." He strode to the centre of the platform where the bauxite was roughly levelled under the hatch.

"Quiet, please!" he called and, after a brief pause. "To introduce myself, I am Lieutenant Commander Moore, Royal Navy, senior officer present. Although this is a prison ship, military discipline and regulations still apply. It is to our mutual benefit that they should. We have ahead of us a very difficult voyage . . . "

"Know where we're going, Sir?" someone called.

"Please don't interrupt. Any time now

they may be pitching down our kit and then it's going to be a proper shambles. We've got to get organised as best we can and as quickly as we can. To answer that question — but no more please — no, I don't know where we're going. My guess is Japan. But it could as easily be Formosa, French IndoChina or even Sumatra or Hong Kong. You're going to be divided into squads. Half army personnel will form A Squad and take the forward section. B Squad will be to my right under the command of Flying Officer Stacey." He indicated Stacey, then Dixon. "Flight Lieutenant Dixon will take C Squad to the left, also R.A.F., and Lieutenant Anderson will be in charge of D, army, towards the stern. Is that clear?" He gave them no chance of disagreeing. "I notice one or two of you are starting to commandeer some of those loose planks that are lying around the place. That's out. The planks will be used to carpet this level section where I'm standing and any over will be used as duckboards to form passageways."

"Fucking officers' platform, I suppose," someone jibed.

11

"The officers will not be on the platform," Moore said shortly. "The platform will at all times be kept clear for the serving of food and for emergencies. And that man who just spoke, hear this! I will not tolerate insubordination. We may be Japanese prisoners of war but we are still members of His Majesty's Services."

But this remark rebounded. It was apparently understood by one of the listening Japanese who laughed and chattered loudly to his nearby friends, no doubt translating, whereupon contagious cackling ran round the tiers of soldiers, very many of whom, good-humouredly enjoying the spectacle below, were lying on their bellies with their shaven heads poking out from their shelves. The cackle caught on and became a babel with incomprehensible jeers being shouted to the prisoners down below and equally incomprehensible jokes and sallies being hurled across the empty space between the Us of Japanese.

"You Majesty's Service like tabacco?" one wag called. "Nippon tabacco, very nice!"

This witticism sparked off a perfect gale of laughter and much activity as other Japanese, up to this point sitting back in their shelves and therefore out of sight, moved themselves forward to join in the fun, adding their own shaven heads to those already in view until there was hardly a vacant space but four rows of parallel black-bald heads sticking out and countless eyes, many bespectacled, grinning down. Conversation became more ribald, a small fraction was in pidgin English but in the main it was meaningless. At the same time cigarettes began to fall. Beginning as a few, these soon became a snowfall which was joined by a kind of hail as sugar sweets were hurled as well. The sweets were hard and stung a little where they struck but the cigarettes, however energetically they were thrown, soon succumbed to the clammy, heavy atmosphere and, often finding unsuspected air currents, drifted in surprising directions.

The effect on the men below was predictable. Briefly held by Moore's undoubted personality, at first they gaped and stood around embarrassed;

but once the cigarettes began to fall order disintegrated and they became a rabble with a fair number grabbing for cigarettes, trying to pluck them from the air or scrabbling for them in the slimy bauxite, trampling over each other, pushing, jostling, arguing, shouting. The greater number simply stood around, their eyes morosely following the paths of the gyrating white cylinders while quite a few shouted contemptuous objections and even seized the legs of others eager for these handouts. An odd fight broke out and a few men fell slithering on the bauxite. Oaths flew, orders had little effect, squabbling and imprecations echoed queerly in the damp, hot, iron hold. All this, hugely amusing the Japanese, caused many of them to come up on their knees, lean forward dangerously, thump their platforms, bellow encouragement and fling further ammunition. Above was babel; below was chaos.

Moore, in the centre of the platform, made no attempt to stem the turmoil. Occasionally he felt the sharp prick of sugar sweets against the bare flesh of his

14

knees or forearms and more than once the softness of a cigarette caressed his cheek before falling to his feet. Only in such cases did he move, grinding the thing to shreds of paper and tobacco with his foot like a man crushing the life from some noisome insect. There was, he realised, no way of stopping what was going on. To attempt to do so would invite rebellion and put such tenuous discipline as still remained under added stress. In any case he did not, as did Stacey yapping uselessly beside him, accept this terrifying exhibition as a total abandonment of self-respect. Men came in many ways — to some this was indeed shameful. But to grab at a floating cigarette was to others a release from tension and uncertainty; or displayed defiance and an intention to survive. The time to reassert control would come. Moore waited patiently.

Inevitably the supply began to thin, the shaven heads to reduce in number, the catcalls lessen and, in moments, all was over. Still Moore waited. By his own indifference he had drawn attention to himself and made a point.

15

"Apparently," he observed, "the supplies of manna are exhausted. And it isn't worth searching for any cigarettes you've missed because once they land on this filthy sludge they become unsmokable." And, in a businesslike tone: "Are there any Sergeant Majors or Warrant Officers?"

"Sir!" said a neat and very tall man close by who had evidently been holding himself in readiness. "Warrant Officer Worboys!"

"Come up on the platform, Worboys, will you?"

Being well done, thought Worboys. Establishing the platform as out of bounds. He climbed up. The shingly ore was particularly friable at the platform edges and his boots sank deep into it. Nevertheless he managed a crisp salute.

Meanwhile two other men were following. Very different types from Worboys, they were in some respects alike. Both were shortish men and both had rather fishy and protuberant eyes. The one who was of the R.A.F. wore only a soft yellowish hat rather Australian in style with one brim curled, a pair of dirty shorts and clogs; his nut-brown

16

skin displayed by its wrinkles that he was well into his forties, he sported a massive, indeed rather ridiculous, jet-black moustache drooping at its ends and he had the surprising manner of a man ready and confident to take over everything. The third man was, by contrast, smartly turned out in good boots, neat socks, long shorts, belt and short-sleeved tunic. He was egg-bald and carried a pith helmet in his hand which he jammed on his head before saluting and announcing himself in a tremendous boom as: "Sergeant Major Rudge!"

"And you are?" queried Moore of the other.

"Toms. Warrant Officer First Class. Harry James Toms, Sir. Number 137713. Regular Air Force, Sir!" Again, for all the respectful and military nature of his words, Toms conveyed that everything was best left to him.

"Is that all the gear you have?" asked Moore.

"Until they release our kit."

"Make a point of getting into something else as soon as they do, will you. Now, will you please take B Squad under

Flying Officer Stacey, Toms. Sergeant Rudge, you will take A Squad under Captain Brimmacombe and Warrant Officer Worboys, C under Flight Lieutenant Dixon. Can you recommend a Sergeant?"

"Kerrison, Sir," said Worboys, without hesitation.

"Sergeant Kerrison!" Moore called loudly. "Will you come up on the platform, please."

"Sir!" The reply echoing from the blackness was satisfyingly crisp and was followed by the slow, steady crunching of resisting gravel curiously softened by the dampness and the muffling effect of the low iron deck above. For some reason otherwise complete silence fell as if a very dramatic thing was about to happen and this change of atmosphere communicated itself to the Japanese who watched with great intent. It was as if it had of a sudden occurred to them that here was an opportunity to discover what kind of men these were who after being so easily defeated had failed to adopt the honourable course of self-inflicted death.

18

Waiting, Moore realised that this was an important time. The devastating first effect of being crammed into this terrible hold after all the indignities which had gone before — the trudging naked through troughs of warm lime liquid like sheep being dipped, the glass rod shoved up each man's anus in full view of rows of giggling Japanese girls — had been that in an instant a man was stripped of the remnants of his personal essence. Used to measuring himself by his relationship to his surroundings and judging himself by his capacity to make and take decisions, he discovered himself, in one awful instant, utterly exposed. Publicly humiliated, dispossessed of all but a few rags, his feet sunk into an oozy shingle and no matter which way he looked about him finding nothing positive on which to focus his attention or give himself guidance he was suddenly a non-being. And in fact, thought Moore, perhaps worse even than the crowding and the bauxite, and what had gone before, was the utter symmetry of these men's tomb with its truncated pyramid of glistening ore sloping with smooth regularity in all directions towards the anonymity of darkness at its extremities; this *harmony* — for it was a form of harmony — bore a frightening resemblance to the barren walls of an interrogation cell. In such a place even the presence of nearly three hundred men in an equal plight merely emphasized the unimportance of the individual.

★ ★ ★

Kerrison proved to be an efficient, if unimaginative, man in his middle thirties. Moore guessed that like Worboys, Toms and Rudge he was a regular — and that was a queer thing when the four officers under whom these N.C.Os. would serve were all wartime servicemen. The man's kit was a trifle bizarre in that he wore corduroy shorts similar to those worn by thigh-slapping Tyroleans, a short-sleeved Air Force battledress blouse and a glengarry. But his boots were cared for and his stockings neatly darned with string and the useful articles he had festooned about him — a water bottle in its webbing harness, a billy-can, a mug and rim-drilled plate, all hung from a broad leather belt — indicated a man who used his head.

"Glad to meet you, Sergeant," Moore said with a smile. "Your service?"

"Army, Sir."

"Seen action?"

"Yes, Sir. All the way down from Alor Star."

This information reinforced growing doubts in Moore's mind.

"Captain Brimmacombe," he said. "On second thoughts I believe it would be better if we split up the services into the various sections. There could be some problems if we're too neatly subdivided. If you will start organising say half your chaps and you, Sergeant Kerrison, will draft the balance . . ."

"With great respect, Commander Moore . . ."

"I could write your objections for you and find them entirely valid under normal circumstances, Captain," Moore interrupted briskly. "But these circumstances are not exactly normal."

★ ★ ★

The movement of the crowded men began. Some, careless of where they went, moved willingly; others for reasons they might have found it difficult to explain foresaw advantages in particular locations and there was much cross-shouting and argument as friends espoused the merit of their choice. Some wished to be close up to the platform but even these gave different motives. Some argued for light and some for air. Some (already secretly pondering on the possibility of the ship being torpedoed) wanted to be near the ladder so, they professed, as to be handy for the lavatories, queer wooden contraptions on the upper deck. Others chose the dark, lower areas out of sight of the Japanese. Some feeling no compulsion to choose anywhere in particular simply sat down where they happened to be standing.

This shifting, barging and calling out reverberating around the iron box, for a while continued to hold the attention of the Japanese but then their interest waned and they began to withdraw like tortoises into their shelves and the four

Us above presented a largely deserted façade from which now and then shot cigarette ends, orange peel and gobs of phlegm.

★ ★ ★

When things had quietened sufficiently, Moore (who had selected a place a little in from the platform and close to the foot of the ladder) gave instructions for hauling the loose planks into place upon the platform and forming walkways as far as they would stretch diagonally from its corners. This was a difficult operation because of the confines of the hold and the crowding of the prisoners. Dixon, meanwhile, assisted by the quietly-spoken, reasoned, impressive Worboys, was constructing, on sheets of lavatory paper a careful irk had donated, a temporary roll of the men who were to be in his Squad; Toms, attended as it were by Stacey, was handing to him small pieces of card, on each of which he first wrote a number, while Brimmacombe, with Sergeant Major Rudge in close attendance, was elbowing through his

23

flock exchanging cheerful and encouraging words.

Of these men the least at home was Flight Lieutenant Dixon. Originally he had been a Sergeant Pilot but success in the Battle of Britain, and more recently continuous action against an infinitely stronger and far better prepared enemy air force which had decimated his squadron, had brought rapid promotion. Yet as he had little experience in an established officers' mess, his social contact with the handful of officers who had survived had been, in hotel, bar and night club, hardly greater than it had been before he had been commissioned. Moreover he was shy by nature and in self-protection had developed a taciturn style which distanced him from all who did not know him well. Dutifully writing down as best he could on the wretched lavatory paper the names which Worboys quietly spelled out to him, he longed only for the opportunity to retire to some quiet spot well down the bauxite slope, there to possess himself in patience until this ghastly experience ended.

Toms, on the other hand, was in his

element, and Stacey for all his continuous complaints was subconsciously more at ease than he had been for quite some time. Toms was a tremendous organizer, a man of fanciful, even preposterous, ideas. Had he not chosen a service career he would inevitably have become involved in theatre; there was hardly a station to which he had been posted that had not sooner or later boasted a Toms' 'Choir' or 'Company'. Stacey was very different. A snob with a carefully researched pedigree, Public School and Varsity educated, he had worked in Japan and then held a minor Colonial post in northern Malaya at the time of the Japanese assault. Local influence and a sudden, if tardy, rush of patriotic blood to the head had enabled him to switch, with a commission, into the R.A.F. and to get himself posted down to Singapore. Here his luck rather deserted him, for when he was evacuated before the Japanese assault, unlike a number of his cronies who were to spend a comfortable war in Australia or some such place, he was put ashore in Java when his ship crept into Tandjeonpriok after being damaged in an air raid. Stacey was not of the Air Force, or any force at all, but a civilian in masquerade. Here, at least, he had a role.

As regards the men in charge of A Squad, Sergeant Major Rudge had been a Quartermaster Sergeant and a rogue. Although he would unquestionably have succeeded as spiv or barrow boy, probably climbing to quite dizzy commercial heights before he was done, he would never have made the change. The Army was for Rudge; for Rudge the Army was the world. He never questioned its rules, its regulations, its hierarchy. Far from it, he saw these rules and regulations, the very hierarchy, as having been framed, as it were, for the special benefit of William Randolph Rudge. They were to him as are the law books and case history to barristers; his bread and butter — thickly spread with jam. Judges come in many kinds but in their wigs look much the same; and Leading Counsels, although *they* at least may be able to distinguish between the good and bad, treat them all alike. And thus did Rudge treat officers. Brimmacombe he had summed up swiftly and accurately. He could have put it in six adjectives: enthusiastic, muddle-headed, chauvinistic, adolescent, conventional and easily manageable. In thinking in these terms Rudge would not have been criticizing Brimmacombe. He no more criticized officers than a skier criticizes slalom poles — they were there, not so much obstacles as indications of the sensible course to take. So, as Brimmacombe made his cheerful, encouraging trudge-about, Rudge was correctly a pace behind him, catching his mood, ever ready to approve and see to things.

* * *

At about seven in the evening a Japanese interpreter appeared by the hatch coaming and barked staccato orders for a party of men to attend on deck and shortly after they had done so the kit came hurtling down. Initially a few individuals dared to mount the platform to reclaim a piece they recognized but soon, as the bedrolls, kitbags, knapsacks, parcels,

27

began to compress into a gigantic and unstable mound, quick withdrawal became a risky business and such attempts were outlawed. The officers stood as it were on guard, casting a wary eye on the latest consignment hurtling from the black above while the Japanese amused themselves trying to catch small items which had broken loose in transit. Worboys and Kerrison, aided less energetically by Toms and Rudge, assumed the role of levellers, swiftly hauling down swaying pinnacles, laying them as curbs or buttresses, trying all the time to leave sufficient level space to prevent the mound toppling en bloc off the platform and on to one of the four walls of men now lining the area. Eventually the deluge ceased, the working party descended and the baffling business of sorting out the ownership of the constituent parts of the pile began. In such hopelessly restricted conditions this took about two hours by the end of which the two hundred and sixty-eight men exhausted by the events of a bewildering and still barely comprehended day, stained by oil and bauxite, lathered in sweat, bitten by insects, hungry, thirsty, jaded, hauling their gear, tripping over each other, cursing, grumbling, apologising, attempted to create for themselves some manageable living space on the banks of sloping ore. But no sooner had they begun to do this than a renewed bellowing from above announced the arrival of food and at once two huge tubs descended into view lowered on ropes, banging against the flex, making the light bulb sway and spin and cast enormous shadows of the tubs which, distorted in shape, raced madly in all directions.

The shouting from above and the weird racing shadows added a layer of unreality to the nightmarish hole with its funnel now relined with the layers of shaven-headed, grinning Japanese re-enthused to study the capers of the curious species in their den below. It was very close to chaos for a while, but in the end Moore's organisation, aided by the utter weariness of the punch-drunk men, held. At least there was no mad rush for food. Rather the prisoners waited to be instructed. Worboys and

Toms acted as dispensers, Rudge and Kerrison as ushers. The squads took it in turn to file up in a ragged fashion with its members holding out the most amazingly varied collection of vessels into which were ladled rice and a pale pink liquid with a faintly fishy smell. Each man turned away, warily balancing his ration as he gingerly trudged and weaved his way back down the sloping, slithery, much-obstructed pile, seeking his chosen oblong. When all had been served and it had been established that the two Warrant Officers' judgement of quantity had been intelligently pessimistic, second helpings were offered and the process wearily repeated. And finally again repeated for a water ration. Then the tubs were hauled away up into the small square of blackness; the business of how to clean soiled utensils or dispose of uneaten portions remained unsolved; in batches of ten the men scaled the long rusted ladder to relieve themselves; and two hundred and sixty-eight men, who were all utterly exhausted, dazed and confused but who were separate human beings, each with his own degree of competency and ingenuity, of courage and resilience, of weakness, of tenacity ... each of these two hundred and sixty-eight arranged as best he could his paltry possessions around him, scrabbled out the most congenial base of squelchy ore and prepared himself for the long days and nights which lay ahead.

3

"WONDER when it's laights out", said Lenny.

"Lights aht?", said Hobby.

"That bluddy thing", said Lenny, thumbing towards the naked bulb.

"'ope they bloody don't."

"Never could sleep wi' laight on."

"There's rats 'ere, Lenny."

"Yeh. Bigguns too."

"They'll be crawling all over us . . . If they switch that light orf."

"They won't switch that light off. Don't be so bloody daft", Mac said.

"Don't see why not," Lenny reasoned. "There's nowhere we can go but up ladder."

"Fat charnse we'll 'ave. If there's any subs abaht."

"Know your trouble, Hobby?", Lenny said. "Too bluddy cheerful by half. That's your trouble."

"Subs," scoffed Mac. "We got no subs. We got fuck all."

"Yanks'll have subs," Lenny reasoned hopefully. "Bound to by now. I mean . . . 'f a girl c'n 've a baby in nine months, the Yanks c'n 've built some subs. Anyway they couldn't 've lost 'em *all* at Pearl Harbour, could they? I wonder . . . "

"What?"

"If we sort 've levelled out a trench for our backsides and built a sort 've . . . well a sort 've pillow for our heads . . . "

"Pillow!"

"You know what some of the Nips use? A matchbox. No really, no kidding. Saw them on the *Yoseda*. They just put a matchbox down, end up too, and put their 'ead on it an' go right off."

"Gawd!" said Nobby. "Thought that was the bloody end, the *Yoseda*. Bloody pleasure cruise compared to this."

"What about *Altmark* then? Remember the fuss they made 'f that?"

"That's what Dixon said."

"He's got a gong, y'know. D.F.M."

"We oughter 'd been in 'is lot."

"Join the Raff and end up in the Navy."

"Knew a bloke who did that," said Lenny. "Well, in a way. There was this long corridor. We were in this queue. Bluddy hours it took. Inching along for hours. Not that they turned anybody down, mind you. An' across the corridor there was another queue. Three in it. Always seemed to be three. When someone came out of door, someone else joined the queue. There was this bloke in front of me. Proper stroppy 'e were getting. So he stops this spud adjutant walking down corridor. 'What's that queue for, mate?' he asks. 'Navy', the cor'pral says. 'That's for me,' this character says. 'Not waiting any bloody longer.' An' he nips across the corridor. An' ten minutes later, 'e's in an' out the door. 'Cheero,' he says, 'I'm in the Navy.' Wonder what 'appened to 'im."

"Couldn't 'ave done much worse 'n us", said Nobby.

"Well, you never know. Might've got sunk. Might 've been on the *Prince 'f Wales*."

"Where did 'e spring from?" asked Nobby.

"Who?"

"'im?" Nobby jerked his head towards Moore who was only a few yards away.

34

"Not a clue. Never saw him in the camp."

"Queer old war, ain't it?" said Lenny. "Bet you're sorry you joined up now. What about this bum-hole?"

They were sharing a macintosh spread over the bauxite. The macintosh was shiny black and very old; had the light been better it would have shown brown at the creases where the glaze had cracked. The macintosh belonged to Lenny Brooks and so he had pride of place in the middle. Clarke was on the left and had to put up with the buttons digging into him; Macavoy was on the right. The macintosh had been found in a shed by Lenny when on a working party in Java; it must have been owned by a very stout Dutchman but even so the three of them had to lie close, their bodies touching, to avoid the outer pair being in contact with the ore. There was a problem at the head where the macintosh reduced in size which had been dealt with in a rather untidy way. Lenny had a shirt folded and refolded and placed precariously on his upturned plate but it wasn't really thick enough and his neck was cricked; Nobby had a knapsack whose webbing and buckles presented problems; Mac had a rolled-up, threadbare towel already soaking up wetness and attracting bugs. The macintosh not being long enough, their heels (and in the case of Macavoy, who was tall, the lower part of his calves) were in the bauxite. Spread around them, forming a sort of weird perimeter, were the balance of their possessions: a fibre attache case, a knotted towel with a stick through it such as tramps are supposed to carry, a brown paper parcel heavily tied with string, a spare pair of boots, a straw hat, two forage caps and a miscellaneous collection of odd items including battered tin plates and cups. Beyond this perimeter they were tightly hedged in by an equally extraordinary assortment or the actual bodies, head or feet of other men. Between each group of men, or each man on his own, there was scarcely room to place a foot.

The majority were lying on their backs, many asleep, two or three who were near enough to the light were reading, one in a distant corner fiercely grinding his teeth, several snoring. Desultory chatting mingled with these sounds as did the distant guttural speech of the layers of Japanese. The ship was moored to a quayside where in fact there was much activity — but that was another world. The iron sides and decks were as efficient baffles against its sounds as were the bulkheads against those of the adjacent holds.

The only movement which took place was when a man, wishing to relieve himself, made his laborious way up to the platform to gather into a group which, when ten in number, was permitted to scale the ladder on to the lower deck whence they were escorted by a Japanese soldier, with rifle and fixed bayonet almost as tall as himself, to the latrine, or, as it was called, the *benjo*.

However, as an exception, there was one man who, most carefully and unhurriedly, was making his way around the hold in the area where there was sufficient light for him to do so without risk of stumbling over bodies or impediments. This man was surprisingly well turned out and evidently, judging by his matching tunic and trousers, of the army. Every now and again he paused to speak to someone, usually another man on his own. He spoke in a low tone but nevertheless with the closeness of the prisoners to each other those nearby could hear his questions and judge from his voice he was well educated. He wore spectacles and his sleek black hair was decently trimmed and altogether he seemed as out of place as a man in a lounge suit down a coal mine.

When he arrived at the head of the trio of Lenny Brooks, Nobby Clarke and Macavoy now busily engaged in attempting in their confined area to carry out Lenny's plan of excavating a hollow for their posteriors and patting the excavated material into a kind of barrow for their heads, he paused for a moment glancing at the macintosh which had been concertinaed into a shape like crumpled up paper in the lower part of their space, then briefly shook his head and passed neatly between their barrow and the feet of a couple of men above them. He was then forced to circumnavigate two men who shared a rattan mat and this brought him up to another man whose pitch was near the ladder's base. This man owned a wicker suitcase whose lid was open and on which he sat sideways so as to be able both to keep his backside dry and guard his few possessions. He was a youngster of nineteen or twenty (and thus several years junior to the perambulator), of middle height, with fine hair of the type which thins early to baldness or near baldness. He wore shorts and home-made wooden clogs the straps of which were made of several layers of edge-frayed linen held in place to the side of the clogs by many tintacks. He was seated, Rodin style, one hand under his chin and elbow of that arm resting on the upturned palm of the other laid on his thigh. Thrown over his bare and bony shoulders, threatening to slip off at any time, was a small, thin blanket. His other possessions were easily calculated. The open wicker suitcase was less than one-third filled and contained a pair of pyjamas, a tunic-style half-sleeved shirt, two books, a pair of slacks, a piece of towel, three bars of soap and two tins, both cigarette tins, one a round fifty 'Players' tin, the other a flat yellow

'Kensitas' tin. Additionally, not in the basket, but between his feet was a pith helmet turned upside down in which were a spoon and fork and an earthenware mug and by his side an aluminium plate.

The newcomer stared unhurriedly at the opened suitcase and then said: "I see you've got some books. Lucky chap."

The young man, whose name was Yates, looked up, quite startled.

"Er . . . yes" he said, unsurely. "Yes, I have."

"Mind if I glance at them?"

"No. That's all right."

The older man, Sutcliffe by name, bent to pick up the books and then, half turning so that the light fell on them, opened them at their title pages, first one and then the other. He held one down beside his thigh, as if dismissed, and the other high. "This one," he said. "I suppose you wouldn't care to sell it to me. I see you smoke."

"No, I don't think so."

"Twenty," suggested Sutcliffe encouragingly. "It's rather trashy."

"Yes, I know it is," Yates said apologetically.

"This one then," said Sutcliffe, semaphoring with the books, throwing long shadows. "Russell's *Power*. Better book of course but rather dull. Might be Russell's power but not much swapping power." He smiled showing strong, perfect teeth. "Fifteen?"

Yates shook his head. The blanket slipped and in his effort to stop it falling on the bauxite, he all but lost his balance. Sutcliffe alertly put out a hand to save him doing so.

"All right then. Twenty," said Sutcliffe as if it were all settled.

Yates stared at the bauxite. It was as if he were ashamed. "No," he said.

Sutcliffe considered.

"I see you don't have a groundsheet," he said. "Nothing like that."

"No."

"I might be able to get you one. But it would have to be both books."

"I . . . I'll think about it."

"Yes. I should if I were you. Not much good having books if you aren't alive to read them." Sutcliffe spoke very crisply, exactly as would a businessman who has made his offer and has other matters

41

to attend to. "My name's Sutcliffe. I'm in . . . " he spoke sardonically " . . . A Squad. One row down. In the centre. Where the light's good. Don't leave it too long making up your mind, old chap, will you? I don't have unlimited means."

★ ★ ★

Moore, who had heard every word, just as he had heard every word of the chat between Lenny and his friends, stared after the departing Sutcliffe, watching him continuing to pick a careful, almost delicate path, amongst the recumbent forms, seeing him pause again and strike up another conversation with a couple of men in Stacey's squad. He was intrigued but disquieted. He believed he could categorize Sutcliffe, that he had had to deal personally with quite a number of men of similar type in his business career. There was a smell about such men. They sat at boardroom tables in perfectly cut suits which showed those tiny differences, the pointed cuff, the extra button, which warned you you were a little behind the times. They were quiet men, economical in speech, attentive to every word, who put any differences of view in a reasonable manner and with a smile. They had a self-assurance which was worrying; it was as if they knew in advance everything which was going to be discussed, as if they knew more about the Company's affairs than you did yourself. And when they had gone, never staying for the boardroom whiskies, you realised that all you knew about them was exactly what they wanted you to know. And you knew something else — that you needed to be very careful, that such men were dangerous.

But here . . . to meet one here. That was extraordinary. Such men were never taken prisoner; such men were rarely in the services at all. Such men stayed well behind the lines, watching, listening, making contacts. You found them in munitions, or food distribution . . . or politics. And by the time the pause between the end of the war and demobilisation was over, you would find they had used that hiatus brilliantly, had struck, cobra-like, and were established at levels it might take you another twenty years to reach — assuming they had left you any chance of reaching them at all.

Sutcliffe had no rank, not even a lance-corporal's stripe. The man was officer material — no selection board would have had a moment's hesitation. It was puzzling.

★ ★ ★

"Excuse me, Sir?"

"What!" The question had startled Moore. He stared somewhat irritably at the young man beside him.

"I'd like your advice, Sir. If I may."

Moore nodded. "Yes. Yes, of course."

"You must have heard . . ."

"What you were offered for your books? Yes. I did. I'm sorry but privacy is in short supply here."

"Do you think I should . . . let him have them?"

"No!"

Moore recognised immediately that he had been too vehement. That he had spoken from instinct, not from reason.

44

But the instinct had been boardroom instinct and boardroom instincts had no place in the crammed hold of a prison ship.

"You don't think it matters all that much not having a groundsheet?"

Moore stared at the youngster sitting so comically on the opened lid of his wicker basket. Only it wasn't comical — that lid could save his life. If he had the strength to stay sitting on it. He was tempted to change his mind, to tell the young man to go and find Sutcliffe before he did a deal with someone else. Two things stopped him. The first the utter certainty that it would not be Sutcliffe's groundsheet which would be provided but one bought for cigarettes — one man might die instead of another so that Sutcliffe should have his books. That was obscene.

The second thing was that Moore had a groundsheet of his own.

"What's your name?" he said.

"Yates, Sir."

"Well, you can share my groundsheet, Yates," he said. And, jocularly, to cover his own embarrassment more than to put

Yates at ease: "And I can share your books."

"I couldn't do that, Sir."

"Why not, Yates?"

"I just couldn't, Sir. It's only meant for one, anyway, Sir. There wouldn't be room."

"Nonsense, man, look at those three!" Lenny and his friends had finished their earthworks and were stretched out in a row testing the result. Their chins almost touched their chests and they did not look comfortable.

"Yes, Sir. But they're all . . . " There seemed no way of putting it.

Moore turned the subject. "Know what this is?" He reached behind him and picked up an object shaped like a small bolster.

"No, Sir."

"It's called a Dutch wife. The idea is you sleep with one between your legs. Supposed to keep you cooler. It's quite large enough for a double pillow. Come on, move your things."

"I'd rather not, Sir."

Moore misunderstood.

"Now listen to me, Yates," he said

46

severely. "There are only so many groundsheets and the like in this hold and one thing you can be sure of is that those little yellow bastards aren't going to provide any more . . . "

"I can sell my books to Sutcliffe.."

"And have someone else ill in your place? Or do you imagine he's going to give you his?"

"No, Sir."

"No. But of course he's quite right. If this voyage, assuming it ever starts, lasts more than a week, a lot of us are going to get sick anyway. But those without something reasonably dry to lie on are going to be the worst. Come on, Yates, no argument."

"But . . . "

"It's an order, Yates."

Yates was overborne. "Yes, Sir," he said and began to move his things.

★ ★ ★

Brimmacombe had led a carefully selected quota to the benjo. There were four wooden structures, two on each side of the ship. These structures (which were raised up to clear the bulwarks) comprised an open trough for urine which, continuing, carried through a series of compartments then re-emerged. The structures were simple affairs of stoutly nailed boarding on framing and constructed so that the compartments hung out over the sea like gun turrets. A continuous parallel step provided access. There were no seats in these compartments and the base was incomplete offering both a floor on which to squat across the trough and a sight of the ship's hull and of the sea through the open strips. For the prisoners there were two of these structures on the port side, one forward with three compartments and one towards the stern with six. The Japanese were supplied with identical facilities on the starboard side but in their case both structures contained six compartments. With the *Dai Nichi Maru* being moored to a quayside where lavatories were available the Japanese used the gangplanks leaving their benjos, which were in any case on the landward side, pristine. The prisoners', on the other hand, were already in use, already clogged, already stinking. A dribble of urine managed to trickle its way through the jam of paper and excreta and drip in a thin, breeze-bent or broken stream, into the oily sea below.

The night was superb, cloudless, humid. There was no moon but the stars blazed in their millions, low above the earth, indifferent to its happenings. Harsh, cold dockyard lights cast a shadow of the ships drawn in a line along the quay and beyond this shadow, across the water, the outline of Sentosa Island could be seen. There was much activity on the quayside with little groups of Japanese soldiers, some in ranks, some loitering at ease, coolies hauling handcarts, a battered lorry loading scrap, a crane lowering strange pieces into a distant hold. The dockyard was untidy, a mess of damaged gowdowns, burnt out buildings grotesquely twisted, piles of junk, anchors, cables, tyres. There were even the remnants of a blown-up half track and included in the line of ships one scuttled, canted, showing only its bridge and funnel, held from turning turtle by massive hawsers.

Brimmacombe took heed of none of this. Singapore had no interest for him — it was too well held. Brimmacombe was impatient for the ship to sail. Brimmacombe had a project. He allowed himself to go no further than to consider it a project but, hopefully, it would later develop into a plan.

His party, carefully selected, was composed exclusively of army men and included Rudge. The open part of the trough was long enough for four men in a row to urinate; the balance, under instruction to take their time, straggled between the hatch coaming and a set of winches across the uneven deck which was booby-trapped with rusting pipes and valves. Behind reared the shabby bridge and super-structure, unpainted, but disfigured with blots of red lead paint where the rust was worst. One scruffy guard, already bored with endlessly shepherding parties of men to relieve themselves, was a little apart, noisily hawking up phlegm, of which his supply seemed endless, spitting it over the side and apparently trying to watch its splash.

"These Air Force men," Brimmacombe was saying. "What d'you think, Rudge? Think any of them would have a go?"

Rudge had no opinion; he sought for one he hoped would dovetail with his Commanding Officer's. Unlike Brimmacombe who had got only as far as having a project, Rudge had a definite plan . . . which was: to become a cook. In the Java camp he had, based on his previous service career, laid claim to be in charge of stores and this had served him well. But the cooks, he had noted, had done even better. Apart from some very limited supplies he (and for the R.A.F. contingent, Toms) had brought aboard, there were no stores under his control and there would be no commissariat wherever they were going. But there would be cooks. And Brimmacombe would have an important say in their selection.

"Not really their scene, is it, Sir?" he ventured. "I mean their job's seeing the aircraft work and that sort of thing, isn't it?"

"Hell of a lot of them for the number of aircraft *we* saw," grumbled Brimmacombe. "Most of them seem to have spent their time rushing around Sumatra like a lot of blue-arsed flies trying to get away."

"Heard a few of them put up something of a show against the Japs when they dropped those paratroops at . . . what was the place called?" said Rudge. This was by way of insurance — one never knew. Wouldn't be a good thing damning the Raffs out of hand and then finding some of them were keen.

"Palembang," said Brimmacombe. "Better edge up a bit." The first four men had shifted from the trough and were doing up their flies. The guard was still hawking phlegm. Behind was a loud distant bang as if something had fallen off the crane. There were mosquitoes in the air. And the smell of the sea mingling with sweat and excreta.

"Worboys looks good material," Brimmacombe went on. "Might have a word with him. And the next thing's to organise some contact with the other holds."

"Captain Fairfax, Sir?" (Fairfax was a medical officer.)

"Good idea, Rudge. We've already got

some sick. Bound to be plenty more. And an accident or two. Any idea what hold he's in?"

"No, Sir. Never saw him go aboard. Probably while we were having that bloody bath."

"Impossible to work 'em out, Rudge, isn't it? Hose you down, walk you through a trough, disinfect your clothes, shove a tube up your backside to check you haven't got the plague or something and then cram you in a hold you wouldn't keep pigs in." He moved two or three paces along the deck; Rudge stayed in close attendance. "Bloody savages. Look at that one." He nodded to their guard. "We could tip him over easy as kiss your hand. That's one thing on our side, Rudge. They're over-confident. Cocky. Had it too easy. I tell you, Rudge, give 'em a few days at sea and with the way they're crammed into their slots if we could control a few strategic points, grab some rifles, a machine-gun maybe, it could be done all right."

Rudge didn't believe a word of it.

"Could well be right, Sir," he said.

"Have a word with Worboys, will you.

Try him out. Better coming from you than me. But do it gently. You know, Rudge. Test the water, eh?"

"Yes, Sir. I'll do that," said Rudge. And he stood beside his Commanding Officer, hoicking his penis out. Stacey stood in approved fashion, hands folded behind his back, belt to his khaki tunic neatly tight, long sleeves rolled up neatly as well showing his elbows, peaked R.A.F. cap at a jaunty angle. All he needed to look the exact part was a flying brevet. He spoke in a voice calculatedly loud enough to be accidentally heard over quite some distance.

"The most important thing, Warrant Officer, is cleanliness. That sounds absurd, I know, in a hole like this. But I've spent a lot of time up-country in the bush and I know what I'm talking about. *Mens sana in corpore sano*. Do I need to translate?"

Toms slapped at an insect on his wrist; his watery, protuberant eyes held Stacey's which were rather strange eyes with a permanent stare to them as if he were continually affronted. His mouth was petulant.

"I could go on," said Stacey when Toms gave no sign of answering. *Fortis posce animum mortis terrore carentem.* Roughly translated that means: Pray for the courage not to be afraid of death. But praying won't be enough here. Nothing like. Cleanliness is the thing."

Bloody arse, thought Toms and, unable to resist it: "I didn't see the bathroom on the way down, Sir."

"I'm not talking about body cleanliness. I'm talking about these!" And, bringing his hands out from behind his back, Stacey displayed with triumph a knife, fork and spoon. "There's obviously no way we're going to be able to wash ourselves. But we *have* to find the way to wash these and the things we eat and drink from. Our plates. Our mugs. They have priority. Priority over drinking even. And we can't rely on the men. Which means that after every meal all utensils are to be collected and rinsed in clean water, sea water if necessary, and then returned."

"Who to?" said Toms.

"The men."

"All two hundred and sixty-eight, Sir?

55

That's going to take some time."

"I'm talking about B Squad."

"Doesn't matter about the other squads?"

"Of course it matters, man! You senior N.C.O.s can sort it out amongst yourselves. But get it organised. Look at it . . . " He waved a still podgy hand towards some dishes on the bauxite near at hand. "Disgusting. The man's made no attempt." Anger seized him. He took a step forward but the slope and the soft gravel rather spoilt the effect. He swayed and all but stumbled. "You! What's your name?" he demanded of the man who evidently owned the offending plate.

"Me?"

"Me, Sir! Yes, you. What's your name?"

The man hesitated. "Witherspoon," he answered. "Deryck Witherspoon." And he spelt out the first part.

"I see. Have you heard what I've been saying, Witherspoon?"

The man nodded.

"Don't nod at me, man!" Stacey blazed. "Answer me. Have you heard what I've been saying?"

Moore had had enough.

"Flying Officer Stacey!" he called out. And when Stacey turned towards him. "Leave it till the morning. The men need rest."

"I beg your pardon, Sir, but . . . "

"You are quite right, Flying Officer Stacey," Moore interrupted. "It's important to get something organised about washing plates and so on. But there's nothing we can do tonight and the men need rest. So leave it, will you please." And he deliberately turned away.

Stacey clapped his hands behind his back again. "Very well," he said determinedly. "We will deal with it in the morning."

But he was talking to nobody. Deryck Witherspoon — whose real name was Harry Tilley — was chuckling with a friend. And Toms was twenty yards away.

4

THE *Dai Nichi* remained beside the quay for two long days. Except for the small groups allowed on deck to visit the benjos, the prisoners were kept strictly confined to their holds. Moore managed a meeting with a Japanese officer who spoke some English but this bore little fruit. His request for water for washing dishes was treated with disdain and apart from the provision of a few score rattan mats pitched contemptuously down the hatchway, nothing was done to improve conditions. Such small benefit as was gained by this minor concession was offset by a rapid multiplication of flies and other insects by day, by the increased audacity of the rats by night and by the steadily rising temperature, made doubly unpleasant by the growing stench of two hundred and sixty-eight unwashed men crammed into an unventilated hold.

The hours crawled slowly by, especially

those of the second day. Through the first there were useful things to do — rolls to be drawn up; kit to be unpacked, rearranged, repacked; possessions to be bartered; an inventory to be made of the pitifully small stock of food which had been brought aboard. There remained even the encouraging, if absurd, optimism amongst some of the men that they had been dumped here purely as a temporary expedient while other quarters were arranged, that it really was not to be imagined that even the Japanese could contemplate subjecting their prisoners to a voyage under these conditions. But by the second day even this faint hope was withering and there was simply nothing to do but queue for the two meals issued, for the ration of drinking water and for the benjo. Otherwise sitting or lying on the sloping bauxite, there was only reading for those well enough placed and fortunate enough to own a book, an uncomfortable game of cards for those with cards, an occasional cigarette for those with cigarettes, the endless discussion of subjects already done to death in the earlier months of captivity and the choice of sleep or boredom. Already the transient interest of their captors had faded — there were no more cigarettes or sugar sweets thrown down, there were no more catcalls; already they were all but forgotten men.

Moore was gradually appraising the quality of those on whom he must rely — the other four officers and his four selected N.C.Os. It struck him how under-officered they were. In the two stern holds, he reasoned, the proportion of officers to men must be greater. On the *Yoseda Maru*, the ship which had brought them from Java to Singapore, it certainly had been. The mistake had been for the officers to have largely stayed together as a group. When they had been lined up on the quay, the Japanese had arbitrarily detailed off a group to go aboard the extraordinary ship which had been converted with endless troughs of warm, limey liquid as a kind of disinfectory and he, with Dixon, Brimmacombe, Anderson and Stacey had been the wrong side of a bayonet. That had been his personal tragedy for within that larger group had been Charles Sandford and Pete Mitchell, two men whose friendship had stretched back beyond the beginning of the war and in Charles' case back to school-days. How curious it was that Charles and he who had so artfully wangled staying together, afloat and into a prison camp, should have been split up by the casual whim of a myopic Jap. Possibly, quite possibly, Charles and Pete were aboard, in one of the two stern holds; possibly they would meet on deck; perhaps even they might be reunited in another prison camp. But what a difference it would have made if Charles with his marvellous capacity for making light of the worst situations, and Pete with that easy-going, rather adolescent yet convincing manner which had enabled him to handle the men on the *Merlin* so brilliantly, had been here to help him.

Well, there was no sense in dwelling on what might have been. For the time being this hot, clammy, fetid hold was the world and two hundred and sixty-eight men were its inhabitants. Some had the boon of friends, others, such as himself and the young boy who shared his groundsheet, had not even that consolation. A few had books, cigarettes or even a little food, but compared with what had been lost these were mere trifles. A thousand qualities which together made up the marvellous tapestry of life had been taken from them with freedom the greatest forfeit of all. All had been lost but life itself. That was the reality — that life at least remained and must be sustained. It had fallen to him, by accident, by the shoving forward of a bayonet, to take on this responsibility. I don't, he told himself, have Charles and Pete to help me — I have Stacey and Brimmacombe, Dixon and Anderson. And four chosen N.C.Os. I must do the best with what I have.

* * *

It was night when the *Dai Nichi* sailed. The Japanese did not bother about blackouts on Singapore. The air was firmly in their control. The sea was another matter. As Lenny Brooks had correctly reasoned, the Americans had not lost all of their submarines at Pearl Harbour. Already the losses of ships were mounting.

The prisoners were not informed when the ship was to sail but there was plenty of advance notice. Apart from a great deal of to and froing between ship and shore, there was the sound of shovelling of coal which could be clearly heard through the bulkhead rust holes between their quarters and the fuel bunkers and the parties climbing to the benjo at first reported a thin column of smoke from the battered funnel and then later, as this thickened, with the breeze blowing from the stern, soot fell continually into the hold. On balance this activity heightened morale and when, at last, the hull began to throb and tremble, relief was the greater emotion, chatter increased and forecasts were carelessly cast about. Few slept at the time of departure. In any case sleep had become a shallow sort of business continually interrupted by men clumsily seeking their way through the narrow, ill-lit or unlit paths between recumbent bodies, and, to the accompaniment of curses from its owner, sooner or later stumbling over a limb or a piece of kit.

At dawn Moore called an early conference of the officers on the platform.

"We're part of a convoy of four freighters, all about the same size and as decrepit as ourselves," he told them. "We've got one old, and I'd say, very outdated destroyer to protect us. We're heading a little east of north which means that we certainly aren't going to Sumatra. And Borneo or the Phillipines are most unlikely."

"How do you work that out?" said Brimmacombe.

"Because if we were, we'd head due west until close in to Borneo and then hug the coast."

"Wouldn't that be a good reason for doing a wide sweep first? Head up north and then turn south east?"

"There are endless alternatives," Moore said. "You could even be right, Captain Brimmacombe. But I doubt it."

"Seems to me," said Brimmacombe, "it'd be a damn sight more sensible even if we're going to end up heading north. I mean, stands to reason, with all the traffic that has to be going between Singapore and Japan, the thickest packs of submarines are going to be hanging about just where we're . . . "

"Just a minute, Captain Brimmacombe," Moore interrupted politely. "If you wouldn't mind." He called: "Warrant Officer Worboys!"

"Sir!"

"Come up here, would you." And when Worboys arrived. "Worboys, I want to occupy the men while we have a discussion up here. I need a full roll of the men with their home addresses and names of next of kin. I want four copies of that roll so that when we get the chance we can distribute three of them to the other holds. Get that going, would you?" He smiled. "Within reason the more noise you make the better."

"Understood, Sir," said Worboys, saluted smartly and turned on his heel.

"That's one of the biggest problems we've got," said Moore. "Privacy. Or rather lack of it. We must try to remember to talk quietly bearing in mind that otherwise everything we say will be overheard, or worse half-overheard, and reported back with trimmings. Also I think we want as far as possible to choose our subjects with care. For example I don't think we want to overdo the submarine business."

Brimmacombe shrugged. Games and noisy, convivial drinking following games, had played an important part in the pre-war life of Freddie Brimmacombe and he had been a big man, steadily growing bigger. But the best part of a year of being prisoner had fined him down. His cheeks, which had been full, were a little hollowed and he had lost a tendency to a double chin. Nevertheless he was still easily the biggest of the five with strong thick wrists and hairy forearms. His eyes were very blue and his hair, which was almost golden in colour, had natural and very close waves. Women had found him manly and attractive.

"No good running away from realities, Moore," he responded, cheerfully enough. "Any man in this hold who says he isn't thinking now and then about how the hell he's going to get out if we stop one's a bloody liar."

"Perfectly true," said Moore. "And

that's one of the things we've got to work out. I'm merely pointing out that there are some things better not dwelt on and some things better not said at all. Anyway . . . I think our possible destination has to be either Saigon, Formosa or Japan itself."

"Why not Hong Kong?" said Stacey.

"Because I can't see why they should take us there."

"Why Saigon or Formosa then?"

"Why even Japan?" asked Anderson.

"To show us off."

"Couldn't that apply to Saigon and Formosa too?"

"Yes, Anderson, it could. But in Hong Kong they've already taken a lot of British prisoners and with all those Chinks to call on, I really can't see it's worth the risk and trouble adding us to them . . . Now. I estimate we're doing about eight knots. If this old tramp can keep that up, it means we ought to make Saigon in about three days, Formosa in about seven and Japan in about fifteen. And I think we've got to assume the worst — that it's Japan."

"If it were Hong Kong?" insisted Stacey.

"If it were . . . " Moore gave it thought. "About the same as Formosa. Seven days. Or maybe six."

"I happen to know Hong Kong," Stacey said with apparent irrelevance. "I stayed there for a couple of months shortly after I came down from Cambridge. An uncle of mine was out there at the time. You may have heard of him." He mentioned a well known diplomat and then went on as if to prove he was not being irrelevant. "They get typhoons in Hong Kong this time of year, you know, Moore. If we run into one of them we won't get to Japan in fifteen days."

"In this," said Dixon, speaking for the first time, "we won't get there at all."

Moore found Dixon puzzling. Through being in a different service and with most of his time in it spent afloat he had not really met any Battle of Britain pilots, merely run across a few on London leaves. As far as he could judge they had fitted in pretty well with the legend they had created, managing a casualness of dress the other services lacked, as often as not over-moustached, usually noisy. But Dixon didn't fit this pattern at all.

Clean shaven, his sandy hair cut short, neat, small, really rather nondescript, he could speak in a normal tone and not be heard by the curious listeners all around them. Moore probed.

"Captain Brimmacombe," he said, "was talking about the problem of how we get out if we stop a torpedo, Flight Lieutenant. Any ideas?"

"Pray?" suggested Dixon.

"Nothing better than that?"

"Not that I can think of. I suppose it depends on how quickly the ship goes down." For the first time to Moore's recollection he smiled. "Pretty fast, I imagine," he said. "How old d'you reckon she is?"

"Turn of the century?"

"And not too well serviced by the look of her."

"No."

Dixon looked upwards. The world outside the hold was a small blue square through which a hot morning sun slanted across one side of the Japanese bunks now, with many of the soldiers on deck, thinly filled. The sun was not yet high enough to pierce the hold itself.

"It depends, doesn't it," he said, "on what we're allowed to do."

"They'll be too busy trying to get off to bother with us," said Brimmacombe.

"Will they?"

"You don't think so?" said Anderson.

"I fought against them. Did you?"

"No," said Anderson. "The first Jap I saw was in Garoet. You know Garoet?" Dixon nodded. "We marched in to give ourselves up. Under Dutch orders. We must have outnumbered them twenty to one. Do you know what my job was?" He laughed, bitterly. "I was in charge of controlling the traffic. There was hardly a Jap in sight and those we did see looked scared to death. We could have taken that town over in five minutes."

"Why didn't you?" said Stacey.

"Because he was under orders," said Brimmacombe. "Like we all were. Or perhaps you weren't. You know what surprises me, Stacey? That you didn't get yourself a suit and a Panama hat and make for the British Embassy."

Moore raised a hand. "Let's get back to where this started, shall we?" he said.

"I think Flight Lieutenant Dixon's right. We sunk a troopship in the Banka Straits and it went down pretty fast but they didn't panic. And they won't if this one starts going down. As for what happens to us, that'll have been already decided. In Tokyo. There has to be a general policy on what's to be done about prisoners."

"And what do you think that is, Sir?" Anderson said.

"I imagine there are parties already detailed to stop us trying to leave the holds until all the Japs have got off first. They won't want us fighting them for the life rafts."

"A jolly outlook, Sir."

"Yes," said Moore thoughtfully. "And I'm afraid that isn't all." He nodded at the hatchway.

"You really think they'd do that, Sir?"

"No, Anderson, I shouldn't think so. But if we get dirty weather they'll have to batten down and, although it's less likely then, we could get torpedoed while we are. So that at least is something we can occupy our minds with. Working out how on earth to knock those hatch covers off again. It's not an easy thing to do from underneath."

"You just push them up," said Stacey.

"Not with a couple of wedges driven in."

"You'd need a sledgehammer," Brimmacombe said.

"Something like that," Moore agreed. "So we'd better keep our eyes open."

"You mean . . . pinch one, Sir?" said Anderson, awed.

"I mean exactly that. On an old tub like this there's bound to be all sorts of bits and pieces that might serve as crowbars. So it'd better be quietly put about that every time a man goes to the heads . . . " he smiled faintly " . . . to the benjo, he's to keep his eyes open. If he spots anything that might be useful, he's not to touch it until he gets our say so. If we had a crowbar the best place to put it mightn't be down here."

"What about light?" said Dixon.

"There probably wouldn't be any. We'd have to provide our own. There's a lot of things like that we need to think about."

"We may not have much time."

"I think we've got a day or two at least. The Japs can give air cover here. If I was a submarine commander, I think I'd look for my pickings where that's more difficult. But you're quite right. We shouldn't waste too much time. Let's assume we're torpedoed while we're battened down, or the ship doesn't sink at once and the Japs batten us down. We've got to have something to smash the hatch open with and some sort of torches. And afterwards, we've got to prevent the men panicking which will mean allowing only so many up the ladder at a time. Then, when we get out, we'll be faced with an open sea and all the ship's rafts and lifeboats gone. Anything that'll float can save lives. These planks we're standing on, the ladders the Japs use for getting to their upper berths, the berths themselves — any that can be broken loose . . . "

"I never heard such nonsense," Stacey said rather wildly. "If the ship's torpedoed we haven't a cat's chance in hell."

Moore shook his head.

"Not true," he said. "That troopship off Banka isn't the only ship I've seen go down and although I know it *has* happened, I've personally never seen one go down, however fast, without there being some survivors. Particularly when the ship's a wreck that can fall apart at the seams . . . "

"I don't agree," said Stacey, his voice beginning to rise. "If we're torpedoed, that'll be the end of it for us. All you're going through all this for is to . . . to bolster up morale. You don't believe a word of it yourself."

"Please lower your voice," said Moore patiently. "And come to the point."

"Yes," said Stacey, a little more under control. "Well, the point is this. We've put up with nearly a year of being prisoners. Come this far. This is a hole, I know. I couldn't have imagined you'd ship pigs in such conditions. But at least they're leaving us alone. But if we start rampaging about the place, trying to steal sledgehammers and crowbars and God knows what . . . and they catch us . . . and they will . . . "

"I think," interrupted Brimmacombe warningly, "you'd better shut up." He moved himself a little nearer to Stacey, calculating that it would be easy enough to hook his ankle and gave him a little push.

"I will not shut up," said Stacey petulantly. "I have as much right as you."

"You do not," said Moore. "You are a Flying Officer only. And you will do what you are ordered to. However, as you don't agree, you are personally excused."

"Personally excused!" said Stacey shrilly.

"I told you to keep your voice down. Now listen to me, Stacey, and please don't interrupt. You got yourself into the services when you didn't have to. And I think we all of us on this platform know the reason why. Having got yourself in, you can't opt out that easily. And certainly not while you're on this ship. As I said at the beginning to the men, we may be prisoners but military discipline still applies. If decisions are made which seem to me to be in the best interest of us all, then you will obey those decisions."

"It only needs someone to let the Japs know what we're up to . . . " Stacey objected.

"Yes," said Moore sternly. "It does. And if that should happen, then we shall know what to do."

"Have a Court Martial, I suppose," sneered Stacey.

Moore nodded. "As you say."

"And?"

"Sentence the culprit." He looked hard into Stacey's affronted eyes. "And don't be under any delusions, Flying Officer Stacey, as to what under the circumstances that sentence would be."

5

AN hour before there had been a heavy rainstorm, a tropical deluge which had swept down through the open hatch. The rain had fallen vertically but the forward motion of the ship had slanted it over those men in Moore's section who had taken up quarters too close to the platform. The rain had fallen without warning causing a sudden stampede amongst those affected and quarrels between them and others a little lower down who did not see why they should be pushed further into the gloom towards the rats. Moore had arbitrated with his award in the latter's favour. Outnumbered, the unfortunates had collected their soaked belongings and stumbled their way down the bauxite and out of sight. Meanwhile a few men had sought and been granted permission to strip and stand naked on the platform and others had been preparing to follow their example when as suddenly as it had started the rain had ceased. Grumbling at their bad luck the men had lain down again to sleep. The hold was lit — there was a curious inconsistency in the Japanese thinking on the extent to which darkening the hold was necessary (the stack poured out sparks interminably in any case) — and there was a slight swell on the sea causing the *Dai Nichi* to roll and the bulb on its flex to sway and throw its light briefly into areas it had not reached before. It was perhaps two in the morning and, after the hubbub caused by the rain had died away there was little talk.

Moore lay awake, listening. There were many sounds. The hum of the engines, the curious vibrating noise of the propeller which he guessed to be out of true, snorings, sleep mutterings and, from somewhere, the whimper of a man in pain. There were small scuttering noises which he guessed to be the rats and the occasional curse and slapping sound of someone who had woken to find one on his chest or investigating his belongings. Now and then a man rose, threaded his way to the platform and climbed the awesome vertical ladder. The expected, dreaded diarrhoea had started and the Japanese had been persuaded to allow men singly to the benjo. There were no sounds of the world beyond the ship except the faintest wash of the swell against her plates.

Moore lay musing on the countless nights he had spent on watch and then later as Captain on his bridge. Old and rusting though she might be, the *Dai Nichi* would yet be carving her way through a tropic sea, creaming the water with her bows, raising the phosphorescence, leaving the boiling trail behind. The tawdriness of her companions would be beautified by the night, their silhouettes rising and falling in the swell. There would be that marvellous sense of companionship, one vessel with another under a starlit sky. It was curious, he thought, how, in the camp in Java, he had thought less of the sea than of home and yet it had needed only to be afloat again, even in a stifling, stinking hold, to feel the grip of it again.

His thoughts turned to home. What time would it be in England now? Nine, ten in the morning. What day was it? With a shock he realised he did not know. The days of the week had lost significance. He tried to work it out. Monday or Tuesday, he thought, Ros would have walked Angie to school and probably be back home. Or gone straight on to the hospital. Charlie would be at his lessons. What might he be doing? Monday morning? Tuesday morning? Tuesday! What did Charlie always call Tuesday? *Black* Tuesday! Latin! That was what they started with on Tuesdays. Latin! He'd been talking about the Monday morning feeling. Oh Mondays are all right, Charlie had said, in that casual way children had of dismissing parents' problems, of using them merely as lead-ins to their own affairs which were of so much more importance. You try starting the day with Latin, Dad! It's like being served up spotted Dick for breakfast instead of egg and bacon! I mean give a chap a chance! But of course that was a year and a half ago — since his last leave. Since he'd seen Ros and the kids. They'd stayed at Torquay. It had been convenient. They'd said their goodbyes on Torquay station. Ros and Angie heading back to Cheal; Charlie to Bovey Tracey; and me to Plymouth. They'd stayed at the Grand. Pushed the boat out to celebrate his command! Ros had complained. Darling they're miserable! Only three days! I mean it's not as if there's a war out *there*! And you'll be so long. Oh blast the bloody war! She hated the war. She wouldn't have minded if she could have played a part, become a Wren or something. But what with her mother. And Angie only six. And Charlie. Well it could have been worse. If they'd moved into London as they'd so often contemplated. At least she would be safe. She and Angie in the country; Charlie in Bovey. He'd be ten now. Ten. And how old would he be when next he saw his father? It was going to be a long, slow war. They'd been allowed to go so far. They might be scruffy dwarfs but they were tenacious little buggers. They'd have to be winkled out of every island. Well, out of the ones that mattered. Not out of Java. They wouldn't bother with the Dutch East Indies. No point. Charles had got that wrong. The sensible thing was to fight them where you had to and cut them off in droves elsewhere. Draw a line on about the twentieth parallel. Well, no, that would exclude the Philippines. The Americans would want to take back the Philippines. It was a matter of pride. And bases. The trouble with Charles was that he was always such an optimist. It never had been possible to have a sensible discussion about the war with him. Wherever he was, that would be the first place to be relieved! If they ended up on Formosa, in five minutes Charles would be pointing out you could hardly have a better base from which to invade Japan. Japan. If it *was* Japan, it'd be cold in winter. He passed a hand across his chin. Might as well grow a beard again, he thought. What was it Charlie used to say? — "Here it comes! Whenever Dad pulls his chin, you know he's put the world to rights again!" Charles. Ten now! About half the age of the lad next to him. Turning half sideways, he glanced at Yates and was startled to find the look returned. They were lying very close. They had begun the night by sharing the Dutch wife. But now Yates was using his attache case as a pillow.

"That can't be very comfortable, Yates," he said.

"It's all right, Sir."

"But surely the edge of it is biting into your neck?"

"It's all right, Sir."

"Look," Moore said. "If it embarrasses you waking up and finding you're lying against me, forget it. If we do go all the way to Japan we'll probably all of us be doing that for warmth."

"It really isn't all that uncomfortable, Sir. I got used to it on the *Yoseda*. When I get sleepy I can always roll something up to make a cushion."

"You aren't sleepy?"

"I've been asleep, Sir. Anyway there's all day, isn't there?"

"Yes, Yates. All day and every day. And a lot of them to come."

"You think it's Japan, Sir?"

"Yes."

"You ever been there, Sir?"

"No."

"What sort of ship were you on, Sir?"

"Destroyer."

"Were you sunk, Sir?"

"Yes.

"Whereabouts, Sir?"

"In the Banka Straits. Know where they are, Yates?"

"They're between Sumatra and an island called Banka."

"Were you in Sumatra?"

"Yes, Sir."

"What were you doing?"

"Getting away from Singapore, Sir."

"You're R.A.F. aren't you?"

"No, Sir. Army."

"Oh." Moore was surprised. "Had you been in Singapore long?"

"Not very long, Sir. Bit of an accident I got there at all."

"How was that?"

"Well, I was taken crook, Sir. At Durban. We were on the way to the Middle East when Pearl Harbour happened. By the time I'd got better my unit had gone on."

"Diverted to Singapore?"

Yates laughed quietly. "That's what they thought. There was a mess up somewhere in the filing system. And there was this aircraft . . . a Liberator taking out some spares or something. And there was room for me . . . and a couple of others. They thought it the best thing to do with us . . . so we could rejoin our units. Only you see, Sir, our unit was in the half of the convoy that didn't get diverted."

"Well," said Moore, "it isn't the worst cock-up I've heard out here but it gets fairly close. So what happened when you got to Singapore?"

"No one wanted to know us, Sir. It was funny really."

"When exactly," asked Moore keenly, "did you land in Singapore?"

"Beginning of February."

"Just before the Japs invaded."

"Yes, Sir."

"But," Moore said, "you must have tried to get yourself attached."

"Not very hard, Sir. No one wanted us. And no one seemed to think Singapore could hold out."

"So you decided to escape."

"Yes, Sir."

"I'm not sure," said Moore, "that didn't amount to desertion."

"We weren't sure either, Sir. But there

didn't seem much sense in just staying there when we hadn't got a unit and no one wanted us in theirs just to be taken prisoner by the Japs."

"I'm still not sure it wasn't desertion," Moore said, "but I have to admit I see the logic. Anyway you got away."

"Yes."

"All three of you?"

"Yes."

"Are the others on this ship?"

"No, Sir." Yates paused. "They died."

"While you were escaping. Or later."

"While we were escaping, Sir."

"And there were only the three of you?"

"Just the three of us."

"Tell me something," Moore said. "When you got to Sumatra and joined up with others . . . is that what happened?"

Yates nodded.

"You explained all this?"

"No."

Moore sat up on one elbow, staring in the half light at his companion. "Are you telling me," he said, "that what you've just told me, you've told to no one else before?"

"Yes, Sir," said Yates.

"What did you tell them?"

"That I'd lost my memory. I was pretty bad when they found me."

"I see," said Moore. "And you've told no one since?"

"No."

"But you tell me now." He paused. "Why?"

"Because it doesn't matter."

"What do you mean?"

Yates hunched his shoulders forward expressively. It occurred to Moore that the boy was quite finely made. That his cheekbones were rather high, his chin under its days of stubble firmly rounded. But his most noteworthy feature was his eyes which were almost frighteningly defensive, the eyes of someone who had been bullied all his life. It was difficult to imagine Yates had ever enjoyed himself.

"You're talking about survival, aren't you?" Moore said.

"Why shouldn't you? You're not ill, are you?"

"Not especially, Sir."

"Say what you mean."

"I've got a touch of Happy Feet."

"Haven't we all. Anything else?"

"I've had dengue fever."

"So have ninety percent. Have you had dysentery?"

"No, Sir."

"And how long were you wandering around Sumatra?"

"Three weeks or so."

"And you haven't had dysentery. You must have the right sort of belly. Why shouldn't you survive?" But he put it more as a denial for he understood what the hunching of the shoulders indicated. Yates had no interest in surviving — he had lost the motivation. Yes, he might die, here in this joyless, damp, malodorous hold — as many men had died in Java. Lain on their patch of concrete, physically sound, or sound enough, but pathologically done for. You visited them, like a parson making his rounds, gave them a cigarette, drew them out, talked about their homes, searched for an interest. But you knew it was vain; you both knew. They had lain down to die and they would die. They were like those kinds of animals which never live long in captivity — which must have freedom. Yet Yates had lived till now.

That was the curious thing. For the men who had lain down to die had done so very early on, had lasted a matter of only months. That sort of weeding-out process had run its course.

There was something puzzling here.

"It must be particularly odd," he said, "finding yourself in a camp with a couple of thousand other men and not one of them of any unit you were part of. You haven't run across *anyone* you knew?"

"No, Sir."

"You didn't make any friends?"

"I don't make friends easily."

"How many of us do?" said Moore.

★ ★ ★

He lay awake for a long time thinking about the boy beside him. His story was of course a nonsense. The Royal Air Force did not pick up other ranks in Durban and fly them six thousand miles to Singapore; they had better things to do with their cargo space. No, that part had been pure fiction. Or perhaps not even fiction, perhaps a mere politeness. You want some sort of background of me? All right, try this for size! I know you won't find it credible but I can't be bothered to dredge up anything more convincing. But the escaping part? Yes, quite likely that was true. Yates was obviously a deserter. There had been plenty of them. Men split up from their units who knew, as all in Singapore had known, that the island would crumble. That it was rotten, crawling with Staceys, its core eaten away by years of fat living, bereft of leadership. They saw it all around them, these men like Yates — the queues at the ports, the gleaming limousines abandoned, the ships crammed with civilians heading for Java, Australia, Ceylon . . . for anywhere so long as it was distant enough from the cruel, sadistic little men who bolted your wrists together with rusty nuts and bolts. They saw it and they said to themselves: 'Why not? What's the difference between them and me? Why, just because I'm in this filthy uniform and they're all smart in their white ducks, should they be allowed to get away, helped to get away, while I've got to stay just to be killed or collared by the Japs? Fuck that for a tale! I'm off!' And down they'd gone to the water's edge in their twos and threes, and their dozens and scores, and stolen whatever was still to be stolen: junks, sampans, motor launches . . . anything that would float. And they'd headed south. And some had been clever and found the mouth of the Inderagiri River and got away along it and eventually to Padang and then Colombo; and others had been less clever and found the Banka Straits and the River Moesi and the Japanese. And as many again had found neither river, had lost their way, or foundered, or been bombed *en route*; and the sharks had eaten their remains, or the Japanese had butchered them on the little islands, or starvation and fever had killed them in the swamps.

But Yates had survived. Been one of the lucky ones. I was pretty bad when they found me, he had said. Yes, well by all accounts, so had been the majority of those who had made that escape by open boat from Singapore. Days under a blazing sun, skin burnt and blistered, hungry, short of water.

And then, at the end, the bewildering

deltas of the Sumatran rivers, brown and swollen by the torrential daily rains. He'd met a few who'd had that experience — the joy of reaching the mainland, undetected, dashed by the impossibility without a guide of knowing what next to do, where next to go, which mouth to try. The impossibility of making headway up stream against the current, the danger of overturning in crocodile-infested water, the abandonment of the craft, the hours, days, of wading through the terrible mangrove swamps, the torment of mosquitoes, the snakes, wild animals, the jungle's din, the awful loneliness. Yes, if Yates had made his escape as one of a tiny and unorganised group it was not so much surprising his companions had perished as a miracle *he* had survived. When they found him he would have been exhausted, fevered, unclear in memory, rambling in speech. No one would have bothered to question him too deeply; anyway more important things were on their minds. He would have had ample time through his recovery to hit upon the simplest of all answers — that he remembered nothing.

But there would be a penalty to pay and for months it would have been paid. A prison camp in Java in which the Japanese had found it convenient to have a quasi-Allied military control was a different thing from a jungle clearing and a motley group of fugitives still hoping to escape and uncertain of their enemy's whereabouts. Yates would have been faced with a decision: to admit he had deserted knowing he would possibly be punished, that he would certainly be ostracized and that should he survive the war there would be retribution; or to stay with his story and by so doing set himself apart from all the others who, however much or little they had done, had at least their experiences to recount in a cloistered life where conversation almost entirely relied on memories. Choosing as he had, he must have been the loneliest of men, always on his guard. And after a while, after a few months had passed, the role he had chosen would have been established. Such new friendships as were made in prison camps would have been cemented; it was no wonder Yates had lain alone on the bauxite, not surprising that the only man who had come over to talk to him had been Sutcliffe feathering his nest.

The contempt which under normal circumstances Moore would have felt for a deserter was dissipated. A popular man he had, until these last few hours, scarcely known loneliness. In the camp it had been natural for three officers off the same destroyer who had known each other so intimately, the only naval personnel amongst nearly two thousand men, to keep very much to themselves. Now, suddenly, he was almost as much alone as the youngster lying beside him. But he would not know the same long-term loneliness. In some new camp he would make new friends while the loneliness in Yates would have become part of him. Dubbed a loner, he would remain one through the long years ahead. And Moore was suddenly aware of a deep sympathy for Yates. As Commanding Officer he had a general duty towards these many scores of men tossing and turning fitfully in broken sleep but as a human being he felt towards this one, morose, unhappy boy, a very personal obligation.

6

"YES?" Sutcliffe said, looking up.
"Do you have a pack of cards?"

"Yes."

"Any chance of borrowing it?"

"No."

Hodges felt his grimy nails digging into his palms. "But you aren't using them," he argued.

"No," Sutcliffe agreed.

"Do you think that's reasonable?"

Sutcliffe looked surprised. "Eminently so," he answered.

"God!" said Hodges. "You're a bastard."

"Not at all," said Sutcliffe agreeably enough. "For one thing if I lent you the cards, they'd be bound to be spoiled in these conditions; for another you probably wouldn't give them back."

"I give you my word." Hodges was desperate. "May my mother drop dead if I don't."

"I wouldn't," said Sutcliffe smoothly,

"want to put your mother to that risk."

Hodges stared amazed. Through his spectacles Sutcliffe returned the look with little difficulty. He was seated on a groundsheet, resting by one elbow on a plump, filled kitbag. There was an opened book beside him, a manual of some sort.

"What's that!" demanded Hodges.

"Since you ask," Sutcliffe said, "it's a Japanese grammar."

"You're learning Nip?"

"Have you an objection?"

"Where d'you get it from?"

"I bought it." Sutcliffe waved an airy hand. "From someone over there. Or to be accurate, I traded cigarettes for it."

Hodges shook his head in disbelief. Sutcliffe fascinated him. His glinting spectacles, his smooth black hair, his unsoiled uniform. He made a new discovery.

"You're shaved!" he called accusingly.

"That's right."

"I suppose," sneered Hodges defensively, "you got the Nips to shave you. You're always chatting them up."

"I really do not see," said Sutcliffe,

more as if he was in an armchair in a London Club than in the hold of the *Dai Nichi Maru*, "what business it is of yours. But since you're curious, I speak to the Japanese for practice. As we are almost certainly going to Japan it could be valuable to be able to make oneself understood. I'm quite sure you'll be having a go at learning it once we get there. I shall just be rather ahead of you. As for being shaved. Yes." He put a hand up to his chin and felt it appreciatively. "For your information I shave every day."

"With what!"

"With soap and water."

"You mean you use your water ration for shaving!"

"No. I drink that. I use what's in my water bottle. Or rather I did until it ran out."

"Then I suppose you got the bloody Nips to give you some."

"I didn't have to," said Sutcliffe easily. "Nor do you. All you have to do when we're allowed to go on deck is catch it from the pipe joints. It takes a bit of time to get a cupful but at least it's hot. Didn't you notice that the pipes leak?"

"No," said Hodges. "I bloody didn't."

"Well, they do."

Hodges went back to cards.

"How much do you want for your pack?" he said.

Sutcliffe shook a dismissive head. "Sorry."

"Thought everything had its price!"

"So it has. But the price varies according to the circumstances."

"Couldn't be much bloody worse than here."

"How right you are."

Sutcliffe beamed at Hodges but in his eyes there was the hard cruelty of the man who knows he is master and enjoys it. A cold fury gripped Hodges but Sutcliffe's calm was an armour saving him from attack. Hodges turned away, stumbling back, threading a difficult path through the booby-traps. When he got back to his shared space, which was between Lenny and his friends and Yates, he said:

"Nothing bloody doing!" He was pale with anger, bitter with disappointment.

"He's got some?" said Farr, who was his friend.

"Too bloody true he has."

"Thought he wouldn't," said Lenny cheerfully. "Bang goes my chance of learning bridge."

"Let's have a look at those cards you've got," said Hodges, angry enough to be determined to find a way.

Macavoy handed them to him, a sorry-looking collection, stained, with creased or missing corners. Hodges riffled through them, lower lip stuck out. He counted them.

"Forty one," he said. "Not so bad. Only eleven short. If we could get some card or something . . ."

He broke off. Worboys descending the ladder had caught his eye. He watched Worboys all the way down.

Worboys went straight to Moore.

"Sir!"

"Yes, Worboys?"

"We'll have to do something about the latrines."

"I don't see what we can do except flush them out."

"They'll have to be done more often.

Once a day is hopeless."

"How often do you think?"

"Should be done every hour."

"They'll never agree to that." Moore got to his feet. "I'll see what I can do."

"Would you like Flying Officer Stacey to come up with you?"

It had been discovered that Stacey's Japanese was very respectable.

Moore smiled thinly. "I'll manage," he said.

He went up the ladder quickly and out of sight. Worboys turned to Yates — it was the first time he had spoken to him.

"In the meantime," he said, "would you be willing to go up with two or three others and see what you can do?"

"Yes," said Yates. "Don't worry about the others. I'll find them."

"What's your name again?" said Worboys.

"Yates, Sir."

"Thank you, Yates."

Toms caught Worboys as he crossed the platform. He was holding a list.

"Norman!"

"Yes, Harry?"

"Flies."

"What about them?"

"They've got to be cut down. We've got three men with dysentery already. It'll be all round the hold."

"It will anyway. But I agree about the flies. Have you any ideas?"

"Ten per man."

"What?

"Ten dead flies per man before they get their ration. They have to produce them!"

Worboys frowned. In spite of Moore's request, Toms was dressed as he had been at the start. Clogs, dirty shorts, curl-brimmed Australian hat. His body glistened with sweat. His black moustache was quite absurd. His eyes were organ stops. Toms was hard to take. All the same it wasn't a bad idea.

"How do they catch them?" he said.

"That's their affair."

Worboys made his mind up. "All right," he said.

Toms had a pencil; he crossed off the first item with it.

"Sing-song," he said. "Every evening."

"I don't think you'll get any support for that."

"Can't just have the bloody men lying there feeling sorry for themselves."

Worboys suddenly understood. These men were vehicles for Toms' energy and imagination. His restless, effervescent nature demanded continual activity. The men could supply it. Instinctively, without knowing he was doing it, Worboys nodded approvingly. In a barracks Toms would be counted a damn nuisance; here he was good value.

Toms misread the nod.

"Glad you agree," he said, making another mark.

"They may not," said Worboys, looking up.

"Bugger them."

Worboys smiled wearily. "I suppose we can try," he said. "What's next on the menu?"

Toms put his hands on his hips. "That Major of yours," he said.

Worboys denied any responsibility for Brimmacombe. "Not my unit."

"Know anything about him?"

"Not a lot."

"Has he seen action?"

"Not out here. Who did? Outside of Malaya and Singapore?"

"We did. At Palembang. And in Java. Damn fool wants to take the ship over."

Worboys smiled faintly. "So Rudge tells me."

"What's more he thinks you and Kerrison will lend a hand."

"Rudge," Worboys explained.

"Didn't try me."

"No, he wouldn't. Brimmacombe would have told him not to."

"Does he think all we can do is fill up aeroplanes?"

"Something of that sort. Don't tell me you want to."

"Man's a bloody fool," said Toms.

"Wasn't on your list then? . . . Anything else?"

"I was thinking we might have debates. Or lectures."

"Lectures!"

"Dixon was Battle of Britain. Moore had his own ship. Wondered what your lot might have to offer . . . "

★ ★ ★

"I'm game," said Lenny. "Coom on Mac. Coom on Nobby. Let's give lad a hand." He stood, carefully pushing himself forward with his hands on the macintosh to do so. It had been discovered that feet transferred ooze which then got into everything. The three of them were now as well organised as ever they would be. The barrow under their heads had been reduced and was covered by Mac's towel; it didn't keep their heads dry but it was softer. Nobby's knapsack, sunk into another hollow, had been pressed into service as a pad for Mac's lower calves and the buttons had been cut off the macintosh (but carefully saved). They had even made efforts at tidiness so far as their other possessions were concerned but had been largely defeated by quite incompatible shapes.

Nobby stood too, but Mac was doubtful.

"Never volunteer," he said. "Never know where it's going to get you."

"Do this time," said Lenny, grinning. "In the shit."

"Someone's got to stay and look after all this stuff."

"I will," Hodge said eagerly, leaning across.

"You stay where you are," said Lenny, holding up a hand. Hodge had terrible halitosis. Stale sweat was one thing, stale breath another.

"You think I'm going to pinch your stuff?" Hodge bridled.

"You'll be for it if you do, mate," Nobby said.

In fact there was little risk. There was an established system that when anyone went to the benjo his neighbours guarded his kit — and there were many neighbours.

"Up we go then!" said Lenny. "Any more for the Sky-lark!"

Yates had been standing silently his spare body at a slight slant because of the slope. His trunk was bare but he held a shirt (which Moore had given him) in readiness. There were half-healed blotches where his skin had blistered and his wrists were still raw where his cuffs had ridden up; he couldn't take the sun. He showed no signs of impatience while they made their minds up and no pleasure, nor relief, when Macavoy grudgingly uncoiled himself, all but losing his balance in his efforts not to soil the macintosh.

When they had gone, Hodges quickly seized the cards. Cards had an irresistible fascination for him. When he'd left Java he'd owned two packs. Somewhere *en route* to Singapore they had been stolen. It was the worst loss of his life. He shuffled them, hastily, as if he could hardly afford the time and then began to deal out hands on the ample space of the shiny macintosh. Farr, who shared his rattan mat, took not the slightest notice. Farr was not interested in cards. In any case he had a griping belly.

★ ★ ★

It was a glorious day although huge cauliflowers of cumulus lying ahead threatened rain. The sides of the ship were lined with Japanese. Many were stripped to the waist, their bodies tough and browned; most wore peaked caps and shapeless green breeches and puttees. The sea had an oily swell and was deep, deep blue. There were two ships of the small convoy ahead, but staggered, and one behind; the destroyer was fussing around, low in the water, two funnelled with raked-back masts, her ensign streaming out behind. There were two men repainting the *Dai Nichi*'s funnel from which coal smoke issued endlessly. Scattered around the deck were many prisoners holding all manner of utensils in which they sought to catch drips of hot water from the leaking joints of pipes. The Japanese took no notice of them doing this. The day was warm, the breeze was pleasant. There was the sense of holiday.

★ ★ ★

Brimmacombe had cornered Moore. They stood strategically near the benjo queue as if waiting to join it when it diminished. The Japanese did not like prisoners standing around doing nothing — but urinating was approved and catching drips of water apparently acceptable.

"Surely at least you could form a navigating team?" Brimmacombe was suggesting.

"With what?"

"You're the Navy man, not me."

"Precisely."

"I would have thought that with a little initiative . . . " Brimmacombe lost his patience. "For God's sake man, there's men with dysentery down there already."

"Are you surprised?"

"They were fit men when we left Java. We were specially selected . . . "

"And some of them were incubating it. We're all fit until we go down ill."

"Men are going to die if this voyage isn't over soon."

"They are," Moore soberly agreed.

"Isn't it better to die in a last go for freedom rather than in that putrid hold? God dammit, man, we're British, aren't we?"

"Your trouble, Freddie," said Moore. "is that you think in battalions, not individuals. Those men don't. They're thinking of themselves, every last one of them. Hoping they'll survive. Hoping that if some frightful plague sweeps through that hold — and it could — it'll pass them by."

"You wait and see," said Brimmacombe.

"You wait until it starts happening. Then they'll be in a different mood."

"From which I gather you aren't getting all that support."

"The first thing in any operation is to settle on your key men . . . "

"Oh, really, Freddie, be your age! You sound just like a schoolboy playing soldiers. Or some damn fool general hundreds of miles behind the lines shoving little wooden things around a map!"

Brimmacombe turned pink but Moore pressed on. Sutcliffe was a dangerous character; so, in another way, was Freddie Brimmacombe.

"Have you ever actually seen action?" he went on ruthlessly, knowing the answer.

"No," said Brimmacombe hotly. "And don't blame me for that."

"I don't. I'm sure you'd lead your men magnificently." Moore meant this. He was thinking that Brimmacombe would be an ideal man to play a small part in a major operation which had been carefully planned — and an absolute menace left to his own devices. His voice said Public School which signified Officer Training Corps. Brimmacombe would have done outstandingly well, ensuring himself an immediate wartime commission; then keenness during training and an enthusiastic adherence to the Rules and Regulations of Parade Ground and Mess would have guaranteed promotion. Poor Freddie Brimmacombe! All dressed up and sent out to win his D.S.O. fighting the Japanese, he had found himself diverted to Java and, almost before he'd unpacked his malaria pills, ordered by the Dutch High Command to capitulate! In a word he had been cheated. He must have felt exactly as he would if he'd been picked to play at Twickenham only to find when he got there the match was being played on another ground.

"But you'll not be one of them?" Brimmacombe said in a hurt tone.

"There are not," said Moore, "going to be *any* of them. Look at the little buggers . . . " He nodded towards the nearest Japanese. "Hundreds of 'em. And all armed to the teeth."

"I am not," said Brimmacombe,

"suggesting . . . Oh, let it go."

It was obviously best not to pursue it with Moore. The only way *he* could imagine waging war was from the bridge of his destroyer — just as Dixon could only from the cockpit of his Hurricane!

Brimmacombe was frustrated. He had parted with precious cigarettes to buy writing materials from Sutcliffe. Already he had sketched plans of each of the two decks and marked out distances. He had calculated the time required for carrying out various operations while different hieroglyphics indicated the strategic positions which had to be controlled. He knew with reasonable accuracy the number of Japanese troops in the tiers above their hold and the disposition of their officers and N.C.Os. From inspection he concluded they were only lightly armed and that their insistence on having their bayonets permanently attached to their rifles would probably prove a hindrance in such close-packed conditions. Moore's discouragement merely underlined his original belief that when it came to hand to hand fighting, there was only one service you could call on.

He turned the other cheek.

"This business of smashing open the hatches? Any new ideas?"

"Yes. Apparently there's a working party from Hold One which has to fuel the boilers. If we can grab anything useful maybe it could be dropped down the chute into the fuel bunkers and then pushed through. Shouldn't be difficult the state that bulkhead's in."

"That's a good idea," said Brimmacombe fairly.

"It was Worboys'. I think we'd better join the queue."

They moved along and joined the end of the benjo queue. Brimmacombe was angry again. Worboys was an army man — and here he was in charge of Dixon's squad and thick with Moore! He should have been under Anderson . . .

"I think tha' should keep back a bit, Sir!"

"Eh?"

"Going to be a bit rich, I reckon, Sir."

Brimmacombe realised that the benjo queue, which was about a dozen men, was shuffling backwards. As it did so it

112

disclosed two other men leaning over the ship's side doing something. In moments the mystery was explained. They were hauling up a bucket. He moved back hastily . . .

* * *

In the hold Anderson threaded his way up to join Worboys and Toms on the platform.

"Where's Commander Moore?" he asked.

Worboys explained.

"There's another man going down with it," Anderson said.

"Where?"

"C Squad. Name's Dyball. Army. We'll have to get Captain Fairfax somehow." He looked around, then called. "Stacey!"

Stacey joined them. He immediately struck his pose. One hand around the other wrist behind his back, arms pulled down.

"What is it, Anderson?"

"There's another man going down with dysentery. Something's got to be done about it."

"My dear fellow," Stacey objected. "I don't know why you haul me up here. I'm not a doctor."

"That's the point. We're pretty sure Fairfax must be on the ship . . . "

"Who's Fairfax? And how do we know?"

"Our M.O. Well, he was on the draft."

"Doesn't follow he's on the ship. Probably got left behind with the others in Singapore."

"We've got to do something, Stacey. You've got Japanese and . . . "

"No, thank you," said Stacey. "They're a funny lot. Anyway what could he do if we managed to get him down here? If he couldn't stop it spreading in Java, I don't see how he can do any better here. If I'd been listened to at the beginning. It's up to *every* man to keep the things he eats with, and the things he eats out of, clean."

"How?" Toms said disgustedly.

"I keep mine clean. They're letting us go on deck. The pipes all leak. Look at them . . . " He waved a hand encompassing one half of the hold. "What are they? A bunch of uneducated

114

louts. Call a spade a spade." There was purpose in this. Moore had given him Toms and Toms pulled no punches. Unlike Worboys who had polish, Toms was rough. A man without breeding. Yet of all the men in the hold the one who made him feel the most uncomfortable. Unable to handle him, Stacey could only retaliate vicariously. "If you think I'm going to stick my neck out for a crowd of idle clods who won't even begin to start to look after themselves, you've got another guess coming. Is that all?"

"You know," said Toms, "I don't mind you sticking it up my arse, but do you have to break it off as well?"

"I think," said Stacey disdainfully, "that is quite the most disgusting thing I have ever heard said."

"That's right," said Toms. "I've never said it to anyone else before." He turned to Anderson. "I'll see what I can do, Sir."

"And I'll come with you, Harry," Worboys said.

Anderson watched them climb the ladder, then said to Stacey who was pale with anger:

"They're a damn good pair of chaps. I only wish we had more of them."

* * *

Moore returned shortly after Yates and Lenny and his friends came down.

"Good of you to volunteer, Yates," he said. "We've got approval to sluice them three times a day."

"I'll see to it," said Yates.

Moore stared at him in surprise.

"You don't have to," he said. "Everyone can take their turn."

"I'll see to it," Yates said. And he picked up his trashy novel and began to read. Whenever Moore was with him he sat on the opened lid of his wicker case. It was only at night he shared the groundsheet. Anderson came across a little later to give him the news about Dyball.

"I hate to admit it," Moore said, "but Stacey's right. There's nothing Fairfax could do even if we could contact him. Even if he's on the ship — which I'm beginning to doubt. All we can do is try to keep the things we eat with as

116

clean as possible. We haven't a pill on the forward half. I only hope it's Saigon."

"How long before we get there, Sir?"

"About four days," Moore said.

7

ON November 3rd, 1942, six days after leaving Singapore, the *Dai Nichi Maru* dropped anchor in the Mekong River off Saigon and some seamen who had been injured when a steam pipe burst were taken ashore. The deck was soon crowded with Japanese soldiers but the prisoners, with the exception of officers who were given dispensation, were ordered to stay below.

"Are we going to dock, d'you think?" Brimmacombe demanded, eagerly enough for Moore to shoot a sharp look at him. Brimmacombe had not made any further approaches but Moore knew from the whispered conferences which had continually been taking place between Brimmacombe and a band of cronies he had gathered around him, that his scheme was not abandoned.

"I should doubt it," he answered sharply. If Brimmacombe had plans, the earlier they were doused the better.

"Oh." Brimmacombe's face had fallen. "Why d'you think that, Jim?"

"Because apart from the bauxite, which is obviously needed in Japan, all we have is human cargo. Japs and us. There'd have been preparations if either were going ashore."

It was a lie; there could be foundries in French Indo-China; the Japanese could still be intending to put some, or all, of the prisoners ashore. But it was good enough for Brimmacombe who had the comfortable mind of the man who invests all who have succeeded with ability and believes slavishly in experts. Moore was a sailor; therefore Moore should know. Besides, Brimmacombe had heard a rumour Hong Kong had been retaken.

He leaned on the rail. Now that there were no immediate decisions to be made he could enjoy the scene which, after the dreariness of the hold and days of empty sea, was fascinating with many ships swinging at anchor and numerous rowing boats and sampans creating a picture of vibrant activity. But his enjoyment was short-lived for almost at once he noticed men in gleaming white suits strolling along the distant waterfront.

"Bastards!" he hissed.

"Uhm?" said Moore who, with this taste of civilization, had become very conscious of his appearance. With his hand up to his chin, he was feeling the long stubble which had yet to soften. Shaving was, for the moment, a reasonably comfortable operation with hot water there for the taking by the exercise of a little patience; but there was no guarantee how long the Japs would put up with prisoners scurrying over their deck with mugs and cans, and a half-grown beard was more presentable than an unshaven face. Like Brimmacombe, he felt a killing envy of the white-suited men. In his whole time as prisoner he had never before felt the loss of his liberty so keenly. The combination of being able to watch ordinary men and women going freely about their business allied to being on a ship riding at anchor with all the recollections that brought, was sharply painful. But otherwise his reaction was quite different from Brimmacombe's for, in a way, the pain, reminding him so acutely that there was more to life than the joyless half existence of the past few days to which, astonishingly, he had found himself becoming accustomed, was oddly reassuring. These strange new people in their sampans, half Malay, half Chinese, this mysterious country, of which he knew nothing, beckoning from across a mere few hundred yards of water, insisted that there was more to life than being prisoner and more to life than memories.

"Bloody frogs!" he heard Brimmacombe going on. "Look at this lot! Turncoat Vichy bastards!"

Until then Moore had overlooked the possibility there could be Frenchmen here. But, even as he considered it, he saw, approaching from behind the *Dai Nichi*'s stern, the smart motor boat to which Brimmacombe was referring creaming the dirty water of the estuary and he knew at once from the attitude and the disposition of the men upon it that it was a naval launch. It came quite close. The uniformed white men manning it looked smart and very efficient; they did not even turn their heads to glance at the rusty, dirty little tramp they passed. From the stern the French tricolour was flying.

He was taken straight back to Gibraltar where, as a First Lieutenant, he had spent the early months of the war in a corvette. They had been based on the harbour and their job had been to sally out to meet the approaching convoys and help escort them through the dangerous strait and on their way to Malta and Alexandria. Sometimes there had been units of the French Navy there as well, calling in from Oran. A smart pinnace flying the tricolour would have been nothing remarkable then, merely part of the busy scene exactly as was this motor boat. And what would they be doing ashore, those men in their smart white uniforms? Why, just those things that he had done in Gibraltar. They'd be strolling towards a favourite café for their morning pernod, contemplating lunch at their favourite restaurant. There would be music. In Gib there had been guitars; here, presumably, there would be accordions. There would be girls in bathing costumes throwing back their hair and laughing, beads of water on their thighs glittering like diamonds in the sunshine. There would be cocktail parties, tennis parties, deep sea fishing parties. There would be dancing, flirting, making love. There would be all those things to do and say which free young men and women do and say with an especial enthusiasm in ports which in wartime know a special glamour. Someone had made a choice. Some general perhaps, some admiral, or some civilian — a choice to go along with Vichy. Thus the Japanese were allies and these white suited men were free. If the general, or the admiral, or the civilian, had made the other choice, there'd be no cafés, no restaurants, no girls in bathing costumes, no music, no making love — there'd be no clean white suits, no baths, no birds to listen to, no trees under which to shelter from the sun, no gardens in which to stroll, no crisp cool beds in which to lie with a perfumed woman. Instead there would be a sloping bank of stinking bauxite ore so crammed with sweating, ill-clad, unwashed bodies that you had to take care where you stretched your limbs, and there would be weevil-filled rice and a fishy-flavoured liquid and insufficient drinking water . . . and lice and crawling things, and flies and rats.

Moore could not be angry with the Frenchmen. Someone it seemed had made a wise decision and, in doing so, provided a very tangible reminder of what life had been and, more importantly, could be again.

"Would you change with them?" he asked.

Brimmacombe's blue eyes widened, glaring in disbelief. "Change with them! Change sides!"

"They didn't change sides, Freddie," Moore said gently. "The sides were changed for them. Are you sure you wouldn't change with them?"

"I certainly would not!"

"You'd rather sweat it out?"

"Yes."

"I wouldn't," said Moore.

He looked hard at Brimmacombe, studying him. The past six days had taken their toll. It was not merely that his cheeks were thinner, his face more angular. It was not that his uniform was dishevelled, his hair long and un-Brimmacombelike under his peaked cap, his shoes scuffed and unpolished. The greatest change was in his eyes and lips. His eyes were indignant, the eyes of a man obliged to treat as normal actions from which his instincts recoiled and accept things which his training utterly opposed. His lips echoed his eyes; a pre-prisoner photograph of Brimmacombe, Moore conjectured, would have shown his lips generous and rather sensual; now they were thinning, muscles were working on them which never had, and probably never would have, worked on them. Brimmacombe would end a tight-lipped man.

"I've had," said Moore, "enough degradation to last me for a lifetime. I could do without having any more of it. I want to save a few of my ideals."

"We've got a job to do," said Brimmacombe. "Those men are our responsibility."

"You're enjoying this, aren't you?" Moore said.

"It's a challenge."

Moore shook his head. "Not to me,

Freddie. Not to me." He turned to glance towards the open hatch. "And not to them. Come on, let's go down. What we're doing to those men below isn't all that different from what those Vichy French are doing to us." But he paused before returning to the hold.

"Take a good look at civilization, Freddie," he said. "It may have to last you a long, long time."

8

AFTER a few hours at anchor, the *Dai Nichi Maru* left Saigon heading north-eastwards into the South China Sea. The weather since Singapore had, apart from the occasional tropical rainstorm, been good with blue skies and sunshine to lighten the scene and light winds to ensure a comfortable sea. But now, as if to punctuate her departure, it changed for the worse. Heavy clouds drew a pall across the sky, the wind freshened, rain fell steadily and the sea grew rough.

Already conditions in the hold were becoming alarming. The dysentery was spreading fast and the queue for the benjos was continuous, requiring at least a ten-minute wait. Men who felt this too long started to use corners of the hold itself, while others, already too weak through their constant evacuations, could not manage the ladder and began to use receptacles. To keep out the rain many of the hatch planks were put in place and the stench from the combination of urine, excreta, dead rats and sweat became disgusting. As the sea roughened, so the *Dai Nichi* began to roll and sea sickness soon became an added torment. As the pitching increased some men found it difficult to stay in their chosen positions and tried to rearrange them but with men now steadily withdrawing farther from the offensive, soiled corners forcing others to edge upwards, the prisoners, already crammed, were packed even tighter and this manoeuvre became all but impossible. Everywhere was a confusion of bodies, legs, arms and heads, kitbags, attache cases, bedrolls, boots and bundles, boxes, plates, billy-cans, mugs and empty water bottles, topees, knapsacks, rolled-up blankets. To play a game of cards men had to move cautiously, edging backwards against their fellows to open up a space. They sat, excruciatingly uncomfortable, on kitbag projections and other curious seatings, canted at angles, hunched of shoulders, knees drawn up, reaching awkwardly with foreshortened movements for their cards and flicking them out again like table tennis players and all the while adjusting to the rolling and pitching of the ship. To read men had to hold their books aloft, higher than the shadows of the men above them, waiting patiently through the dark periods when the bulb swung the other way, searching hastily for their place when it swung back again. Serving food became a nightmare operation: the swinging tub had to be caught and steadied before it tipped; the men, threading their way up in file, found balance problematical and returning with their rations, one in each hand, a lottery. Raising one foot to clear a recumbent body, two plates aloft like a parson holding up the Sunday collection before the altar, swaying to the rolling of the ship, sometimes they stumbled, even fell, casting their rice and thin pink soup across another unfortunate, ruining his book, his small tobacco store, filthying his few articles still clean. Even when a return had been accomplished without mishap, the men had to corkscrew themselves down to a sitting position, somehow wedge their plates on the sloping base whilst allowing for the roll not to slop it on their bedspace, and, fumbling one-handed for their irons, avoid inconveniencing a neighbour with an equal problem.

Permission to go on deck except on a benjo visit was, for unexplained reasons, abruptly halted and, in consequence of this and the spreading dysentery, the benjo queues lengthened until there were never less than fifty men in line, some using the excuse to breathe fresher air, others in such need now that having reached the end of the line they merely returned to its beginning. It was not cold on deck, merely grey, wet and depressing. With land soon lost from sight the sea was a black-green heaving mass; threaded and crested white under a lowering sky and there was no clear horizon. Their convoy was larger now with freighters, oil tankers and two escorts; it was difficult to count its number, partly because of the *Dai Nichi*'s bucking and rolling progress, partly because the guards to the benjo queues, a novel feature, occupied themselves with rifle butts bruising the ankles and buttocks of those who showed too great an interest.

★ ★ ★

There was, once again, no light now at night and the night was very long. Occasionally a tiny flare announced that some fortunate man still supplied with matches had lit a cigarette, or, more likely, a butt. Briefly a profile or two would be illuminated and eyes caught by the glow would flash. Then the light would vanish to be replaced by a stab of red which moved mysteriously, brightened, faded. Each brightening would show the spectral outline of a head. Then the stab would vanish, pinched out by expert fingertips and, after a moment, a faint thud would indicate the closing of an airtight tin to which the end had been returned.

The rats were rampant in the dark. By day they had come to be something of a diversion and men would cheer their nimble progress along the web of a steel joist which formed part of the ceiling of the hold and if the ship pitched too suddenly and one fell on to some unfortunate individual there would be wild, if slightly hysterical, cheering while the victim slapped his hands and jumped about. But by night the rats were not cheered. They were hated. They took to lying on the chests of sleeping men and were big, and whiskery, and stank.

The night was full of sound: snores, fartings, grinding teeth, moans, mutterings, rat scutterings, coughs, whispered conversations, wet bowel explosions, the hiss of urine, the trudge of uncertain boots, the clack of clogs, cursings and apologies, the slow regular clump, pause, clump of weary feet in the Sisyphean torture of the vertical ladder, the shift of bodies, the clatter of some plate dislodged, the cries of pain, some sudden, unexpected, some regular from positions which could be pinpointed.

And, enclosing all of this was another sound, the sound of the sea against the *Dai Nichi*'s hull. The hull was rusted and time-thinned and its joints uncertain. The sea, forced its way through these joints and through suspect rivets, trickled down the inside of the hull filling the bilges beneath the bauxite. The waves thumped and the *Dai Nichi* groaned and creaked so that not for one moment of the endless night could a man, awake, forget that only thin plating lay between him and the black-green, cold and boundless sea. Each man thought of submarines and imagined how it would be: the sudden clang of the torpedo striking, the searing terror of its explosion, the dam-burst power of water pouring in, the panic, shouting, fighting for the ladder as the water rose. Of death in darkness. And, although there was no sense in it, each man shifted at the thought as if to inch nearer to the ladder and give himself a better chance.

★ ★ ★

It was on the third night Yates broke his silence.

"Sir," he said, "are you awake?"

"Yes, Yates."

"How old are you, Sir?"

Surprised, Moore told him. "Thirty-seven."

"Thirty-seven?" Yates seemed to weigh it. "I'm twenty," he said. "You could almost be my father, couldn't you, Sir?"

"I suppose I could."

133

"Have you always been in the Navy, Sir . . . You don't mind my talking?"

"Of course not. No, Yates, I was in the R.N.V.R. Royal Naval Volunteer Reserve."

"Yes, I know." There was a trace of irritation in his tone; as if he was sensitive to being told things he already knew.

"I had my own boat, you see," Moore went on.

"What sort of boat?"

"A sailing boat. Do you know anything about boats, Yates?"

"No, Sir."

"Then you did very well getting to Sumatra. Would you care to tell me about it?"

"Yes, if you like. The only thing . . . "

"I give you my word," said Moore, "nothing you tell me will ever be used in evidence against you." He could have bitten out his tongue at the absurd choice of words and added quickly: "But I can't vouch for anyone else who hears."

"It's all right, Sir," came a voice from the blackness. "Who's going to give a bugger if we get out of this."

"Not too many, I imagine."

"They'd better not," the voice insisted. "We'd have 'em all for garters. Eh, Ben?"

The invisible Ben agreed.

"Off you go then, mate," the voice encouraged.

"But quietly," Moore advised.

"That wasn't what I was going to say, Sir," Yates said. "I mean when I started. It doesn't matter. What I was going to say was that the only thing about my getting away from Singapore . . . Well I didn't get all the way to Sumatra from Singapore by myself. Well, I mean, with the other two."

"How did you get away from Singapore?" Moore asked quietly.

"Well, we were down at the waterfront, me and these other two. There were a lot of boats about, dozens and dozens of them. We'd got ourselves into civilian clothes, just shirt and trousers and got rid of all the army stuff and we'd got some supplies we'd scrounged, tinned meat and milk . . . that sort of thing. And we'd pinched a rowboat and got a tarpaulin to use as an awning and a drum we'd filled with water. Our idea was to row it out to one of the bigger boats . . . there were launches and junks and all sorts of things, just there for the taking . . . and switch to one of those. But we weren't very happy about it because none of us knew anything about boats and we knew it was a long way to wherever it was we were going to and we didn't really know that because all we had was an atlas we'd pinched from a school we'd passed. Then we saw this boat being provisioned, all in the open, and we guessed it was being got ready to get people away, civilians we thought. So we thought if we could get ourselves on that and hide somewhere . . . Well, that's what we did. We waited till it was dark and climbed on board up a ladder hung over the side. There were a couple of men but they were doing something to the engine, I think, and talking and they didn't hear us . . ."

"Just a minute," Moore said. "What sort of ship was this?"

"Oh, it was quite a big thing, Sir. Sort of thing they used for ferrying people out to some of the islands I suppose. Had a funnel and an awning at the front. Launch, I suppose you'd call it. Anyway it was big enough to have a lifeboat so we climbed into that and hid ourselves. What we thought we'd do was stay there for a couple of days and then make ourselves known when it was too late to off load us. And that's what we did. We wouldn't have if we could have helped it, though. Because we'd picked the wrong boat. It was filled with people that were thought too important to have been caught by the Japanese." Yates laughed mirthlessly. "Staff officers for example. Well we had to come out because we had no water and they didn't take long to work out what we were doing. There was this Colonel . . . oh, well, never mind."

"I can imagine," Moore said.

"Yes. Either the Japs were going to get us or once we were somewhere safe we would be dealt with as deserters. But we were lucky or at least I was. We got torpedoed. Right in the bows or I wouldn't be telling you this because I was in the stern. I think a lot were killed outright and the boat went down so quickly there wasn't time to launch the lifeboat which got all tangled up with ropes. But there were some of these life-rafts, a pile of them at the back and I don't know if they weren't fixed or if someone managed to untie them but when the boat went down one of these was floating loose and I got on to it with one of these staff officers and a couple of the crew."

"Any idea where you were?" Moore asked.

"More or less, Sir. We'd been sailing past this island called Sinkep. I think the idea was to go through the Banka Straits where you were sunk because that was the quickest way to Java."

"Then you hadn't a chance anyway. You'd have run straight into the Japanese fleet that was covering the invasion of Sumatra. Go on."

"Well we just drifted on this raft, Sir. We hadn't any food and we hadn't any water. And the first day one of the crew who'd been hurt in the explosion died and we took his clothes off him and used them to help cover us from the sun. And then the Staff Officer died, which left me and this other man. We pushed them over the side when they died. I think we were frightened we might start eating them and then afterwards we were sorry we'd pushed them over. It rained sometimes, always in the afternoon, but we hadn't anything to catch it with." He laughed as he had before. "We tried everything. We used to lie there on our backs with our mouths open. And then after it had stopped we used to wring our clothes out and let the water drip into our mouths. There wasn't any way of saving it. And then, one night, we ran aground . . . on the edge of a mangrove swamp."

"You could hardly do anything else," Moore said, "most of that part of the coast of Sumatra is a mangrove swamp."

"We thought we were lucky, running aground," Yates mused. "But we didn't think we were for very long. You ever been in a mangrove swamp, Sir?"

"Not really. I've been on the edge of them. And even in a little way. Nightmarish places."

"That's right, Sir. Stinking mud and lots of snakes — only we didn't know that then because it was dark. And all these weird mangroves like . . . well snakes too, in a way. All sticking up through the mud. There was a moon and it was quite bright. Looked like a petrified forest really. Horrible."

"And by now you were both pretty done in."

"Yes. We were all blistered by the sun and the blisters had burst and started ulcerating and we hadn't eaten for days and apart from the rain . . . well we tried drinking the water in the swamp but it was salty so we spat it out again. Anyway we explored a bit until we came to some . . . well I suppose they were trees. Might have been overgrown mangroves for all I know. They had great roots growing out of the mud and we tied the raft to them and climbed up and there was room to lie down on them they were so big. Much more room than we've got here. And we fell asleep. There were millions of mosquitoes and it was all very eerie but we got to sleep all right. And then the next morning we talked it over and decided we'd walk along the edge of the swamp until we came to something."

"Why didn't you go along the edge in

your raft, you clot?" said the voice from the darkness, as if to remind them its owner was still listening.

"We didn't have any paddles and we reckoned we might have got blown out to sea again," said Yates.

"Good thinking," Moore said. "Must have been a dreadful business wading through that muck. Or did you swim it?"

"Did both, Sir. About three or four hours we were at it and then this other fellow got bitten by something. We thought it was probably a snake, we'd seen enough of them. We couldn't do much about it but hope; we hadn't a knife or anything like that. Anyway we kept going for a bit but then he had to stop because his leg started swelling up and hurting. So we found one of these trees and I helped him get up on it . . . on the roots. And then I left him. Well, I couldn't do anything else. The only hope for both of us was to find a village or something. We'd only both of us have died if I'd sat there just keeping him company!"

"It's all right, Yates," Moore said

reassuringly. "There was nothing else you could do."

"That's right," confirmed the voice. "Push along as p.d.bloody q. as possible. Right, Ben?"

"Right," said Ben.

"All the same . . . " Yates began, then stopped. "Well, I did," he said. "Waded along as fast as I could which wasn't very fast until I couldn't go another step. Then it poured stair rods and I managed to get a bit to drink. And I pushed on. Then it got dark. And that was another night and I kept thinking about this other fellow and wondering how much his leg was swollen. But there was nothing I could do. And all next day I kept on wading and swimming. I never saw anything and I thought of turning back and trying the other way but I knew I couldn't make it. So I just kept going, slower and slower. And my back was hurting. And I was just beginning to think it didn't matter much when I heard this river ahead of me. And I thought . . . well there must be fishermen. It was about an hour before I got to it. That was the longest hour of my life. I hoped there'd be a village. But there wasn't. There wasn't anybody. But at least I could drink all I wanted. It was very muddy . . . muddy as chocolate. But still . . . And I found some roots. I don't know what they were. But I was starving. So I pulled one of them up and ate a bit of it although it tasted horrible. And then I just lay down in a sort of daze. I'd stopped thinking about the other fellow. About anything really. It was all like being in a dream. There were a lot of mosquitoes and I thought I heard animals, monkeys screeching anyway. And fish kept jumping in the river. They must have been very big ones, the noise they made. And they made big rings in the water. You could see them in the moonlight. It was beautiful really, in the moonlight. But lonely. I never realised it was possible to feel so lonely. Anyway, I finally drifted off to sleep and then some voices woke me. It was very early in the morning. No sun. Mist lowdown over everything. But there were these voices. Three men in the middle of the river. I shouted to them. They didn't hear me for a long time. I expect it was just a croak, the best I could do. But then they saw me and came across and tied up their canoe and started jabbering. Of course I didn't understand a word. Anyway to cut a long story short eventually they took me in their canoe and paddled me a long way upstream to their village which was built on stilts over the river. And gave me something to eat. Rice and I think it was fish. They didn't know a word of English. I tried at first to tell them about this other fellow. But after a bit I gave it up. I thought he must be dead anyway. And nothing would have persuaded me to go all that way back for him."

"Don't blame yourself," said Moore.

"Well, I don't really," Yates said. "I told myself I'd tried. And I did."

"So what happened?"

"Oh, I was ill, Sir. With some sort of fever. I was there about three weeks, four maybe. But I got better. And they took me farther up this river. It was called the Hari. There was a town called Djambi. We didn't get as far as that, not then. But we got to another village where there was a Malay who spoke a bit of English and a couple of Australians trying to do the same sort of thing as I was. I think they were deserters too although they wouldn't admit it. This Malay told us he'd get us up to Djambi where apparently there was an escape organisation getting men away to Padang and then India. We got to Djambi. There had been an escape organisation there." He paused, then added bitterly. "But it wasn't there any longer."

"But the Japs were," guessed Moore.

"Yes, Sir. We'd been shopped for blood money. End of story."

* * *

It was a long time before Moore was to sleep. Yates' tale had stirred many thoughts. It had been, he reflected, a curate's egg type of story, part true, part false — and much left out. But the interesting thing was that the youngster had wanted to talk of his experiences at all. He was a queer lad — a deserter whose only concern had been for himself, who had, admittedly with an excuse for doing so, left a man in a mangrove swamp to die; and yet now, having volunteered for perhaps the most noisome job imaginable, the cleaning out of the obscene, even dangerous, benjos, quietly, efficiently, uncomplainingly, picked his way around the hold three times a day, seeking, and finding, volunteers to help him with the task.

You could of course postulate that his conscience was troubling him, or believe that what he was about was building a store of mitigating credits. But Moore accepted neither of these arguments. In this fearsome hold conscience would have a poor ranking amongst the affections and present fears always vastly outweigh far-distant imaginings however grave those imaginings might be. There was something deeper, an inner yearning, perhaps for help, perhaps for self-expression, perhaps simply for companionship.

Whatever the reason, Yates had told a story which in peacetime would have ranked with the sagas of internationally known explorers. Ill-prepared, untutored, not especially selected for his aptitudes, he had survived an experience which had encompassed all the dangers which such explorers might as a maximum expect to face, to finance which large sums were raised and as a reward for facing which they were lauded, knighted, granted an at least transient notoriety. Yet Yates' experience was merely one of many, and one which any one of the men around him might have been called upon to face and would, no doubt, have faced with an equal endurance. Or else it was an experience which a dozen of the men around him might, for all he knew, be able to equal if not cap. And then again there was this voyage. It seemed unlikely that since the days of the slave ships men in such numbers would have been required to endure similar privations. Possibly, probably, perhaps even in this convoy, the Japanese transported other prisoners in equally appalling conditions but he had never, outside the slave ships, heard or read the like. The nearest comparison had been the *Altmark*, the *Graf Spee*'s auxiliary, boarded in Jösing Fiord. What a wave of patriotic fervour the releasing of those merchant seamen had enthused! Why, the releasing of those men, starved, confined, maltreated, had seemed a greater triumph than the sinking of the *Graf Spee* herself. And what had been the truth of it? The truth had been that the men had been well fed, well treated and were in such excellent health when released, that all the ambulances, pressmen, doctors, photographers, sent post-haste to meet them had to be sent home again because there was nothing much these men needed to have done for them and there was nothing much to say about them which hadn't been already said not penny plain but twopence coloured! No wonder '*The Altmark*' was the standing joke here on the *Dai Nichi*. Yet the *Altmark* would live in the annals of British history and the Dai Nichi and her like probably not rate a mention. Would those who survived this trip and the balance of their captivity and spoke of this evil, rat-infested charnel house even be believed? Was it even possible to convey the horror and the degradation of such a voyage?

He realised that he had been granted an opportunity such as few men had granted to them in a lifetime. Under normal circumstances Brimmacombe would have had an active war and afterwards would have been justified in believing he understood the behaviour of men under stress; Dixon, a Battle of Britain pilot, stating his views would have felt entitled to be believed; Stacey would have cited his wide experience, background, Varsity, Public Service; the N.C.O.s — Kerrison, Toms, Rudge and the splendid Worboys — could have talked about their many years of handling men; he, himself, who had commanded a destroyer and studied men's behaviour through long and stressful convoy service, in sudden fierce action, would have felt he knew how men really ticked when the chips were down. Now, he realised, he was just beginning to have an inkling.

Yates. Yates was a mystery. They slept like two men in a single bed, breathing each other's breath, sharing a life identical in its privations and its fears. Their backgrounds, presumably, were poles apart. He had a Lieutenant Commander's rank, his sole, and possibly only temporary, advantage — that and a few more possessions . . . a decent pair of boots, a pullover, a Dutch wife . . . He started to chuckle at the thought of his Dutch wife but was brought up short by more mysteries. Why *wouldn't* Yates share it as a pillow? And how had Yates come by the few things he owned? A wicker attache case? A pair of pyjamas? Two books? Strange items for a man cast all but naked on the Sumatran coast and then sold penniless for blood money to the Japs.

Lying motionless in the dark, hearing the thud of the waves against the plating and the various sounds of the many men around him, his nostrils filled with the stench of sweat and ordure, his limbs aching, his skin sore from the base on which he lay, a disturbing hint of discomfort in his bowels, Moore pondered. Yates was just an other rank. The man he happened to have found himself adjacent to. It could have been that North Country lad, Lenny something, or either of his two friends, or the two between — the one who loved cards and the other who did not. It could have been Sutcliffe who, most extraordinarily, could treat this hold as a market place; or Brimmacombe seething with his absurd escape plans; or Stacey still trying to justify himself; or the self-effacing hero, Dixon D.F.M. Or any of the other two hundred and fifty odd. But it was Yates. And after a week sleeping as close to him as he had slept to Ros all he knew of him was this one adventure, that he had the capacity to take on something very unpleasant and stay with it and that he had an aversion to sharing a pillow!

There are, he told himself two hundred and sixty-eight men in this hold and every one is different from the rest. All share an equal problem and each has different equipment with which to deal with it. Some will die unless the voyage ends in Formosa; even if it does, I think some will die. Others will survive. Some will die from physical weakness but some will survive in spite of physical weakness. It is what happens. If one could analyse, understand clearly across the entire spectrum of these men, how knowledgeable about the human race one would surely become. An impossible dream, of course. But if one got to know a stranger, really got to know a stranger — got to know him better than perhaps one had ever known a man or woman before? A stranger with whom one apparently had nothing at all in common: age, background, experience, interests . . . surely that would be of value? Of mutual value? This boy, this unhappy boy, friendless, guilt-ridden, disingenuous, touchy, puzzling . . . Am I to lie beside him for however many more days and nights we have to endure and know no more about him, and for that matter him about me, than when we started? Can two human beings share an experience so unreal, traumatic, awful, and at the end of it wave a vague hand in parting with nothing learnt? Am I supposed to stand on the so-called dignity of rank and refuse, if it is wanted of me and I have the capacity to give it, true warmth and comfort to a lonely, troubled boy? Am I one day to tell my wife and children that I shared long-drawn-out hell on the same groundsheet as another human being and we never gave each other comfort?

"Yates," he whispered. "Are you still awake?"

"Yes, Sir."

"Tell me about yourself. Do you mind?"

Moore felt the stirring beside him in the dark; as if the question made Yates uneasy.

"We've a long night ahead. Many long nights," Moore said encouragingly. "Talking will help to pass the time."

"I don't think anything I can tell you will be very interesting," Yates said. "I haven't done much."

"Where did you live? Before you were called up?" he asked.

"I wasn't called up. I joined up."

"I'm sorry," Moore said, "I misunderstood."

"Because I deserted in Singapore? Well, of course."

Moore thought that was probably the end of it, but after a long pause, as if Yates had wanted to think about it, he went on:

"What I mean is," he said, "you'd be entitled to think someone who deserted wouldn't have joined up in the first place, wouldn't you? But then you see I didn't want to join up. It was just that it was

153

the easiest thing to do. I didn't join up for the reasons you did. I mean I wasn't patriotic or anything like that. It was just that . . . well I was sick of Rupert Brooke!"

Moore could think of nothing to say which wouldn't have been absurdly trite.

"I suppose," Yates resumed after a pause through which he had seemingly been awaiting a comment, "you thought it was just the thing to do."

"To join up? Yes, I did."

"Would you do it again . . . Sir?"

"Yes."

"Even knowing you were going to end up in this lot?"

"Yes. I think so. But I wouldn't have ended up in this lot."

"What would you have done?"

Moore chuckled. "Gone up the Inderagiri instead of the Moesi."

"Simple, isn't it? When you know." There was another pause. "I'm going to have a smoke. D'you mind?"

"Good Lord, no!"

"Like one?" Out of embarrassment, Yates spoke almost insolently. "It's all right. I can spare it."

"No, thank you, Yates."

"Or share it?"

Moore had never shared a cigarette. Not even with Pete or Charles. They had agreed that to do so would be a concession to lowered standards.

"Yes," Moore said. "If you don't mind."

There were many small sounds before the cigarette was lit: Yates's sitting up, the rustle of his wicker basket lid, the tinny noise of his fingers scrabbling for his container, the small rasp of its opening, the reversal of these sounds. With shocking suddenness Yates's face was illuminated in the yellowish flare, his fine hair untidy across his forehead, the corners of his mouth down drawn, the shadows of his sucked in cheeks exaggerated. Moore knew how Yates lit his matches, with his fingernail.

"Don't you ever do yourself an injury? Lighting them that way?" he asked.

He received no reply. He should not have asked. A smoke was too precious to be interrupted with chat. He felt reduced. Faults he had never noticed in himself were occurring all too frequently. He lay back with his head on the Dutch wife, smelling the tobacco smoke, listening to the sea thudding against the plates. He was particularly conscious of the fact there were men all around and very close. Not so much because of the noises they made or the smell of them, but through an animal sense of contact. He wondered if it was how swarming insects felt.

"Ready?"

He saw the brilliant red of the cigarette form an arabesque.

"Take it at the bottom end," Yates said, as to a tyro. "But don't move it till I say. Okay, Sir?"

"As you say." He felt for the end below Yates fingers, his own like a pair of scissors open, closing carefully.

"Got it?"

"Yes."

"Okay."

The cigarette was dry at its end; he had been prepared for wetness. He hoped that when he returned it he would have done as well as Yates.

★ ★ ★

"Whereabouts did you live, Sir?" Yates asked when the smoking was finished.

"In the country. In a small village. It's called Cheal Down."

"Funny name."

"Yes. We just call it Cheal. It's not far from Winchester. Where did you live?"

"Oh, in London. In a hotel."

"In a hotel!"

"In Highbury. Know where Highbury is?"

"Yes. But I've never had occasion to go there. How long were you living in a hotel?"

"All my life. More or less. When I wasn't at boarding school."

"Do you know," said Moore, "I think you're the first" . . . he had nearly said *boy* . . . "the first youngster I've ever met who was brought up in an hotel. I mean outside those who have parents who spend a lot of time travelling. Or perhaps yours did?"

"Ha!" It was not a pleasing laugh. "The only travelling they did was backwards and forwards from their bedroom."

"What did your father do."

"Called himself a Captain. He was my

157

stepfather anyway."

"What d'you mean, he called himself a Captain? What sort of Captain?"

"Indian Army."

"But you don't think he had been a Captain?"

"Bloody sure he hadn't. I'm not even sure he'd been in the army at all."

"He must have talked about it?"

"Nothing you couldn't have got out of Henty. Or Kipling, maybe. He was always reading Kipling. And E. M. Forster."

"And Rupert Brooke apparently?"

"Yeh!" There was scorn in it. "Especially once the war had started."

"But your mother? Didn't she talk to you about what he'd done?"

"Don't know how much she knew. She married him after he came back."

"From India?"

"Yeh." And after a moment. "Captain Legette. That was a good name, wasn't it? I mean, impressive? Straight out of the Foreign Legion!"

"It could have been."

"Often used to wonder why he hadn't chosen the Foreign Legion rather than the Indian Army. It's much more romantic, isn't it? And you're much less likely to be tripped up."

"Was he ever tripped up?"

"No, I don't think so. Or maybe they didn't want to trip him up. I mean it wasn't much of a hotel and he was . . . well, a personality, I suppose you'd say. To them, that is."

"Tell me about the hotel."

"Waverley? Oh it was pretty big. A lot of houses in a row all joined up together and holes knocked in the walls so you could get from one bit to another. It was owned by a Mrs Latta. She had goitre. Eyes like a Pekinese. Like Warrant Officer Toms's really. There were a lot of steps up to the houses but no one ever used them. You came in the side back door. Unless you were entertaining royalty." (This was evidently a hotel witticism.) "That's where she sat. Mrs Latta. In a kind of cubbyhole. Watching everyone come in and out. She liked my stepfather. I think she felt he gave tone to Waverley. There was a sort of semi-basement lounge where everyone read the Sunday papers and it was bad form to talk before eleven. Except in a kind of whisper. And there was this big dining-room and everyone jockeying for better tables when someone died or went away. And there was a billiard-room, and a dance-room, and a card-room, and a tennis court. There was even a swimming-pool. Big round thing like a huge tyre filled with freezing cold water and about an inch of leaves."

"It was quite a place," Moore said, "your Waverley."

He felt the rustle of a shaken head. "No. Not really. It smelt of food. You know the smell, Sir? Sort of hot and thick. And a lot of the rooms were only attics. Thirty bob a week, they cost. All in. Mine was less."

"And you didn't like living there?"

"Well, in a way it was all right. Quite fascinating. It had all come together accidentally, you know. She bought a couple of houses. And then another a bit further down you couldn't get into from the first two. Then the one in the middle when it came up. I think she ended up with seven. And just knocked holes through. There were corridors everywhere, and lots of staircases. And different levels. I used to go exploring."

"Did you have others to explore with?"

"Not really. There were only a few of us kids as they used to call us. *Kids*. And we were different ages. And went to different schools."

"Boarding schools?"

"Mostly."

"What kind of people lived there?"

"In Waverley? All sorts. There were quite a lot of young chaps and girls. You know, Sir, twenties to thirties. It was cheap and they didn't have to bother and they all piled into a motor car one or other of them had and went off all laughing and joking. Six or seven of them maybe. And there were some older men who weren't married. *The Commercials* my stepfather used to call them. Some of them were funny. Funny peculiar. One particularly. There were a few old ladies living on their pensions. And then there was what they called *The Core* which was those who were married and had the best bedrooms on the first floor."

"And your parents?"

"Second floor. But front!"

Moore had the picture. A lonely boy living his holidays out in a rambling, second-rate hotel with pretensions to be something more which would have been a hot-bed of intrigue, gossip, transient affairs and jealousies. A stepfather who without the means to be one of its leading lights substituted a legend and false rank and, perhaps even, name. Every inner London suburb owned at least one such hotel to cater for the lazy, the transients, the lonely, the ill-equipped: a population by necessity inward-looking whose members seldom, if ever, mingled with those who owned their own houses, nurtured their gardens, lived what, rightly or wrongly, was termed a normal way of life. A life such as he lived with Ros. Yes, Charlie went to boarding-school and not because it was wartime . . . he would have gone to Bovey anyway . . . but because he had decided that was the best education one could give one's son. Not because he was a nuisance, something under one's feet to be endured through the holidays and thankfully parked out somewhere as soon as school term began. Only . . .

"You don't talk about your mother,

Yates," he pointed out.

"No," Yates agreed. "There isn't much to say about her."

"Is that why you joined up?" Moore asked, changing the subject. "To escape from Waverley?"

"Not really."

"From Rupert Brooke, then?"

"Well, I'd left school, you see," Yates said. "So there was a lot more time for it, wasn't there?"

"What was he like, your stepfather? To look at, I mean?"

"Captain Legette? Oh, he fitted the name all right. Tall, slim, good-looking, dark. Very dark. I always suspected he'd got a touch of the tar-brush he was always accusing others of having. He'd been to India all right. If you want to know, I reckon that's where he started."

"You think he was Anglo-Indian?"

"We used other words."

"And he was always throwing Rupert Brooke at you?"

"Blow out, you bugles, over the rich dead! There's none of these so lonely and poor of old, but, dying, has made us rarer gifts than gold!"

"I don't know that one," Moore said.

"D'you think this lot around us would share my stepfather's sentiments, Sir?" said Yates sardonically.

"Hardly, I think." said Moore.

9

WORBOYS made his way up from a dark corner of the hold.

"May I speak to you, Sir?" he asked.

Moore put down Yates's novel. "Yes, Worboys?"

"On deck if you don't mind, Sir."

"Of course."

Moore could not but be impressed by Worboys who somehow achieved the miracle of balance, dignity and cleanliness in what was daily becoming little more than a cesspit. There was, he had long appreciated, an utter dedication in Worboys which was almost religious in its content. On the whole Moore felt he had done well in his inheritance of N.C.O.s. He had rumbled Rudge but the man was a professional. Kerrison was efficiently unimaginative. Toms's repertoire of sing-songs, lectures, quizzes and the like had, after a limited initial success, mouldered on the soaking bauxite with fly-swatting its sole survivor; but the man had tried with all his heart and even now, disappointed, a little baffled, he was continually making rounds, sitting down with groups, joshing them, telling them jokes, still trying.

But Worboys had *presence* and that was an important thing. He conveyed, to a degree no other prisoner had matched, a sense that a man should have inside him qualities which nothing could destroy. Tall, long-limbed, straight, composed, self-disciplined, he was an example of inestimable value. Nor did it finish there. Practically, he contributed much, with the ideas he propounded never fatuous. With no doctor and no medicine in the hold, it had been Worboys who suggested making charcoal pellets from the dampened scrapings of burnt wood as a stomach palliative. It was Worboys who noticing some discarded tarpaulin amongst the junk which littered *Dai Nichi*'s untidy deck had dropped it into the coal bunkers thence to be smuggled through an enlarged rust hole in the bulkhead; now, with the drinking-water ration cut to half a pint a day, it was at least possible to catch some of the precious rain which poured not infrequently upon them. It was Worboys who had organised the *borrowing* of some paraffin (discovered in the store at the base of the derrick mast where Yates was allowed to keep the bucket and ropes he needed for his benjo cleaning) as fuel for the cloth torches Moore had ordered to be made. He was fertile in ideas yet intelligently economical in proposing them.

★ ★ ★

The sea was calmer now, dull grey under a level, leaden sky. The day was mild. A long line of men queued for the benjos and a few others, risking the wrath of their captors, were scurrying around catching the drips of hot water from the leaky pipes. A continual flow of prisoners alternately climbed or descended the hold ladder but very few Japanese were about and of these most were brief benjo visitors.

Moore and Worboys dared make their way to the ship's rail and lean against it.

"Yes, Worboys?" Moore said.

"We're going to have our first death soon, Sir."

"Thomas?"

"No, Sir. Glenister. I don't think he's got very long. How are we going to handle it?"

Moore stared across half a mile of water at a rusty oil tanker scarcely larger than themselves. "Depends on what our friends allow us to do, Worboys, doesn't it?" he said.

"Will you speak to them?"

"Yes, of course. I'll have Stacey interpret."

"If he agrees to."

"He'll damn well have to! He's the only one who can speak enough Japanese."

"I think Sutcliffe is getting on with it pretty well, Sir."

Moore turned his head sharply. There had been something in Worboys' tone his ear didn't fail to catch. "What exactly are you saying, Warrant Officer?" he asked very deliberately.

"I don't know if I'm saying anything, Sir," Worboys responded calmly. "But I don't really like that man and I don't really trust him. He spends altogether too much time talking to the Japs for my liking."

"He spends a lot of time talking to Flying Officer Stacey."

"Yes, he does, Sir. But . . . " Worboys broke off.

"Oh, come on, man!" said Moore almost irritably. "This isn't the time or place for niceties. If you've got something to say, then say it. And you needn't worry what you say about Stacey, anyway."

"Very well, Sir. I think Flying Officer Stacey spends time with Sutcliffe because they're of a kind and because Sutcliffe has a lot to offer. Cigarettes, books, even food. You've got to hand it to him, the man's a bloody miracle." It was the first time Moore had heard Worboys swear.

"No," said Moore. "I don't think it's quite that. Stacey is the worst kind of snob. The kind who looks down on people who haven't enjoyed his advantages from a level he likes to pretend he has attained. Sutcliffe is a mystery man who, I suspect, has had an education rather less than Stacey's but who has every intention of reaching levels far beyond Stacey's wildest dreams. I don't think they're of a kind at all but I think getting thick suits both of them. Stacey's found someone who will listen to him he doesn't think he's lowering himself to talk to and Sutcliffe is quite determined to be fluent in Japanese and Stacey, after the Nips themselves, is the best person to practise it on."

"Why is he so keen, do you think, Sir?"

"Oh, that's perfectly obvious. It'll make life easier for him as a prisoner and afterwards he won't feel his time's been entirely wasted. Don't be under any misunderstandings about our friend Sutcliffe, Worboys. I've met his type before. From the moment they wake until the moment they sleep, there's only one subject on their mind."

"Themselves."

"Correct. They'd shop their own grandmother if it helped to clinch a deal."

"Would they shop their fellow prisoners?"

Moore hesitated before replying, then nodded. "That's quite a point you have there, Worboys. He'll know where the torches and the paraffin's hidden." He thought about it. "You'd better hide it all somewhere else."

Worboys shook his head. "It's impossible to hide anything without someone seeing it being hidden . . . "

"And there's damn all new to talk about. Yes. It's a problem. Well we'll have to think of something. After all Sutcliffe isn't the only possible Judas we've got. Meantime we still haven't got anything that'll really do as a crowbar."

"We have, Sir," said Worboys quietly.

"We *have*! What, man?"

"Two lengths of pipe with flanges on them. All we need now is enough nuts and bolts to screw them together."

"Good God!" said Moore quietly. "How absolutely splendid. But who? And where?"

"Where, Sir? In the coal bunker. Only prisoners go there now. They're quite safe."

"Can we get them through?"

"We just pull them through. The hole's already made. Covered with an old piece of plate and some coal pushed over it."

"You deserve a medal, Worboys! And

if we both get through this, by God I'm going to see you get one."

"I didn't do it, Sir."

"Maybe not. But you kept it to yourself. Who got the pipes?"

Worboys smiled. "Yates. Who else?"

"Yates!" Moore slowly shook his head. "You know, Worboys," he said. "People are baffling, aren't they? Take our hold. Two hundred and sixty-eight men. You see them in uniform, lined up on parade, and what do you think?" He shrugged. "Two hundred and sixty-eight soldiers. Or airmen. Or seamen. All pretty much the same. Wanting the same things. Food. Money. Beer. Cigarettes. Sex. You look at their faces and start making judgements. That one's a mean one, you think. That one looks reliable. He's a bit weak. Might be a bully, that one. So you go on. Getting it wrong all the time. Or most of it anyway. It isn't just Sutcliffe who's a mystery, you know. We all are. We've all got our little boxes other people can't see into. That maybe we don't even know we've got ourselves. And then we get into this situation . . . which nothing could have prepared us for. And how do we react?"

"How do we, Sir?"

Moore shook his head. "I don't know, Worboys. That's the whole point. I just don't know how *we* react. I only know how *you* react, and to a degree how the other officers react. And the other N.C.O.s. And just one or two people I happen to sleep near enough to. So far as they're concerned, I've got a slight idea. Lenny, Nobby, Mac!" He chuckled. "I could give you a character study of those three that mightn't be too far out. Farr and Hodges. Same thing. And, of course, Yates! But now you show me I'm wrong even so far as he's concerned. Now you tell me he's stolen two pipes and hidden them in the coal bunkers! What the hell are the other two and hundred and fifty capable of, I wonder? God, Worboys, I'm thirty-seven years of age. Been through school, training, everything. Been a Company Director. Chairman even. Commanded a destroyer. I thought I knew how to read men. And Yates has stolen two pipes and hidden them in the coal bunkers! Yates!

Why, of all people, Yates?"

"Because," said Worboys simply, "he's the only one who could."

And suddenly Moore understood. "You!" he exclaimed "You asked him to! . . . *Yes*, of course!" He stared at the tanker again, fixing his eyes on it as it slowly pitched and rolled as if waiting for it to perform some particular manoeuvre before he spoke again.

"Funny lot, our friends, aren't they?" he said. "If you step out of the benjo line one day, it's a crack with a rifle butt; the next, you can walk about as if you own the ship and they just don't give a damn. One day you can fill your mug with water from the drips, even turn a winch stop cock on if you're quick and don't mind the risk . . . and the next you go so much as near a pipe, or look at the convoy . . . Baffling! But Yates. Yates can do what he likes now, can't he? Because they're used to him! Used to hearing him going around the hold calling for volunteers! Used to seeing him come up three times a day with three different men to clean out those filthy benjos! Used to seeing him giving instructions, taking a rest himself, strolling around . . . why shouldn't he, by God? He's just part of the furniture to them. Yet rather special. That's the way their minds work. If he picks up an old piece of pipe they've just replaced . . . well he's probably going to use it as a plunger to clear out all that bloodied diarrhoea and rags and paper, isn't he? And if he carries it somewhere . . . well there's a reason. Has to be. He's part of the furniture." He paused. And for a long time was silent. "All the same," he said, "it's a damn brave thing to do."

"Getting back to Glenister, Sir" Worboys said.

"Yes," said Moore ruefully. "We're getting casehardened, aren't we?""

"A lot died in Glodok."

"We rather thought we were escaping that, didn't we, Worboys? Going on this draft." He pulled at his young beard. "Well, he'll be buried at sea of course and I know all about handling that. But whether the Japs will let us have a burial service . . . I'll do what I can. How many men do you reckon are on the danger list as well as Glenister and Thomas?"

"About half a dozen, Sir. And more than a third have symptoms."

"Have you?"

"No, Sir. I haven't passed a stool since Singapore."

"Try and keep it that way . . . More than a third! And we aren't halfway yet. And already we're living in a sewer! But what can they do? They haven't the strength to climb the ladder . . . "

"And they haven't the speed." It was a rare interruption.

"There was a Greek philosopher," said Moore. "His name was Menander. He said something very true. 'We live not as we would but as we can.' We have to face the reality that three benjos can't cope with our problem. I doubt if twenty could. It's going to get worse and worse down there and there's nothing the bloody Japs are going to do about it. And not much they even could do about it short of putting us ashore at Formosa. We've got two hundred and sixty-eight men of whom two are dying, half a dozen are on the danger list and about eighty can't control their bowels. Already they're starting to use old tins; soon it

176

could even be the dishes they're eating from. We've got some rope, haven't we?"

"Yes, Sir." Worboys knew what was coming. He would have made the same suggestion.

"I want an area roped off. Right at the lowest, farthest point. But only those who simply cannot hang on are to use it. God! What a suggestion to have to make!"

"I was thinking, Sir," said Worboys. "If we could get permission to have the worst cases brought up on deck. Put some of the hatch covers in position, rig up an awning if we can. Then set aside one of the benjos just for them?"

Moore nodded. "That's a very good idea. A very good idea indeed." And grimly: "And it will have the advantage that when they die we won't have the same problem fetching them up from the hold as we're going to have with Thomas . . ."

"What is it, Sir?" Moore had suddenly broken off the conversation and was alert, staring at one of the escorting destroyers.

Moore did not at once reply. He was

feeling the bristling in his scalp he had always felt when his senses warned him danger threatened.

"Is something up, Sir?"

"Very up!" said Moore. A destroyer was circling hard, turning away from and ahead of the convoy, smoke pouring from her funnels. A signalling lamp was flickering from her stern. Moore looked quickly towards the *Dai Nichi*'s bridge. A man was speaking, urgently, into the voice-pipe. Another was staring out, staring at the destroyer which was heeling over with the steepness of her turn, turning back towards the convoy to head in the opposite direction. Moore looked quickly round, across the *Dai Nichi*'s deck, seeking the second destroyer. There was the sound of running footsteps. Alarm was communicated quickly. The benjo queue was breaking up, the men talking excitedly to each other; others with mugs had stopped collecting drips. The second destroyer suddenly came into view, passing in front of *Dai Nichi*'s bows. The first had finished its turn and was streaking in the reverse direction exactly parallel but beyond the convoy's limits. Of a sudden the *Dai Nichi*'s speaker system crackled into life. Staccato commands in Japanese rasped the air. Sounds of the movement of men, barked orders could be clearly heard issuing up the hatch well. Two seamen came running, racing up the short ladder towards the bridge, their boots ringing on the iron treads . . .

It was then it happened. There was a sudden, muffled thud and immediately from the rusty tanker not half a mile away a huge column of smoke and flame. The speed of the conflagration was incredible. One moment she was a small, tired oil tanker pushing her way through the grey and relatively calm sea, and almost the next, it seemed, she was a ball of flame from stem to stern as oil hurled skywards by the explosion fell back on the stricken ship bathing her in fire. And then the oil gushing from her set the sea itself on fire so that she was fire ringed by fire, all in moments, the heat from her intense even across the distance. And her end came as quickly. There was not even time for Moore to see a single member of her crew attempt escape; there was no hope of escape for a single member of her crew. Old, rusty, used up, she could not resist the sea pouring in through the huge rent in her side which had all but blown her apart. She toppled sideways, her bow reared up in the air, and she was gone, plunging out of sight leaving only the ghastly boiling, flaming oil spreading across the cold, grey sea to show where she had been and a smell of burning and a spreading stain of jet-black smoke across the sky.

Worboys spoke just two calm words: "Good God!" But his face was white as lard.

* * *

Japanese soldiers poured up from below making a tremendous commotion and lined the rail to gaze, giggling and jabbering, at the awful pyre already dropping clear astern. Moore, with Worboys, elbowed aside but otherwise ignored, stared at them, amazed that all they seemed to see in this fearful tragedy was entertainment. He did not notice an earless N.C.O. coming up from behind until the latter seized one and then another of his fellow soldiers, sent them sprawling to the deck, belaboured them with his rifle butt and kicked them where they lay. In the midst of this an officer arrived, quickly appraised the situation and started rasping orders. The N.C.O. ceased kicking his fallen comrades and turned his attention to the untidy, uncertain benjo group, screeching at them, thrusting at them with his bayonet, driving a deep wound in the leg of one unfortunate. The man cried out, blood pouring from his thigh, only to be slapped about the head by a second N.C.O. Then, while some Japanese started hastily to withdraw back to their quarters, others, apparently under instructions, came hurrying up from below and, under orders from officers (of which by now there were several), began to herd the prisoners towards the hatchway coamings. Minor pandemonium reigned while a dozen Japanese bellowing unintelligibly swung their rifle butts and the prisoners raggedly retreated and at the same time other soldiers started lifting up hatch planks from their pile and putting them in position over the hold. Moore, surprisingly unnoticed, realised the danger the prisoners were in and, ignoring the screeching Japanese, shouted orders to them to go back down. This action deflected Japanese attention towards him but in turn an officer intervened and Moore, with Worboys in attendance, was able to restore some kind of order amongst the prisoners who began to lower themselves over the coaming.

Some were pale-faced, shaken, descending in silence, others vociferous, angry, berating him. In the meantime the hatch covers (planks with iron bound ends) were now being rapidly, and efficiently, placed into position and the hatch opening steadily closed.

A distant boom behind Moore's back told him that depth charges were being hurled but there was no time for him to turn. His entire concentration was on encouraging the men to get down the ladder while it was still available; he had not the least doubt that any who failed to do so would be either bayoneted or shot. He felt appalled at assisting in condemning men to a hold from which the chances of survival should a torpedo strike must be negligible — but the alternative was *certain* death. The soldiers dropping the hatch covers into place, evidently practised in this task, were winning the dreadful race but, when there remained only two to position, an officer stepped forward ordering them to pause. Through all of this performance the soldiers had continued their screeching and their wielding of rifle butts as if no officers were present and they continued to do so until the last of the prisoners had left the deck. Only now did Moore turn towards the Japanese officer to object and was at once rewarded by a staggering blow from a rifle butt behind his legs which sent him sprawling on the rusty deck. Cold with shame and anger he staggered to his feet; but it was not a time for protest. He nodded to Worboys, standing with fists so clenched the knuckles paled. "Go down," he said.

"There's nothing we can do."

Worboys lowered himself over the coaming and went down hand over hand. Moore followed. He could see

Japanese watching him as he descended
. . . and then the final hatch cover cut
them off from sight.

* * *

Had it not been that with the hatch
covers in place light was essential if
only for the Japanese, there would
have been chaos; as it was there was
turmoil. All but the very sick prisoners
were on their feet, stumbling amongst
their gear and against each other, many
struggling to approach the ladder as if
once those arriving were down they
could escape. Curses, shouting, orders,
mingled, echoing around the iron clad
hold. Something very near to panic
reigned.

Many men have known the trepidation
of being in a convoy under attack. The
knowledge that somewhere close-by in
the deep, cold water, malevolent eyes are
watching through a periscope, deciding
on another target, strikes cold into the
heart of the most courageous. At any
instant there may come that terrible
explosion, that awful inrush. But at least

under normal circumstances (if being at risk of immediate torpedo attack can ever be called a normal circumstance), at least each individual knows that should the worst occur all that can be done to save him will be done while even the stoker deep in the bowels of a ship has a task, a duty, to occupy his mind while he shovels away with one eye on the escape ladder.

But the men in Number Two Hold of the *Dai Nichi Maru* knew no such comfort or distraction. They were not merely helpless but specifically rendered helpless by the ruthless closure of their only possible avenue of escape. Looking upwards, they could see the Us of Japanese, jabbering and gesticulating, organising themselves as best they could in preparation for the worst. But the Japanese could escape more quickly through the bulkhead doors and amidships stairs — they did not have a single iron ladder leading up to the dead-end of a battened-down hold. Nor did they have to face the probability that should escape be necessary there would be a party specifically assigned to make sure that the last to have the chance of escaping would be the prisoners.

Moore, as his feet touched the raft of planks, understood this. Having been under threat of torpedo attack for most of his time afloat, having several times been subject to actual torpedo attack, having *been* torpedoed and sunk, he was conscious that the fear he was himself experiencing had a colour to it he had never known before. It is hope which holds fear in check and the only hope left was that the *Dai Nichi* should not be singled out; should it be, then panic would surely follow. Men would crush each other to death in a mad scramble to mount the ladder for all that it led to nowhere. Those who reached the level of the waiting Japanese on the lower deck, whose discipline he guessed would hold, would be clubbed or bayoneted off the rungs to fall back on the yelling press of men below. It would be ugly; it would be hellish. He knew, that for all the business of organising a crowbar, the chance of it being of value was small.

Yet small though it was, the possibility must be milked.

"Quiet!" he shouted. "Pull yourselves together! And listen!"

They obeyed — not at once — but after the order had been shouted several times and Worboys, Toms, Brimmacombe and Anderson had elbowed their way through the shrill crowd of those most frightened who had occupied the platform.

"Move back!" Moore shouted. "Get off the platform! Off it, I say! Every one of you!"

Reluctantly they did so, cursing those immediately behind who objected to giving way. Finally the platform was cleared.

Moore steeled himself to be silent long enough to create a telling break between his speaking and the previous discord. But as he waited through what seemed endless moments a sudden dreadful drumming signified the explosion of a depth charge perilously close. In spite of his resolve Moore found himself turning his head towards the plating and knew that in doing so he had thrown away control.

Shame filled his soul; at the supreme moment he had failed . . .

And then, even as the first faint

murmuring started he was rescued.

"If," said a broad Lancashire voice from nearby, "they do that too often it could be dangerous." It was miraculous; there was even laughter.

"It could," said Moore, seizing on it gratefully. "So I wouldn't get too near the sides if I were you."

After Lenny Brooks's sally it was feeble yet it served a purpose. Tension remained but its edge was just that trifle blunted.

"Now," Moore said swiftly. "Listen to me. And no interruptions. To scotch any rumours, what has happened is that one of the tankers in the convoy has been torpedoed. Obviously we are at risk of being torpedoed too. On balance I would say that we're a less inviting target than other ships in the convoy. In fact," with a forced grin he very much doubted was convincing, "I shouldn't think any self-respecting submarine commander would consider we're worth wasting a torpedo on. We have two destroyers to protect us — a funny thing to say, I know, but that's how it is. We are closing rapidly on Formosa which means we'll shortly be under air-cover. By tomorrow we certainly will be. I think we have every chance but if the worst comes to the worst our only hope of survival is through self-control. Trampling on each other in a mad rush for the ladder is the one sure way of making sure that none of us survive. If the ship is hit and sinking, the Japanese are sufficiently well-disciplined to abandon her in an orderly fashion and in accordance with orders they will have already received. Those orders — it's no good beating about the bush — will include leaving a party behind guarding each hold for as long as they dare to do so. Until they too have left, any man who starts to climb that ladder will be shot before he's halfway up it. Make no mistake on that. They didn't put those hatch covers back for nothing. They put them back to keep us from getting under their feet while they get away. If we're hit all we can do, all we *must* do, is hang on to our courage and wait. When that waiting's over — and it'll be a long wait because there's a lot of them and they don't have that many exits themselves — when that waiting's over we too must have a plan.

We will do this. D Squad being nearest will organise the battering-ram I am going to christen Susie." (Saying this within earshot of the Japanese was a risk but one that must be taken.) "Meanwhile B Squad will start to climb the ladder with strongest men leading. Flying Officer Stacey and Warrant Officer Toms will choose the leaders. Susie will be passed up to them."

"We do have . . . Susie?" someone asked.

"We do. Never mind where. C Squad will follow B. A Squad will follow C. D Squad will follow A . . . " He broke off, as another reverberation shook the ship, and then a second in close sequence. Both were more distant. "It seems, Brooks," he jested, "they're taking notice of your concern . . . As I was saying, D Squad will follow A. Exceptions are as follows. One. Sick men will have priority. When I've finished, officers and N.C.O.s in charge of squads will organise bringing the sick as near the platform as they can. Two. N.C.O.s will follow their squads up. Officers will remain except for Flying Officer Stacey who has a good command of Japanese and may possibly be able to intercede if there's trouble up top. Three. Nothing, repeat nothing, is to be taken with you. I don't care if it's a photograph of your sweetheart or a can of M & B you've had stashed away for a rainy day, I am not going to have the escape ladder cluttered up with parcels! But what you can do . . . and don't start doing it now, we've plenty of time as we've got to allow our friends to get comfortably away. What you can, and should do, is put on all the clothes you can, within reason, manage to swim in. The China Sea isn't the Caribbean. Finally, once on deck, don't jump overboard unless she's going down very fast and you've got to get clear of the suction. You'll be far better advised, if there is the time, levering out a piece of timber from our friends' sleeping quarters to hang on to. All that's on the assumption they've locked the bulkhead doors behind them. I shall go ahead with a couple of men to check on that. If they haven't locked the doors, you get off the ladder at lower deck level which will be altogether easier. Now. Questions, please."

There were many questions. Moore did his best to answer them. Most of what he had said was pretty much nonsense; if the *Dai Nichi* was torpedoed the chances of survival were minuscule. Still the chance *was* there; as he had said to Stacey, it was rare when none survived a sinking, however swift, however spectacular. But the more important purpose was to quieten down the men, to discipline them, to give them hope. With each passing minute he felt the tension easing. It was a while now since they had felt a depth charge's shudder; some, braver spirits, were returning to their area of bauxite while others had begun complaining of their bowels . . .

★ ★ ★

Glenister lasted one day longer than expected and died on Armistice Day. His death had the effect of reducing the fear of death through sinking. Tension remained and every over-heavy slap of a wave against the *Dai Nichi*'s side, every shudder of her bows, every change of engine note or shaft vibration, caused a tightening of the shoulder muscles and ice within the stomach; but the perpetual apprehension was broken — immediate fear is a more powerful force than the most dreadful imaginings. More than this, Glenister, in his dying, brought home to every man the true gravity of his situation.

For many hours after the oil tanker had been sunk the hatch covers remained in place so that soon to visit the roped off area became a commonplace and what had been a fearful stench became not merely appalling but an unremitting reminder of the sickness which was remorselessly spreading from man to man. Glenister was dead and Thomas by his shrieks announced that he was dying. Apart from these, scattered throughout the hold were a handful already too weak to move about without assistance. To these discomforts was added the growing shortage of drinking water at a time when bodies through loss of fluid demanded more. Such as there was was eked out at fixed intervals and thinking of hot mugs of tea, or frothing pints of beer, began to become a major pre-occupation. Food, which since the earliest days of captivity had been the predominating obsession, was now demoted; the very sick had lost the desire to eat and there was now plenty for those retaining appetite. In turn the knowledge of sufficiency lessened drive and the unappetising, and absolutely unvarying diet of weevil-ridden rice and pinkish, fishy-flavoured soup completed the equation. No longer did men scrutinize the ladlefuls dished out to them to check that the rice was tightly packed into its measure; nor did they glance, as for months they had, at their neighbours' plates to satisfy themselves they had been fairly served. Apart from a few tins kept by to tempt the really ill, the small stock of rations brought aboard had been exhausted as had cigarettes except in the hands of the very crafty, very frugal or exceptionally well-disciplined.

Thus the situation had compacted to almost entirely basic limits: to breathing, eating, sleeping, drinking, urinating, defecating — to, in a word, survival. Glenister's dying underlined the word. At the beginning of the voyage he had been, it was pointed out, as fit as any.

★ ★ ★

Moore, accompanied by a reluctant Stacey, sought and made contact with the Japanese Commanding Officer who proved to be a surprisingly young, slim man of aristocratic bearing whose features were markedly less Oriental than those of his compatriots. A model of impassivity he listened in silence as Stacey interpreted (although Moore suspected no interpreter was necessary) with not one muscle of his face, nor any movement of his lips, giving the least clue as to his reactions or intentions. Through the whole of Moore's monologue he remained attentive yet relaxed, an impressive, and Moore admitted to himself, a handsome man. When the hearing was over, he enquired, through Stacey, Moore's minimum requirements for the burial of Glenister and then, without any indication as to whether or not any of these would be met, by a brief nod dismissed them to the hold.

Two hours later, some of these requirements having been already met, the Japanese interpreter leaned over the coaming and shouted that the corpse should be brought up and that twelve men would be permitted to attend.

★ ★ ★

Peter Glenister's body was hauled up from the hold by means of the pulley rig on which the food was normally lowered. Once on the deck (which was empty to receive it except for the prisoners who had pulled the rope, the Japanese interpreter and one officer) it was placed on a board and covered with a Union Jack which the Japanese provided. The twelve prisoners consisted of all five officers, of Kerrison (in whose section Glenister had lived), and of six other ranks, army and air force, including two men who had been his friends. Excepting for Moore, who had trimmed his beard as best he could, all the men had shaved and all were reasonably smartly turned out in a hotchpotch of clothes, boots and forage caps borrowed from around the hold.

Under instructions from the Japanese officer the body, on its board, was carried to the stern of the ship and laid on the deck. The prisoners were then called to attention, where upon the most astonishing procession marched out from amidships. This consisted of the Commanding Officer and eight further officers each of whom wore immaculate uniforms, dazzling white gloves and swords. Following this group, equally immaculately dressed, were four buglers and, behind them, a number of soldiers each carrying a tray laden with sweets, rice balls, fish and novel delicacies.

When the group were alongside the body, they came smartly to attention and turned to face it. The Commanding Officer nodded and the interpreter instructed Moore to read the burial service. When he had done so, the buglers were signalled to play, the Japanese officers brought their swords to the salute, the Union Jack was removed, the board raised and tipped and Glenister was slipped over the taffrail into the sea. Then, in turn, each of the Japanese officers took items from the trays and cast them after the body which floated for a few moments as it drifted astern and then quietly vanished beneath the waves.

The Japanese parry then withdrew and with no further comment nor ceremony the prisoners were curtly instructed to return below.

10

BRIMMACOMBE came to complain about Dixon. "The man's not pulling his weight, Jim. It's too bad."

"What's he supposed to do?" said Moore.

"Not just lie on his backside looking at the sky. Does he think he's still in his Spitfire?"

"Come off it, Freddie," Moore said gently. "You can do better than that."

"It's what it is all the same. The man gets a medal and thinks that's the end of it."

"I don't imagine he thinks that way at all. It takes all sorts to make a world. Maybe the kind of man who's the right material for a fighter pilot isn't the kind you'd pick for this sort of situation."

"That's balls!" said Brimmacombe, "And you know damn well it is, Jim. At least he could go round his lot occasionally. Try to cheer them up."

"He's shy," said Moore.

"Shy!" Brimmacombe was disgusted. "Then he's no bloody business being a Flight Lieutenant!"

"They made him one for what he could do in his Spitfire; not what he could do in a prison ship."

Brimmacombe shook his head. "When you accept a commission, you accept responsibility."

"And I expect he did. When he was doing those things for which he was given his commission. Look, Freddie, I'm disappointed in Dixon. I won't pretend I'm not. Half the men down here are R.A.F. He's the one genuine officer they've got and you're quite right, he's not pulling his weight. But then I don't believe he has the strength to. Not in *this* situation. In another one it might be different. Let's leave it there, shall we?"

"H'm!" said Brimmacombe expressively.

He was sharing Moore's groundsheet; taking the opportunity while Yates was on top with his second benjo party of the day. This had been delayed to allow the burials of Dyball (who had been found to be dead by the man sleeping next to him) and Thomas who had died an hour or two before. There had been another ceremony and again boards and Union Jacks had been provided; a Japanese officer had attended and thrown rice balls after the corpses. But there had been no buglers and no procession.

"You've heard the latest rumour?" Brimmacombe asked.

"Which one, Freddie?" Moore had come quite to like Brimmacombe. They had reached an unspoken agreement not to discuss plans for taking the ship over; in any case, Moore was fairly sure that, although nothing would have allowed him to admit it, Brimmacombe was losing heart. Moore felt sympathetic. The idea, however absurd it might have been, had been a brave one — as had Toms's quizzes and sing-songs. Both men had depended on enthusiasm; but enthusiasm depends on vigour — a fading asset.

"We've retaken Sumatra!"

"As well as Hong Kong?"

"It's all round the hold."

"Yes," said Moore chuckling. "I know. Any idea how it started?"

"They've got a wireless going in Hold Four."

"Must be powerful!" said Moore. "With metal all around us. And in the middle of the China Seas. How has contact been made with Hold Four?"

"Through the stokers."

"I thought they all came from Hold One."

Brimmacombe shrugged. "Well you know how it is. In Java the Americans had landed at Cheribon and were advancing on Batavia."

"There were even those who swore they had heard their guns. Curious how the human brain reacts when conditions are hard to bear, isn't it, Freddie? It builds its apprehensions into realities. The man who heard those guns had heard them; the man who first said Hong Kong had fallen has it on the best authority. Same now with Sumatra." He made an end of rumours. "How's Anderson?"

"Not good."

"I hope he makes it. There's a lot of quality in that young man."

"When should we reach Formosa?"

"Tomorrow. Even today perhaps. But there's no guarantee we'll even anchor. They may intend to run up through the Formosa Strait. In fact I hope they do. It would be a damn sight safer."

"I was wondering whether if we do dock, they'll let the sick go ashore. Think it's worth asking?"

"Anything's worth asking. But I think I know the answer in advance. Any man we can persuade them's dying might be allowed ashore. Might. On the other hand they could look on it that there's hardly an easier way of getting rid of dead prisoners than simply pitching them overboard. And so far as those who aren't as bad as that are concerned — Anderson for example — I'm not sure they won't have a better chance of survival by sticking it out until we get to Japan. I wouldn't imagine Formosa's exactly a healthy place for a sick prisoner to be."

"How many days, do you reckon? To Japan?"

"From Formosa? Four? Five? It can't be much more than . . . what? Nine hundred-odd miles? Nautical. And we're doing eight knots, I'd say. Of course it depends on the weather. Nothing to say we won't run slap bang into a typhoon."

"Could she weather one? This thing?"

"Oh, I imagine so. Tough things ships, you know, Freddie. But that's a point."

"What?"

Moore looked upwards. The hatch opening was no longer square, but a narrowed oblong. Approval had been obtained for some of the worst of the sick to be removed from the hold and housed at deck level. A crude tarpaulin awning had even been provided to shelter them from the hot sun which had broken up the previous day's cloud layer. There were about a dozen men from each of the two forward holds and two medical orderlies discovered to have been in Hold One were doing their best to give them comfort.

"Well," said Moore, "I wonder. If we hit a typhoon, we'll have to get all those chaps down again. And that won't be a picnic!"

★ ★ ★

A few yards along, Lenny Brooks was playing bridge with Nobby, Mac and Hodges. Lenny was partnering Hodges whose halitosis was, if anything, even worse but Lenny had got used to it. Because of the bauxite's slope Lenny was about a foot higher than Hodges; Nobby and Mac, being edgeways to the slope, kept shifting themselves, sometimes sitting sideways on, sometimes facing the play and resting an elbow on the bauxite or otherwise propping themselves to save tumbling over Hodges. The cards were the original forty one leavened by eleven more made of brown paper. The standard of the game was not of the highest; Nobby was finding the bidding baffling and would have much preferred solo or crib; and almost every card was by now recognisable from its back.

Lenny was declarer. With his bright, sharp mind he had picked the game up reasonably well; in the long run he would develop into a far better player than the card-maniacal Hodges. Mac had known the game; it didn't really interest him but there was nothing else to do now apart from the twice daily meal, sleeping and benjo trips. Even smoking was a memory; the last shared dog-end had been consumed.

Lenny played a card, putting it carefully down on the shiny black macintosh around which they squatted; he kept his finger on it as the ship rolled in the freshening sea. There were all manner of problems in playing. The cards were inclined to slide away and there was only room to stack all the tricks into piles and count them at the end of each hand. Muscles ached from their constriction and interruptions were frequent as one or other of them went aloft. But nevertheless they now played by the hour. Farr, shut out by Hodges' back, took not the slightest notice. He was now one of the very sick. This was another reason why the others played cards so much: from a new-born superstition. As Lenny put it: "A rubber a day keeps the squitters away!"

Nobby put down a trump.

"It's clubs, not spades!" snapped Hodges.

"'aven't any," said the gloomy Nobby.

"Yes, you have."

"No, I ain't."

"And I bloody well say you have."

Nobby searched, and found a brown-paper club lurking behind a brown-paper diamond. He made the exchange. "Sorry." He did not object that Hodges had read his hand from the reverse side of the cards. As Lenny said: "Tha' gets used to things. Even bluddy Nips!"

Lenny played the hand out and made his contract.

"Rubber!" he said enthusiastically marking the score with a pencil stub in tiny figures in last year's diary he had somehow retained. He did some arithmetic. "That makes sixty-three thousand four hundred and twenty quid you owe us." They played for a pound a point; and Hodges now refused to play with anyone but Lenny for a partner.

★ ★ ★

From where he lay, Dixon could watch the derrick mast swaying like a pendulum against the sky. About four-tenths cloud, he mused, and the weather's changing. He was observant about such things which was one of the reasons for his survival while so many were being shot down. In the air he had come alive, the freedom it offered being balm to his anxious nature. He had always yearned to fly but, the only child of a woman widowed early in her marriage and with limited means, had assumed he would never have the opportunity. When he had volunteered shortly after the outbreak of war it had been with little hope that he would be accepted; returning home, accepted, the medical examination over, with nothing more to do but await his calling-up papers, he had still been as disbelieving as a man who has just been told he has inherited a fortune from an unknown relative. He had told himself it was a foolish dream, that he would never even go solo let alone qualify; but he had been a model pupil, quiet, reliable, unshowy and not particularly popular with his contemporaries. The day he wore his wings for the first time was unquestionably the proudest and the most important day of his life.

And there was more to it. The instinct urging him had proved itself; he found in flying more even than he had imagined. Earthbound he was a limited man, uneasy, apprehensive, inclined to periods of despondency; but the moment he was in the cockpit with the ground staff fussing, passing him the harness straps, wishing him good luck, his soul took flight. He had his straps fastened so tightly that only the essential parts of his body, his hands, his feet, his head, could move; this was not for specifically thought-out reasons but because then he was truly one with his machine. He became crisp, alert, self-confident and unafraid. In a word he had found his metier. More than that he had found himself a career. For as long as they allowed him to, he would fly. What happened after that was unimportant.

Now, his head pressed back as far as was comfortably acceptable, watching the swaying derrick mast and the rebuilding clouds, reliving his Spitfire days against the Germans, his Hurricane days against the Japanese, he found a comfort few would have guessed. He possessed an advantage none of the others had: he could project himself through the hatch opening, up into the sky to a freedom not one of them had ever known. Present time to Dixon was like a shadow which would one day pass. He understood that more was expected of him than he gave but lacked the motivation even to feel guilt. He was more content than most for he knew his future. Time would pass and he would fly again; the present was merely something to be endured.

★ ★ ★

To Sutcliffe, as Moore had correctly judged, the present was not something to be endured but something to be used. Fortunately he possessed the rare quality of being a genuinely good listener while combining the ruthlessness to dismiss out of hand any subject which was not of interest with the skill to divert the speaker into other channels. And Sutcliffe's pre-war philosophy had included principles that ignorance on a subject should either be camouflaged or freely admitted and that the man who is believed to be exceptionally knowledgeable but has the candour to admit his lack of knowledge on a particular topic, is usually respected above his worth.

Sutcliffe was self-educated. A bastard who had never known his father and had come to despise a blowsy mother, he had progressed by scholarship to grammar school where he had envied all the advantages his contemporaries possessed, be they material possessions, background or human relationships. Envy is a form of praise and far from deriding those things he lacked and feverishly searching for substitutes, Sutcliffe had quite early on resolved to have them all in plenty. Nothing in his upbringing had brought out any latent softness and he felt not the least obligation to society; the world was for the rich and successful; rich and successful he would be. Although he had his blind spots, Sutcliffe was in many ways a far-sighted man and he had foreseen the glittering opportunities offered in the East. Coupling this with a belief that lack of social background would be nothing like the obstacle it would be in England, he had decided to begin his upward climb to power and riches in Hong Kong. To his disgust he had discovered that who your father was and where you had been educated mattered a great deal in a British Colony, especially one so circumscribed; he had moved down to Singapore only to find things much the same. Acutely intelligent, with a commanding personality, Sutcliffe could have done well enough but his jealousy of those around him whose flabby way of life he both despised and envied, drove him to seek short cuts; money earned illegally is usually more quickly earned and by manipulation of company matters (of which he had a brilliant understanding) Brian Sutcliffe was soon on the way to achieving his ambitions. Unfortunately, as is often the case with such men, Sutcliffe over-valued his own abilities and underwrote those of others and especially those of Chinese businessmen. This was a foolish thing to do. Certain minutes were discovered to be forged, Sutcliffe was arrested, tried, found guilty and sent to prison from which he was only released against an undertaking to join the services when the Japanese were bicycling down Malaya. Having climbed into uniform he as promptly climbed out of it again and via the payment of a handsome bribe secured a passage on, by coincidence (although they did not meet), the same ship which dropped Stacey off in Java. Climbing back into the uniform he had shrewdly not discarded, Sutcliffe once more became a member of His Majesty's Forces intending this as a stop-gap while he bought, out of the considerable funds he carried with him, a further passage to Australia or Colombo.

But in Java, Brian Sutcliffe's luck ran out. The Japanese bombed and blockaded Tjilatjap, the southern port, and the only one from which escape was latterly possible; Sutcliffe learnt a bitter lesson, that there can be times when even money cannot buy the one thing needed. He analysed his situation carefully: he could choose civilian status or be a private soldier. As to the first option, this was filled with peril. He spoke no Dutch, he had no contacts and there was nothing to guide him as to what the Japanese might do with a strange Englishman with an unlikely story wandering around the country. As to the second there was such a hopeless confusion of men from various units who had escaped in penny numbers from Sumatra and Singapore scattered around the island, that, he calculated, it would be a reasonably safe and wise thing to fall in with a large unit and be taken prisoner en bloc. He thereupon did several things: he changed his name (which had been Richard Worsley) to Brian Sutcliffe, changed (at a sickening discount) all his Malay dollars into guilders, buried his passport in a tin box in a carefully memorised location, joined a group of men from a unit other than his own (which in any case was as far as he was aware barely represented in Java) and awaited captivity.

Unlike his fellow prisoners, he had nothing in particular against the Japanese. What they were attempting seemed to him a supremely sensible thing to do provided they could succeed in it, which he rather believed they would. Biased against the Colonials he had found so irritating in Hong Kong and Malaya, and contemptuous of an army which, outnumbering the enemy three to one, had succumbed in a matter of days, he was far from convinced the Allies would triumph; a great believer in compromises when these made sense, he imagined that some sort of solution would be worked out and he resolved from his first days as prisoner to play it down the middle, to use the wasted years as best he could and to avoid, so far as possible, trouble with his captors. As regards the latter he was peculiarly well suited. The Japanese have an instinct for condescension and are impressed by strength; Sutcliffe frankly respected them and was able, through his wealth, to present an impressive image as compared with the majority of those, his considered inferiors, who shared his captivity.

For Stacey, Sutcliffe had little but contempt — but the man had family connections which one day might be useful and could, in the meantime, offer information on subjects in which Sutcliffe was poorly versed such as conduct in society, colonial politics and life in Public Schools and Universities. With little difficulty, this being anyway a favourite subject of Stacey's, he had guided him into the latter but having had half an hour of Trinity Hall, was now efficiently withdrawing with: "Incidentally, Lawrence, which came first, Oxford or Cambridge?"

"Oxford actually. I believe Merton was the first college. Peterhouse was the first at Cambridge."

"Really? And what about yours? Where did that fit in?"

"Trinity Hall? Founded in Edward the Third's reign, you know. Thirteen fifty, actually."

"Remarkable!" Sutcliffe said. "Oh by the way, I heard Toms talking to Dixon about it."

"About what?"

"Trinity Hall."

"What would either of them know about Trinity Hall?" Stacey snapped indignantly. "Toms is nothing but a lazy, ragged, filthy lout. I should think Council School was about the limit of his education, if he had any at all. As for Dixon . . . well he's D.F.M. isn't he? Speaks for itself, doesn't it?"

"Toms was saying the Raff had taken it over."

"Yes, well of course that's the sort of half truth you might expect from someone of his calibre. And the motive for saying it is about as transparent. Anything that smacks of culture is anathema to men like Toms. It makes them want to reach for their revolvers. If his kind ever had their way they'd throw the universities open to the hoi polloi. There'd be nothing worthwhile left. As for taking it over . . . yes, I had to go back to report to the Commonwealth Relations Office my views on the proper role of the Malay Police in the event of an emergency and Sir Charles had just come back from lunching at the Travellers' Club with his son who was a freshman with me and he passed on what they were doing there. Quite appalling. Marching up and down in their hobnailed boots. Singing their filthy songs. Scrawling graffiti in the lavatories. Doesn't bear thinking of. Which, of course, is why Toms brought it up."

"You mentioned Sir Charles . . . "

"Kimpton. Third baronet. He was an Old Wykehamist as well."

"And he's in the Commonwealth

Relations Office?"

"In it? My dear fellow, he *is* it!"

"Cigarette?"

"Well, that's very good of you."

Stacey accepted the cigarette casually as if it were of no particular account and leaned forward gracefully to accept a light from the match Sutcliffe struck. He made no effort to conceal his enjoyment from the jealous, hungry eyes around them, but leaned back comfortably against the kitbag they were sharing as a prop, drawing in deeply, exhaling the smoke in a long, thin stream, then letting the cigarette smoulder, wasted, held between his fingers.

"Was he ever in this part of the world. In the Far East, I mean?" Sutcliffe asked off-handedly.

"Sir Charles? Yes, I believe he was. Yes, that's right. Financial Secretary to the F.M.S. That was very early on in his career of course. Still I get the point. If when all this lot's over you'd like an introduction, I'd be only too pleased. I mean it's not what *he* can do, so much, is it? It's what those he knows might be able to. This property idea of yours . . . Do you really think Hong Kong?"

"My dear chap," Sutcliffe said. "I think everywhere."

"But Hong Kong. You don't think that China . . ."

"Frankly, no. I think the Chinese will be only too pleased to have the status quo restored. But it doesn't have to be Hong Kong."

"I should have thought Malaya, Singapore especially would be . . . well, safer?"

"Possibly."

"If you did choose Malaya, I do have useful contacts and . . . well, I could be very interested myself."

"Could you?" Sutcliffe's tone was bland. He chuckled. "But we're thinking a long way ahead, aren't we? We've got to get through this boat trip first."

Stacey felt the shiver up his spine. For a little while the ever-present fear of a torpedo attack had been diluted. It was one of the several reasons why he spent so much time with Sutcliffe; the man seemed comfortingly impervious to the apprehension which dogged his own mind.

"Presents problems, this hold, doesn't it?" went on Sutcliffe cruelly.

"I don't follow you?"

"Well, how do we get out quickly enough? Moore's battering ram would hardly be any use against the bulkhead doors."

"Wouldn't it?" said Stacey nervously.

"Good Lord, no. They're fixed with clips. They'll just shut them behind them. No." He cocked an eye at the hatch covers partly masking the opening. "It'll have to be that way out or not at all if the worst should happen. This battering ram? What exactly is it?"

"A couple of pipes bolted together."

"Well, I suppose that's about the best they could do. The Japs are no fools. They'll have taken care there's no crowbars left around. By the way, what's happened to the torches?"

"How d'you mean?"

"They've moved them. I suppose that's not a bad idea, looking at it one way. But I think *you* ought to know at least, Lawrence. Being in charge of a section."

"You're absolutely right!" said Stacey.

"I'll go and ask Moore now."

"Oh, I shouldn't do that," Sutcliffe responded easily. "Much better to wait for an opportune moment. Anyway, it's time we did some work."

And he reached for his Japanese grammar.

★ ★ ★

On the top deck Yates was helping. When the sea was calm they could work in pairs alternately, one pair hauling up the bucket, the other standing by. When the sea was rough they had to work all the time and use two buckets because the rolling of the ship swung the bucket against its side, spilling much of its contents.

Yates took the bucket and, leaning over the bulwark, hurled it at the sea, jiggled the rope to edge it, took the strain as it filled, and then with a word to Halsford who was helping, started to haul it up. At first the sea was sloping away quite steeply and the bucket well clear of the plates but by the time it was halfway up the sea had levelled and was rising and the bucket, swinging in, smashed against the side. Yates watched it carefully and, using his experience, gave a jerk at the crucial moment, saving a proportion of the loss. "All right!" he called and, hauling very swiftly, the two men brought it to deck level, and Halsford, letting go the rope, quickly came round and grabbing the handle heaved it up and over the bulwark rail and clanged it on the deck. Gardiner, one of the second pair, picked up the bucket and, with Taplin watching the rope did not get snagged, carried it the several yards to the benjo. The queue of thirty or forty men curling in a line from round the hatch coaming, across the deck and towards the wooden structure watched the proceedings in impatient silence, the head of it keeping well clear to avoid the back-spray when the bucketful was hurled at the clogged-up mass. The beginning of the queue could not be seen being masked by an awning stretched across the pair of lowered derricks and hanging down on both sides which protected the sick in the 'hospital' from the sun.

These sick, of which there were about two dozen, were lightly dressed. Some wore only soiled towels wrapped around their midriffs, some merely shirts, a few wore shorts. None were quite naked. Most were lying down on blankets laid on the hatch covers, but a few were sitting up, heads in their arms or staring dully at the sea. One had a cup of water and, dipping in a piece of rag, was patiently swabbing filth from the back of a leg, craning his neck to see what he was doing. All were unshaven and thin-faced; the bodies of some were already skeletal. Some were very ill indeed, too weak even to totter to the benjo cabin reserved for the hospital, and had to be helped by the orderlies who were kept far too busy doing this properly to attend to all their other duties such as washing these men's soiled legs which were crusted with diarrhoea, blood and mucus. Across the deck, drawing a vague, broad line from hospital to benjo was a trail of filth which Yates would thin with a bucket or two of sea water before he went back down the hold.

Halsford was, comparatively speaking,

a regular, helping Yates once on most days, but Gardiner and Taplin were strangers both to Yates and to each other. Yates had no set method of organising his team; when the time came he would get to his feet and call: "Volunteers for sanitary fatigue!" and if none came at once from close at hand would commence a perambulation, stepping unhurriedly over recumbent bodies, circling round groups, carefully testing each foothold like a climber before moving on, repeating his cry at intervals. He never failed to raise his three volunteers although the time to obtain them was sometimes lengthy. Already, for all that the sense of risk was greater down below and for all that the weather was still mild and the air cool on deck while the hold was fly-ridden, hot and its stench appalling, its curious *cosiness* was starting to make men loath to quit its false security. And, as well, a superstition was beginning to grow that the longer you were able to stay down in the hold, the greater were your chances of survival. Men openly discussed the frequency of their benjo visits, even lied, understating their number as cancer victims sometimes lie to themselves and to others about their symptoms. Moreover it was physically possible to contain the number of motions by keeping still and men worried that climbing the now fearsome ladder (from which more than one man had already fallen) and going through all the unpleasant paraphernalia of queuing for and using the benjo would start them off again.

Gardiner hurled the bucket of water down the urine trough but this had no effect at all as from the first of the cabins it was completely blocked and the water merely mingled with urine and slopped so that he jumped back in alarm to avoid it. Patiently Yates, who had been watching, yanked on the rope, drawing the bucket with an uneven drumming sound on the deck and having been through the process of refilling it, carried it himself to the farthest cabin just vacated by a hospital patient, and, accurately hurling its contents in one bolt, dislodged a great clog of filth and paper, which oozed unwillingly along the balance of the trough, flopping off its end to splatter on the ship's side as it rolled once more to starboard. The stench arising from this operation was sweetly disgusting and the air filled with filth droplets. "You see," said Yates to the watching Gardiner. "You have to start that end, work backwards through the three compartments and finish with the trough. If any of them aren't clear, you merely waste your time."

"Get on with it for Christ's sake!" pleaded one of the benjo queue. "I'll shit myself if you take much longer."

"You bloody well try doing it three times a day, mate!" said another.

"All right, all right." said the first. "I've done it. I know what it's like. I'm just letting him know, that's all, ain't I?"

Yates took no notice of this conversation. He had heard it all before just as he had brought up empty buckets, and soaked himself with spilled salt water, or soaked himself with salt water to remove the back-spray when the wind was blowing hard. His hands were raw from hauling on the rope, his knuckles bruised. He was unmoved by the compliments but he knew a quiet pride in doing what he'd taken on. He felt usefully employed and positively more self-confident as do all men efficiently engaged on an essential task. Also he counted his blessings. As Moore had surmised, he enjoyed a much greater freedom on top deck than any of the other prisoners; the Japanese now expected him to collect water from the leaking pipes, some gave him cigarettes and even the leavings of their better food; on one occasion a seaman had brought him a towel and soap and a bucket of fresh water. He did not run the benjo cleaning for these perks but appreciated them when they came. He could not, in fact, have explained why he had taken on the job (which he had done impulsively) but he would have fought against anyone else replacing him. In such manner did over one thousand men, mostly in the prime of life, drawn from all over Britain (and in a few cases from elsewhere) and drawn from all social levels; officers and other ranks, husbands, fathers, bachelors — in a word a complete cross-section of society — grapple with a predicament of quite unimaginable horror for which their previous lives, however harsh, had in no way prepared them.

Some assumed responsibilities, some sought profit in the experience and some concentrated on being untouched by it. Some anaesthetized their minds in cards. Some fantasised in projects. Some escaped into another life in books, others in dreams or recollections. Some found relief in faith; others in numbness, lying by the hour, comatose, quiescent. Some fixed their minds on visible objects: one counted the lice crawling from a piece of clothing heated by the sun, another the number of times the derrick mast swung into view while a friend was absent at the benjo. Some talked, some listened and some slept. And some, who were very ill, who had never prayed before, called on God to deliver them from the convulsions in their bodies, the blood, the diarrhoea, the awful, griping pains, the fouling of their skin, the gross indignity, the hopelessness, the fear of death too young.

This was how it was in Number Two Hold of the *Dai Nichi Maru* moving in slow convoy northwards, and how it was no doubt in the other holds. This was no doubt how it had been on other rusting, insanitary freighters crammed with prisoners the Japanese were senselessly transporting from one dreadful place of captivity to another often to be sunk *en route* with total loss of life, and this was no doubt how it would continue to be until there were no freighters left to carry on this witless folly.

11

THE *Dai Nichi*, a one island ship, constructed on the Clyde, had a straightforward layout with bottom holds and 'tween and main decks above. Steel bulkheads completely separated the holds and the two decks vertically, and in the latter there were bulkhead doors allowing access from one deck to another and into the midships superstructure which housed the bridge, living quarters, messrooms, stores, engine rooms, fuel bunkers and interconnecting stairways. The thwartships superstructure was pierced only by narrow passages (off which were located the coal chutes) along which no prisoner was allowed to pass.

Thus, so far as both prisoners and run of the mill Japanese soldiers were concerned, there was an absolute separation between the two halves of the ship. On the sole occasions when prisoners from forward had been allowed at the stern (when funerals had taken place) precautions had been taken to ensure the two groups did not mix. This meant, of course, that Moore had no way of knowing how the health of prisoners in the stern holds compared with that in the forward holds, nor how many, if any, deaths there had been.

★ ★ ★

Towards late afternoon on November 12th the *Dai Nichi* reached Takao in south-western Formosa and anchored in its exceptionally well-protected land-locked harbour. With forward movement ceased and the harbour sheltered from all breeze the hold temperature rose sharply. Moore sought permission for the men to be allowed on deck. This was at first refused but after twenty-four hours (during which two more men died) it was granted. Yet, except for short periods, the majority remained below.

"Curious, isn't it?" Moore said to Brimmacombe. "It's become home to them."

Brimmacombe stared moodily at the surrounding land. "Lord, what I'd give to get ashore!" he said. But there was no mention of escape; Brimmacombe's project had finally foundered on the bedrock of reality.

"You may do for all we know." Moore nodded to the distant quay. "There's a lot of activity going on." And even as he spoke he noticed a lighter pulling out and heading towards them.

"By God, I hope that's for us," Brimmacombe said with feeling. And then, abruptly: "You know Dixon's gone down with it?" Moore nodded. "Come on like an express train in his case," Brimmacombe continued, almost with relish: "Odd, isn't it, how differently it takes people. How about you, Jim? You okay still?"

"Managing," Moore said.

"Managing?"

"If you must have the details, six times today. That isn't bad."

"It isn't good."

"Well considering," Moore answered grimly, "that some of those poor devils are up to every ten minutes which, according to my arithmetic, is two hundred and forty times a day, it isn't bad."

232

"No one lasts at that rate."

"No. They pass out everything — including themselves."

"It's the ghastly hiccups that get me. Why do they get hiccups?"

"Dehydration."

"Is that it? — Yes, makes sense. Especially in this heat: on half a pint a day. And the bastards know it's going on. And do bugger all! Absolutely bugger all!"

Moore looked at Brimmacombe who had given up wearing his cap — presumably to protect it from the bauxite. How different a man he was from the spruce blustering Major of that first hour in the hold. For all his efforts, his uniform was stained by the bauxite and an attempt to have some amateur cut his hair had misfired leaving him with a mat rather perched on a too-shorn scalp. But the greater difference was his manner. He had matured astonishingly considering it was still only twenty-two days since he had left Java and his eyes now held the disturbing look of pain and indignation common to many of the prisoners.

"You know," Moore said, "that they've

had deaths themselves?"

"It *is* heading this way, that lighter," Brimmacombe responded.

Moore smiled. "That's exactly how they feel about us," he said.

"They'll pay for this," Brimmacombe said. "If I get through this lot, I'll make it my business to ferret out who organised this death-ship if it's the last damn thing I do."

"You won't, you know," said Moore. "You'll be so grateful to be able to soak yourself in a nice hot bath, to wear clean linen, to pour yourself a drink, to order what you want to eat, to listen to music, talk to a woman, watch a play ... My God, how we took our lives for granted! D'you know one of the things I miss most of all, Freddie? The feel of drying my body on a freshly laundered bath towel. You know, one of those thick rough ones. The kind you find in a golf-club locker-room but never at home. Isn't that a curious thing to miss?" For a moment he thought of Ros, and the perfumed warmth of their bathroom, and the soft, smoother, matching towels she always chose. "In any case," he went on, "you wouldn't get near whoever it was who organised this trip. It was probably some movement sergeant in an office in Singapore who'll have long since been posted to Borneo and died of cholera."

"There have to be records," said Brimmacombe stubbornly.

"Do there? Easy things to destroy, you know."

"*We* will be the record then. All those of us who manage to survive. And that'll be enough."

Moore shook his head. "They won't believe you. You couldn't put it over, Freddie. None of us could. Not what it was really like." He chuckled. "I say, old boy," he mimed, "you did have a rough time, didn't you? Reminds me of what it was like down in our Anderson shelter when that bomb landed just along the road and someone knocked the jerry over."

"There's bound to be a war crimes court."

"Oh, yes, Freddie. Bound to be. They'll collar one or two. Tojo and Takahashi and a few of the more important ones. But this fellow . . . Fujito or whatever his name is — the one who was in charge of that fancy-dress funeral, which, mind you, I appreciated — they won't bother with small fry like that. They won't bother with the *Dai Nichi Maru*. Even if she doesn't get torpedoed or doesn't fall apart of her own accord before the war is over, all they'll do is change her name and you'll never hear of her again. This trip will not have happened. Not this trip nor any other like it. *We'll* talk about it. For a year or two when the war is over, we'll meet regularly on the anniversary of the day we boarded her. You and me and Dixon and Anderson if they survive. Even Stacey. Why not? We'll meet for a few years in a row and go through all the do-you-remember stuff. But you know what, Freddie? We won't even believe it ourselves. We just will not believe it. And after a bit the reunions will fizzle out, like they always do. Because we'll have turned our attention to far more important things. To our careers, to our wives, our children, grandchildren. To our mortgages, and our golf handicaps, and whether Arsenal will win the F.A. Cup again."

"Well, I don't agree," said Brimmacombe. "There are a thousand men on this ship . . ."

"Who, like you, will be thinking about soaking in a tub and getting round a whacking great steak and chips. How about that? A good steak and chips washed down in Guinness! Come over to Dublin with me when the war is over. I know . . ."

"I'll join you in Dublin when I've seen justice done. And not before. There!" Brimmacombe thrust out a massive hand. "Shake hands on that!"

And Moore realised what had happened. That the abandonment of the escape project had left a vacuum. Really, he mused, the man's quite like Toms!

"All right, Freddie," he said, taking his hand. "I'll leave you to decide. And if there's any help I can give . . . if you find someone who would like corroborating evidence, you can rely on me."

"We *will* meet again, when it's all over? We will, won't we?" said Brimmacombe with a sudden boyish eagerness which warmed Moore's heart.

"Oh, yes," Moore answered. "We'll

meet again. We'll need to. Because we'll have shared something that other people would never understand. And we'll want to talk about it. Not at first. There'll be too many other things to do. But later. When things have slowed. When we've got time. When we've retired perhaps. Then we'll want to talk about it. Then we'll want to meet again." He leaned over the bulwark rail to take a better look at the lighter which was drawing up alongside. "Well, Freddie," he said. "Stay close. Maybe that's come to take us off. She's certainly come for some."

"What makes you so sure?"

"Because her deck is clear. She's not bringing cargo; she's come to collect it. And if it were the Japs, they'd have been getting ready."

"Do you think we'd better go down? Get our kit together?"

"I think," said Moore, "we ought to be on our toes to do just that. But first, I want to see . . . "

He had no time to finish. Stacey was of a sudden at his side. "Jim!"

"Yes, Lawrence?"

"Ten sick men can go ashore."

"How d'you know?"

"Fujimoto says so."

"Where is he?"

"I don't know. I didn't see him."

"How d'you know then?"

"Sutcliffe."

"Sutcliffe?! What the devil has Sutcliffe got to do with it?"

"He was taken along to see him."

"Taken along to see . . . Sutcliffe! I don't believe it. Where is he?"

"Back in the hold."

Moore turned to Brimmacombe. "Freddie! Would you mind going and fetching me Sutcliffe. Quickly. I'll go and have a word with the orderlies. Find out which are the worst. Ten! Are they mad? We've got two dead already . . . "

"Five," said Stacey.

"Five?"

"Philtrip's just died. And Number One hold's bringing up two more."

Moore closed his eyes in pain. "God," he said. "When's there going to be an end to it?" He opened his eyes again; they were filled with anger. "And the bastards say we can send ten men ashore! As if . . . " He broke off "Stay here," he ordered. "Wait for Freddie."

He quickly picked his way to the hospital. The deck was burning hot, there was an oppressive clamminess in the air and not a breath of wind. The hospital sick had been collected more tightly together but even so for some there was no protection; they had been given insufficient tarpaulins to protect them all. He called to one of the orderlies: "Laverack!" The man came over. "It is Laverack, isn't it?"

"Yes, Sir."

"How many . . . " Moore nodded his head. "How many are you looking after?"

"Twenty-eight, Sir. Sorry, twenty-seven. Crocker died about ten minutes ago."

Crocker had died ten minutes ago and he had been talking about steak and chips and Guinness with Brimmacombe and it hadn't been worth Laverack's time to come across to tell him.

"Listen," he said. "I've heard that we can send ten sick men ashore. Could you . . . " He hesitated. "Could you pick ten out?"

"Which ten?" said Laverack, brutally. "They're all going to die."

Moore stared at the men on the hatch covers. At their soiled bodies lathered with sweat. Even as he watched one of them cried out and the second orderly called: "Laverack!" and Laverack went quickly across and together they raised the man easily, helping him up by lifting him under his armpits, extricating him from the crowded, emaciated bodies amongst which he had lain, hauling him out. The man had no strength. He made no attempt to walk. The orderlies pulled him like a half-empty sack across the deck towards the benjo, his feet slithering along behind him. He let out a sudden bloodcurdling shriek which stopped the orderlies. The other men on the hatch covers took little notice. The shriek stopped as abruptly as it had begun. The man sobbed. From between his legs flowed a vile slime — greenish, bloody. The orderlies made a wheel, hauling the man back. They put him on the hatch covers, lowering him on to his shrunken buttocks. His filthy shanks were horribly emaciated. The man fell back, turned his head sideways as if he were searching for a pillow. The second orderly fetched a bucket and vaguely swabbed the man's anus area with a soiled rag. The benjo queue looked away, not wanting to see.

Laverack came back to Moore.

"Is he one of the ten?" he asked with hatred.

"He's going to die, isn't he?" said Moore.

"They're all going to die."

"No," said Moore, "they're not. Pick out ten. The fittest ten. Do you understand me, man! The fittest."

"Pick 'em out yourself, Sir," said Laverack. "I'm not having that on my conscience."

* * *

Sutcliffe was waiting with Stacey and Brimmacombe. Staring at him, Moore made a terrible discovery. That he had never loathed any man so much as he loathed Sutcliffe at that moment. He stood, Sutcliffe, relaxed, his black hair smooth and tidy, his spectacles glinting in the sun. He was well turned out.

He seemed astoundingly unchanged in manner or appearance.

"Is that right?" Moore demanded angrily. "That you've been with Fujito?"

"Fujimoto actually. Yes."

"How did that come about?"

"I was sent for."

"By who?"

"The interpreter. O'Hana."

"Why?"

Sutcliffe shrugged insolently. "I was talking to some of the troops, practising my Japanese, and apparently Fujimoto saw me from the bridge."

Moore glared at Sutcliffe. "They give you food, don't they?" he accused him.

"When they have food over. Sir."

"What do you talk to them about?"

Sutcliffe grinned. "Women," he said. "*Chimbo genki*. That sort of thing."

"What does that mean? What you just said?"

Sutcliffe's heavy eyebrows raised. "That you've got a rather useful penis. Sir." Moore could have struck him.

"And I gather," he managed ironically, "that Fujimoto volunteered we could send ten sick ashore."

"Not exactly, Sir. I suggested it. Not ten. Just the sick."

"Did you," said Moore sarcastically, "talk to him first about the usefulness of *his* penis?"

Sutcliffe merely smiled.

"What did he want you for?" demanded Moore.

"To tell me he was our father and our mother. And that he was sorry that we were so uncomfortable but that the men who died had become honourable by dying."

"He told you that in Japanese!"

"O'Hana translated. But I gathered most of it."

"I don't believe you," Moore said.

Sutcliffe shrugged. "Will that be all then, Sir?" he said.

"For the present, yes . . . No! Come back!" Sutcliffe had already turned away.

"Yes, Sir?" He conveyed surprise.

"Didn't he ask you any questions?"

"Questions?"

"I said questions!"

Sutcliffe nodded. "Since you ask, yes. He asked me if I smoked." He put a hand to his pocket and pulled out a packet of cigarettes. "Would you care for a cigarette, Sir? Only Japanese, I'm afraid."

Moore's eyes blazed with anger. He grabbed the packet of cigarettes from Sutcliffe and hurled it into the sea. Sutcliffe blinked. For a moment his eyes were very hard; then the control was totally restored.

"Well," he said, "I would have thought that rather an extravagant thing to do. Particularly with so many sick men who might have enjoyed a smoke."

"Get out!" said Moore.

"Yes, Sir." Sutcliffe saluted in the American fashion and crossing to the coaming lowered himself down into the hold.

"Damn!" Moore said. "What an exhibition."

"I think you did well," said Brimmacombe. "I wouldn't have thrown his cigarettes. I'd have thrown *him*!"

Stacey was looking at the small green packet, a fortune floating off in the tide.

"We'll talk about it later," Moore said. "I'm going to see that bloody Jap."

"I'll go," said Stacey. And when Moore stared at him amazed, explained: "As he doesn't speak English, or at any rate pretends not to speak English, it's not much good you going, is it, Jim?"

"I'll find O'Hana."

"There isn't time."

Moore watched him go. "I was telling Worboys, only the other day," he said to Brimmacombe, "that the one thing this trip has taught me is that I'm a lousy judge of people."

★ ★ ★

Stacey was soon back; his mission had been fruitless and for his pains he had suffered a minor beating-up of which he was as proud as a new boy at school who had been through an initiation ceremony. The lighter had meantime been brought alongside and lay banging against the stern of the *Dai Nichi*. There was a complete lack of interest by the Japanese in the forward prisoners who were allowed to roam their permitted areas of the ship without let or hindrance mingling with the troops who thronged the deck. This laxity produced a sense of freedom which contained elements of both guilt and disbelief. However it was partly explained when it was reported that prisoners from the rear holds were to be sent ashore and replaced by others. No one could fathom the reasoning behind this exchange and after a time it came to be dismissed as yet another rumour. However, at half past five, the lighter was seen to be loading up with men and at the same time the forward prisoners were unceremoniously instructed to return to their quarters except for those in the hospital, those using the benjo or those required to act as bearers for the dead.

The sun was low as the lighter set off shorewards. Once it had left the bearers were instructed to move through to the stern with their charges and there they waited until a second lighter arrived with the replacement prisoners who proved to be Americans who had been working in the Formosan stone mines. In due course the bearers returned, some of them having managed to have conversations with the new arrivals. No one knew how much of what they recounted to accept as fact and how much as fable. The one certain truth was that sixteen corpses had been taken ashore.

12

STACEY'S motives for attempting to obtain an audience with Fujimoto had been entirely subjective. While the esteem of those, the great majority, whom he considered beneath him were of small account, he was inordinately anxious to be held in respect by those who mattered. In the hold these numbered three: Anderson, Moore and Sutcliffe. Of his fellow officers he had dismissed Dixon as being jumped-up from the ranks and Brimmacombe had impressed him as no more than a second-rater, admittedly Public School but certainly not of the purple. On the other hand Anderson, Stacey's instincts advised him, had an acceptable background while Moore exhibited that natural self-confidence and assurance which Stacey associated with those with whom one chose to mingle.

This left Sutcliffe.

In civilian life Stacey had met men like

Sutcliffe and been at once envious and impressed. In the modern world one was obliged to make exceptions for men of political or financial power, for notables in sport, theatre, the arts, letters and, occasionally, the professions. Such people dazzled Stacey for their station in life was, he assumed, invariably due to personal ability. Stacey was devoid of skills, baffled by commerce and in the company of such men, singularly ill at ease; incapable of dispassionate judgement, he took them at face value. In this he shared a quality with Brimmacombe, that of believing that if a man had succeeded he must be brilliant. But whereas Brimmacombe took this view out of an unenquiring mind, Stacey did so as a form of self-defence; if brilliance was not an absolute requirement for success he would have had to face his own reality.

Gullibility is of course concomitant with such an attitude and Stacey was easily deceived; the man in the Rolls-Royce was to be assumed acceptable until disproved — and here, in this hold crammed with men who possessed little but the ragged shirts and shorts they lay in, Sutcliffe stood out. By comparison he was very much the man in the Rolls-Royce: rich, powerful, glossy and secure. It had needed no more than a few bland lies for Stacey to be convinced that here was someone of outstanding qualities who, one day, would be of international substance. To give Stacey credit, his attachment to Sutcliffe was only to a degree materialistic. Today's cigarettes and tomorrow's possibilities were considerations but of greater importance was the companionship, and as he assumed, esteem, of one of the two men in this place who overawed him. Hence his willingness to risk a beating by emulating Sutcliffe.

To Sutcliffe, Stacey's exploit, while being transparent and absurd, was satisfying; the insecurity of his nature, which he masked well, demanded continual adulation and the knowledge that one's actions are being copied is very reassuring. He greeted Stacey on his return with unfeigned pleasure.

"Sorry about that, Lawrence. It was a noble effort. You'd have been all right if you'd got as far as Fujimoto. He struck me as quite a gentleman. I daresay he's involved in all the coming and going."

"What can you expect when it's an uneducated savage you have to deal with?" Stacey said. "They don't even speak the same Japanese."

"There are different Japaneses?"

"Absolutely. I doubt if the kind of people I had to deal with in Japan would have been able to hold an intelligent conversation with that rabble." He pointed a thumb up to the galleries. "It's much the same sort of thing as a Cambridge don trying to set up a discussion with a Hoxton barrow-boy. I really think Moore has let us down pretty badly. If he'd done what I suggested at the beginning, refused to accept these conditions, insisted on seeing Fujimoto . . . and, better still, had me go along with him . . . " He shook his head and sighed. "Of course, it's not entirely his fault. I mean he's never had any dealings with the Japanese except at the opposite end of a gun."

"But you think it's too late now?" prompted Sutcliffe.

"Oh, yes. Absolutely. It was bad enough being a prisoner. But once we accepted these conditions, we hadn't any face at all. Anyway look around you. Toms! Look at him! A senior N.C.O.! What an example for that lot up there to judge us by! That's almost the worst thing about this trip — the company one has to keep! Who'd have ever imagined having to spend week after week crammed into an unspeakable hold with such a rag, tag and bobtail bunch of men. I'm not a snob, don't misunderstand me. I'm sure amongst this mob we've got down here there are some excellent men. But you've got to admit we've certainly got our share of Yahoos and Weary Willies . . . "

Sutcliffe let him ramble on. He understood. Stacey was more relaxed. He had made his mark; proved himself. And, for the moment at least, there was no risk of submarines . . .

★ ★ ★

In the dim glow of the lights permitted whilst in harbour, Worboys spotted Moore quitting the benjo.

"Sir!"

253

"Yes, Worboys?"

"There's someone you ought to listen to, Sir."

"Oh?" Moore looked at the man with Worboys, a good looking man with a neat, thin moustache, dressed in shorts and singlet. "What's your name?" he said.

"Gray, Sir."

"Corporal Gray," Worboys qualified.

"You're in our hold aren't you, Corporal Gray?"

"Yes, Sir. In Flight Lieutenant Dixon's section."

"Yes, I thought I recognized you. Well?"

"I was in the bearer party. I managed to speak to some of the new lot."

"In the stern holds?"

"Yes, Sir. They're mostly Americans."

"So I heard. They've been working in the stone quarries. Did they have a bad time of it?"

"Yes, Sir — very bad. A couple of them showed me their hands with missing fingers where the Japs had chopped off rings. And there were other things. But it wasn't so much

254

that I felt I ought to tell you, Sir. You see, as well as the Americans there are a few other odds and sods . . . I mean . . . "

"Odds and sods will do. Go on."

"Well one of them got sunk on the way from Hong Kong to Japan."

"Where?"

"Not far from Shanghai, Sir."

"Shanghai! How the devil did he end up in Formosa?"

"He got picked up, Sir. I'm not very clear on it. We didn't have much time. But apparently the ship he was on, which was called the *Lisbon Maru*, got torpedoed near some islands and he managed to swim to one of them. He hid for a few days but then he got caught and put on another ship which was sailing here."

"Interesting. Go on."

"Well as I say, Sir, we didn't have much time, but he told me what happened when the *Lisbon Maru* got sunk. What the Japs did about the prisoners, I mean."

"What did they do?"

"Covered the hatches with tarpaulins,

255

Sir. And when men cut their way out, shot them."

"I see," Moore said grimly. "Anything else?"

"Yes, Sir. Apparently quite a lot did get off the ship in the long run. It seems it took more than twenty-four hours to sink. When they got off and tried to swim ashore, the Japs used them for target practice."

"Are you sure of this, Gray?"

"I believed him, Sir."

"Why didn't he get shot?"

"Quite a lot didn't, Sir. Several hundred. Out of about two thousand or so. Apparently they gave up shooting them when they realised some of them were bound to make the islands anyway."

"You mean when they realised they weren't going to be able to hide the fact they'd left two thousand prisoners battened down to drown or die of suffocation."

"Yes, I suppose so, Sir."

Moore thought about it. He had come to terms with the possibility of drowning; it was one of the inbuilt risks you took when you joined the Navy. But suffocating slowly — that was something else. Instinctively he breathed in deeply, filling his lungs with the clean, tangy air. For the moment, standing on a ship's deck rocking peacefully in the slight harbour swell on a hot semi-tropical evening with the moonlight drawing a long broken, glittering shaft across the sea, it was still good to be alive. Good to be alive for all the gripings in his belly, for all his sweat-soaked clothes, his broken nails, his unkempt hair, even for all the horror of the hold with its stink, its rats, its lice, its bugs, its slime, its dying men. But to finish there amongst a seething, crawling mass gasping for air in the pitch darkness of a sealed and abandoned ship was a horror beyond belief.

"Tarpaulins!" he said to Worboys. "I never thought they'd go that far. Not even these swine." He turned back to Gray:

"Have you any idea when this ship . . . What d'you say she was called?"

"The *Lisbon Maru*."

"When she was sunk?"

"October the first."

"Six weeks ago. Sailing from Hong Kong to . . . where? Shanghai?"

"No, Sir, Japan."

"Hugging the coast. Uhm." He dismissed Gray. "Thank you very much, Gray." But then he smiled and said: "I suppose it would be too much to hope you haven't mentioned this to anyone else?"

"Only to one or two friends, Sir."

"Good. Try and keep it that way, will you?"

★ ★ ★

When Gray had gone, Moore said: "Well, of course it'll be halfway round the hold by now."

"Better to speak to them, Sir?"

"How? With all that bloody audience we've got? If we do it piecemeal, it'll take for ever. And if we broadcast it, there's bound to be *one* of the buggers who'll twig! Better just let it run round like all the other rumours. What's more important is how we knock off a set of hatch covers that are held down by tarpaulins? Standing on a ladder.

258

Holding on with one hand. We'd never do it, would we?"

"No, Sir."

"And there's another thing. We'd have to try to do it in the dark."

"But if one man was lower on the ladder. With a torch . . . "

"Burning up precious air? Full of problems, isn't it? Well there's only one thing for it. We've got to get a knife from somewhere. A long sharp knife. Something than can slip between the hatch covers."

Worboys nodded towards a couple of Japanese chatting and smoking close by. "Are you thinking of a bayonet, Sir?"

Moore shook his head. "Not really. A bayonet 'd be too thick. What we really want is a good old carving-knife." He smiled wryly. "Just like the one I used to carve my Sunday joint with." He cocked his head at Worboys. "Well?"

Worboys stood very straight. "It could be done, Sir. They must have them in the galley."

"Exactly. Somebody has to get into the galley of a four-thousand-ton tramp that's crawling with men who look quite different and speak a different language and beg, borrow or steal a carving-knife. Quite a proposition. But it has to be done."

"You really think there's all that risk, Sir?"

Moore put his hands on the ship's rail, finding it wet with condensation. "Look," he said. "Across that way. China. About, what? Hundred and fifty miles? Right. How was the *Lisbon Maru* sailing from Hong Kong to Japan, tackling it? By hugging the coast. Because that was safer than making a dash across open sea. But she *still* got sunk. Only six weeks ago. Now us. We're already into the Formosa Strait which narrows in parts to about a hundred miles. Are you telling me there aren't other American submarines just waiting for a troopship like this? Of course they are. It's a natural." He looked at Worboys directly:

"Let's call a spade a spade. Our chances of being torpedoed in the next few days are very real. Better than one in ten. Better than one in five even. And if we are, and we're sinking, they'll sling those last few poor devils on the hatch covers into the sea or, more likely, pitch them back into the hold, batten us down, put on the tarpaulins, bolt the bulkhead doors behind them and abandon ship. They did it on the *Lisbon Maru* and they'll do it on the *Dai Nichi Maru*. And if we haven't got our carving-knife we'll either suffocate or drown. Which brings us right back to Miss Hay again! How do we tell them what we want with all that shower listening in?"

★ ★ ★

It was Toms' idea. "Why not have a sing-song, Sir, and slip it in?"

"Think we could get away with it?"

Toms stood arms folded across his hairy chest — a favourite pose. His hair had receded sufficiently to leave him with a high gleaming forehead and hung lankly down towards his ears paralleling his huge moustache. His eyes although protruding were set into strongly marked caverns and their lids were lizard-like in

261

his moon-shaped face.

"Nay bother!" he said. "You can get away with murder so long as it's in rhyme. Remember the Glodok concerts, Sir?"

It was true. Moore remembered how a line of Japanese officers had sat listening, watching, insulted to their very faces, baffled. Even the interpreter had been baffled. Learning a language was one thing; learning a vernacular quite another.

"If," Toms urged, "you could say a few words first Sir? A lead-in as you might say . . . "

Moore smiled. There was, he reflected, much of a *barker* in Toms; he could so easily be imagined selling gimcrack at a market stall. Anyway, why shouldn't he have his fun? He'd tried hard enough.

★ ★ ★

"All right, Toms," Moore said. "Start us off!"

Toms mounted the platform, put two fingers in his mouth and whistled. When Toms whistled the effect was usually remarkable, here, unexpectedly, in the half light of the *Dai Nichi*'s hold, it was dramatic. The piercing blast silenced any chatterers and awoke the sleepers. The rats scampered into their holes, the Japs stuck their heads from theirs. Even the very sick were stirred from contemplation of their problems. After a moment or two of silence, a babel of conversation broke out. Toms, the showman, held up a commanding hand.

"Fear not!" he cried. "We are not being sunk! We are going to have a sing-song!"

There were objections, groans, even half-hearted boos. Toms was not dismayed. Arms akimbo he made a complete turn on his platform as if to ensure none had been overlooked.

"Come on you miserable shower!" he bawled. "Let's be having you! Let's show these jewels of Asia what we're made of! And there's a prize! Twenty coffin nails! Know what that means? No, course you don't! You want to get some in! I was cutting barbed wire before you was cutting milk teeth! Twenty cigarettes to *you*. We're having a competition! A treasure hunt! And the first man who brings the treasure to Commander Moore gets 'em! Twenty fags!" He shook his gleaming head. "Never knew there was still such treasure in the world, did you? Right! We start with a chorus of 'Beyond the Blue Horizon' and then I hand over to my colleague, the one and only Commander James Trevelyan Moore D.S.O. R.N.V.R. and all the rest of it!"

And to the air of *Auld Lang Syne* Toms burst into song:

"We're here
Because
We're here
Because
We're here
Because we're here . . . "

and, surprisingly, perhaps because of the lowered tension through being in harbour and freed from imminent danger of submarine attack or perhaps because something was sensed, Toms obtained a modicum of support which swelled as more and more men joined in.

Moore watching the Japanese (many of who had come to the edges of their platforms and were peering down to see what was going on below) noted that as soon as the singing started some, analysing what was happening, even perhaps reassured an insurrection was not about to break out, withdrew.

When Toms came to an end of his endless dirge, Moore signalled for another song and Toms led the men into 'Here's to good old beer . . . ' which went on for a long time. With each succeeding verse more and more of the shaven heads withdrew. Satisfied, Moore had Toms bring the song to an end on rum 'which warms your balls and bum.'

"Very good," said Moore. "Now we come to the treasure hunt part. You don't have to sing if you don't want to, but you have to listen and pick out the word from each song that counts. If you pick out the right words, you will find you have an instruction. Or rather, an offer. You don't have to accept that offer, but I hope some of you will want to. When you've decided you know where the treasure is, and how to get it, come and tell me. Quietly so that no one else who might be listening can overhear you and stop you finding the treasure and bringing it to me. Now we'd better get on with it. We may not have all that time." He turned to Toms beside him. "Ready, Warrant Officer Toms?"

"Ready, Sir."

"You will join in only when I raise my hands like this," Moore said. He raised his hands, palms upwards. "Understood?"

There was scattered agreement. Moore was convinced; it had been put over. Enough of the men knew this was no mere sing-song.

"Off you go then," Moore said.

Toms broke into song, surprising few by the quality of his voice; in Java he had played a leading role in the fortnightly concert parties.

"The dusky night rides down the sky,
And ushers in the morn,
The hounds all join in glorious cry,

266

The hounds all join in glorious cry,
A hunting *you* will go," he sang.

Moore raised his hands and led the prisoners:

"A hunting we will go,
A hunting we will go,
A hunting we will go,
A hunting we will go."

"Fine," said Moore raising his hand. "Good start. Right, Warrant Officer Toms. Next clue please."

"Where are you going to, my pretty
    maid? (Toms sang)
Where are you going to, my pretty
    maid?
I'm going to the cookhouse, Sir, she
    said,
Sir, she said, Sir, she said,
I'm going to the cookhouse, Sir, she
    said."

Moore had this chorused, then signified a pause. Toms sang

"What are you going for, my pretty
    maid?
What are you going for, my pretty
    maid?
To see if the cat has kept out the
    mice,
To see if the cat has kept out the
    mice,
That's what I'm going for, Sir, she
    said."

Moore rebuked Toms. They were, by
now, making a concert turn.

"I think you got that wrong, Warrant
Officer!"

"Did I, Sir?"

"I think you did, Warrant Officer."

"What did I do wrong, Sir?"

"To see if the cat has kept out the
mice!" said Moore, with heavy irony.

"Isn't that right, Sir?"

"It certainly is not. Not how it goes
at all. You don't catch mice with cats in
Community Songs. You catch them with
carving-knives. Carving-knives, Warrant
Officer, Toms. Surely you remember
that?" And he sang:

"Three blind mice,
See how they run,
They all ran after the farmer's wife,
She cut off their tails with a carving-
    knife . . . "

Moore stopped and raised his hands:
"Carving-knife! Carving-knife!"

'Carving-knife! Carving-knife!' was dutifully
echoed and Moore completed it (racing
through the words to underline their
insignificance): "Did ever you see such a
sight in your life, as three blind mice?"

"Again. Sir?" said Toms.

"No, I don't think so, Warrant Officer.
Try something new."

"All through the night?" suggested
Toms.

"Splendid," said Moore. "Very appro-
priate. Silence, please. And listen."

While the moon her watch is keeping,
    (sang Toms)
All through this night;
While the rest of us are sleeping,
All through this night.
To the galley gently wheeling,

Urgently we are appealing,
For the thing you must be stealing,
Somehow tonight."

And Moore echoed: "Somehow, tonight,"
and, raising his hands, had it repeated . . .

★ ★ ★

"Absurd," said Stacey. "Talk about a sledgehammer to crack a nut!"

But Sutcliffe was impressed.

"Actually," he said, "that was quite clever."

"Why not simply pass the word around?"

"For several reasons. The time it takes. Who do you start with? How do you stop it getting garbled so that you find yourself ending up with a chopper instead of a carving-knife? Besides, dramatizing it is bound to whip up more enthusiasm. How about it, Lawrence?" — he could be very cruel. "How about you and me forming a team to creep down into the galley and steal a carving-knife?"

"This is ridiculous," said Stacey, wriggling out of answering. "Here we

270

are crammed in this stinking hold, men dying all around us, liable to be sunk the moment we stick our nose out of harbour, short of drinking water, unable to wash our plates, our clothes, ourselves, rats crawling over us while we sleep, flies crawling over us while we're awake, still not even knowing where the hell we're bound for and all Moore can do is play charades! What's he want a carving-knife for anyway?"

"Yes," said Sutcliffe thoughtfully. "I wonder why he does."

* * *

Yates was the first to volunteer, followed almost immediately by Lenny Brooks.

"No," said Moore to Yates. "You're too valuable doing what you're doing already."

"I'd still like to have a go, Sir."

"So would I. The answer's no. That's final." He spoke to Lenny. "It's a very dangerous enterprise." He broke off. Several men were approaching, the nearest of whom was Kerrison. "Sergeant Kerrison," he said. "Get Warrant Officers

271

Toms and Worboys. Have them see those men go back to their places. Take their names. I'll come to them later. And for God's sake try to calm them down. There's too much . . . " He sought for a word and failed to find it. "Too much buzz," he said.

"Yes, Sir," said Kerrison. "But I'm afraid Sergeant Major Rudge is out of it."

"Dysentery?"

"I think it's malaria, Sir."

"Malaria!" Moore said. "As if we haven't got enough with dysentery, we have to have malaria too! And the rest! Right. Off you go." He turned back to Lenny. "Now," he said. Sit down, Brooks. You'll be less conspicuous." Brooks looked around for sitting space. "Sit on Yates's lid. Move that ridiculous pith helmet. Pith helmet!" He echoed it in disgust. "Probably be snowing when we get there."

"Tha' doan't mind?" said Lenny to Yates. The wickerwork lid already had broken strands through being sat upon.

Yates shook his head, brushing the thin hair from his eyes. If anything he had put on weight. For those with appetite, there was now plenty of food; it was only water which was in short supply. Moore wondered if everlastingly being sprayed by diluted blood and excreta had an inoculating effect; Yates even out-Heroded Worboys; he had yet to pass a motion since leaving Singapore. What a thing to be considering! What a thing to be jealous about! Another man's motions! Who'd ever have believed it?

"Now," he said to Lenny who had gently lowered himself on to Yates's lid. "You're quite clear on what we're after?"

"Yes, Sir. Tha' wants someone to slip into galley and pinch a carving-knife."

"Tonight. You're willing to have a crack at it?"

"Aye."

"By yourself?"

"Me an' Nobby an' Mac."

Moore shook his head. "Three would be too many. Two would be better."

"Me an' Mac then."

"Know anything about a ship's layout?" Lenny shook his head. "Well, I could help but there may be others better qualified than you are, Brooks. We might have an ex-merchant-navy cook for all we know."

"Or a perfessional safe breaker," put in Nobby who was listening and much relieved to have been let off the hook.

"Or, as your friend says," Moore agreed, "a professional safe-breaker. We seem to have most things . . . "

* * *

Moore didn't get an ex-merchant-navy cook; nor a professional safe-breaker. Nor did he accept Lenny and Mac. Instead he found two men, one of whom, having been a joiner's mate, knew a thing or two about opening locks and had several keys he'd made out of flat bits of metal which had been useful on working parties in Java, and the second, a Geordie, had been a riveter and knew how ships like the *Dai Nichi Maru* were put together.

13

THROUGH the night waking hours a positive relationship had grown between Moore and Yates which did not apply through the long days when they were merely two men sharing a groundsheet each with his own way of filling time between voluntarily accepted duties. Indeed with Yates absent collecting his men and sluicing out the benjos, collecting water drip by drip to wash himself, shaving, queueing up for and eating his food, queueing for his miserable water ration, delousing his clothes and similar pursuits and Moore continually dealing with complaints, continually encouraging the sick and dying, continually playing to the best of his ability his role as senior officer while doing what he could to look after himself and contend with his worryingly increasing visits to the benjo, they saw comparatively little of each other.

But by night the hold sank into a kind

of torpor. It was never still and it was never silent but apart from those with fevers or those suffering the awful pains of advanced dysentery or the nagging pain of peripheral neuritis and other vitamin deficiency diseases, the balm of sleep brought a measure of oblivion. It was not a constant sleep and it was a restless sleep; there were too many benjo visits, too many benjo visitors, stumbling their way through the darkness. There were the rats, and the lice, and the bugs. There was the stench and the heat. There were eyes which smarted painfully and thighs which itched to distraction and feet which burned. There was the nagging, everlasting thirst. There were the cries of men in pain, the grinding of teeth, the snoring and farting, the sickening explosion of motions being passed, the trickle of urine. There were the nightmares and, at sea, there was the fear of submarines. There was the yearning for cigarettes. So many wants and discomforts joined together opposing sleep and yet nature would not be entirely denied and, in a considerable measure, sleep won the battle.

Yet the waking-hours were many and of necessity a bond was forged between these two superficially dissimilar men lying closer than husband and wife and sharing a bitter experience. They often talked in a way which would, under normal circumstances, have seemed very strange. "What would you do, Sir," Yates might ask, "if this was all a dream and you suddenly woke to find yourself in England?" And before he could answer (and Moore did not at all mind answering and did not find the question peculiar) Moore would have to set the parameters by a series of questions. What month of the year was it? What day of the week? What hour of the day? What was the weather like? Where, in England, could he choose to be? And, having got these preliminaries settled, he would launch into a long and detailed depiction which was always agreeable and invariably autobiographical. Nothing would be omitted. Should it be a day with his family on his yacht, that day would begin with the selection of the gear, the packing of the food and drink, the drive down in the car . . . should it be an evening at the theatre, the type of play would be defined, the audience would be described, the friends accompanying them would be selected. Or should it be a simple summer afternoon at home, Moore would draw a careful picture of his house, his garden, his family and his pets.

'We're lucky to have a splendid old apple tree,' he might say. 'And when it's a decent day we take our tea out there. It's not a bad view. It doesn't have water and really a perfect view must have water in it somewhere. But it's not a bad view. There's a valley below us and the slope on the other side is one of those which are mostly pastureland with big clumps of trees, copses really, scattered over it . . .'

Or it might be winter and the family inside: 'It's a very old house. We're lucky to have found it. The rooms aren't all that big and the ceilings are low. There are oak beams everywhere. It's a 'Duck or Grouse' house really. We've got one of those fires with a chimney you can stand up in. We could burn quite big logs on dogs if we wanted to but then of course you have to leave the ash and my wife's rather too tidy a person for that . . . '

Yates seldom interrupted these narratives which would go on quietly by the hour. If they were broken by a benjo visit, Yates would be waiting for Moore to return and settle down, when he would prompt him with a: "You were talking about your daughter being rather good at the piano for her age . . . " or wherever it was Moore had got to and so it would continue as if it had not been interrupted.

Yates was far less communicative about himself and Moore realised there was a part of his nature he was deliberately holding back. Equally he realised the degree to which he was exposing himself. But there was much gained by both of them. To Moore there was a greater reality in talking about his peacetime way of life than in the silent sentimental brooding which would have been the necessary alternative. He understood, moreover, that there were positive reasons behind Yates's unwearied attention; that his recitals were not sought as diversions or anodynes but that Yates was genuinely absorbed and sharing vicariously a way of life he had never experienced and always longed for. Occasionally Yates would let slip a remark which strongly underlined Moore's judgement and at the same time told him more of Yates's background than might have been discovered by many hours' research. On one such occasion Moore had been recounting part of a weekend spent with friends and when he ended Yates had told him quietly, not looking at him, but staring up at the iron deck not ten feet above their heads:

"I once spent a weekend with a friend. Well, not really a friend, someone I knew at school. He lived in the country. Place called Woodford. When I woke up I could hear the birds singing outside the bedroom they'd let me sleep in." And Moore had thought that would be the whole of it but after a few moments Yates had gone on: "His mother brought me a cup of tea. She caught me out of bed. I was at the window looking into the next-door garden watching a squirrel. I thought I'd done wrong, being up, I mean, before she'd brought the tea. No one had ever brought me a cup of tea in bed before and I suppose it would have been disappointing for her that I wasn't in bed sort of waiting for it. I mean after going to that trouble."

How simply, Moore had thought, this one small anecdote had drawn a comparison between the life Yates had lived and the life which he had lived, the life he was carving out for his own children. A little boy so embarrassed by not knowing the form of ordinary, normal living, that the incident of being caught out of bed when a cup of tea was brought to him had been graven on his mind. And how much it went towards explaining Yates's motivation for cleaning out the benjos. With sudden intuition, Moore realised that Yates was trying to associate with people and with what he had seen from a distance as a normal way of life, a life that was to do with the warmth, love and kindness he had been cheated out of sharing. This, this abominable chore, was Yates contribution to society. How extraordinary that it had needed a voyage in a cesspit to offer him his opportunity! Yet, not discarding this discovery, Moore sensed there was even more to it. Yes, Yates yearned to be a part of what he believed to be a fuller, deeper, rounder way of life and his benjo-cleaning was a contribution — but, more than a contribution, it was an expiation! Yates was obsessed by guilt! But guilt of what? Of his desertion? Moore shook his head. No, there was no guilt there. Of his escape from Singapore? Of his leaving a man perched on a mangrove root to die and not even bothering to go back later to see if he was really dead? Possibly. Yet even this was not convincing. Then what? Moore could not conjecture. And he did not probe. If he was to learn, he would learn in the fullness of time. One thing was sure — Yates would expose his inner self spontaneously or not at all.

★ ★ ★

"Why do you need a carving-knife, Sir?" Yates asked.

Moore explained.

"And why has it got to be got tonight?"

"For two reasons. The first is that we have no idea when we are sailing.

We might be here for several days; we might leave tomorrow. When we leave we head northwards up what is known as the Formosa Strait. Now we will either first sail due east so as to hug the Chinese coast or, more likely, we'll go up the Pescadores Channel — the Pescadores being a group of islands which belong to Formosa, and therefore the Japanese. Without any question there will be American submarines both in the Formosa Strait and hanging around the Pescadores Channel. Shipping is funnelled into it. Once we're clear of it, it's more or less open sea all the way to Japan. I won't say it's safe but it's safer. So we are, as you might say, just entering our period of maximum risk. And there's the bonus that if we just happened to be sunk off the China coast by no means all of it is under Japanese control and we might not only save our necks but get back our freedom too. But I think it'll be the Pescadores Channel and, should we get sunk, with a bit of luck some of us could reach one or other of the islands."

"You must have a map, Sir," Yates said.

"I've got a map, Yates. But I've learn't it all by heart anyway. And the other reason? This was built as a merchant ship, not a troopship. We've got about two thousand extra men living on a ship designed to accommodate . . . what? Twenty, thirty men? It'll have a galley designed for just that sort of number. Which means that that lot's food and our food, such as it is, is being cooked somewhere else. Lord knows where and it doesn't matter. What matters is that it isn't in the galley. It's common knowledge that the Japanese navy doesn't like the Japanese army and I imagine the merchant navy likes them even less. So I don't think we'll find many soldiers wandering around the galley. And some of the crew have gone ashore. I saw them leaving on the lighter. So apart from the fact we might very well need that carving knife in the next forty eight hours or so, there never will be a time it's likely to be easier to pinch it."

He had not been talking only to Yates. Lenny Brooks had moved over and, sitting on Yates's lid, arms round his knees, chin almost touching them had been listening engrossed. A small, neat man with tight short hair and a tiny moustache, there was something very economical about Lenny Brooks.

"Should 'a let me be one of them you know, Sir," he said.

"Why you, Brooks?"

"Because I'm little."

Moore smiled. What a valuable man, he thought. What a rare man. Perhaps I should have let him. Yet he had no proof Lenny Brooks was better than good average. He merely happened to be a neighbour. The rest, save for a handful, were as much strangers as they had been three weeks before. Excepting in this: that he had learnt that their spirit was remarkable. Apart from those dangerously ill, there was no despair. It was not surprising some had died; what was surprising was that so many still lived. Only a few days now, and then, God willing, they would reach Japan. Others would die before then. But most would live. It was their spirit which had kept them going this far; it would be their spirit which would see them through.

★ ★ ★

A sudden commotion woke Moore from
his uneasy sleep. There was shouting and
there was brilliant light. His immediate
thought was that it could not have
happened here, that they could not have
been torpedoed inside harbour. For quite
some seconds he could see nothing except
the dazzling light directed at him and
he turned away from it, rolling on his
groundsheet. Now he could see the light
bathing a shocked, frightened Yates who
was sitting bolt upright, and, searching
deeper into the recesses of the hold,
illuminating metal ribs which had not
been seen before, picking out prisoners
alarmed, hastily struggling to their feet,
casting elongated shadows.

Moore turned back, shading his eyes,
and now he saw that there was a second
light probing in the opposite direction and
he realised that there were two spotlights
placed at the edge of the 'tween deck
immediately above them in such positions
as to ensure that no portion of the hold
was dark. And he saw something else,
that there were Japanese soldiers armed

with rifles with bayonets fixed looking down on them. The horrifying notion that it had been decided the prisoners should be massacred filled his mind. He got quickly to his feet, forgetting the slope and the bauxite, and, twisting his ankle in its shaly substance, all but falling. There was not too much noise from the men in the hold and such as there was was uncertain, disbelieving. But there were orders being shouted in Japanese, evidently to the soldiers lining the edges above, for they suddenly, if raggedly, came to attention, their rifle-butts ringing on the steel deck, their left arms smacking against their breeches. A second order and their right hands thrust the muzzle of their rifles forward and the bayonets glittered in the spotlights.

"Commander Moore!"

Moore recognized the voice: O'Hana's. He made his way to the platform. The hold was now quiet, only the moaning of some man too deep in pain to be concerned with these proceedings broke the deathly stillness.

"What is this?" Moore demanded of the interpreter standing warily by the 'tween deck's edge, looking down at him.

"All men come up!" O'Hana ordered.

"Come up? What for?"

"All men come up!" shrieked O'Hana.

"All men can't come up," argued Moore. "Some men too sick."

This appeared to baffle O'Hana. He half turned to an officer, one of the eight who had attended Glenister's funeral, and there was a considerable exchange before O'Hana shouted: "Sick men stay down. All men not sick come up. Speedo!"

For the umpteenth time Moore wondered how a race which seemed so lacking in ordinary common sense could have won so many battles. The demand was ridiculous. Some men were too ill to be left alone and many were borderline cases; others were too weak to climb the ladder. It would take hours to organise. "You must send a doctor down," he said. "He must decide which men are fit enough."

"No doctor!" shouted O'Hana. "All men come up!"

Moore looked at the officer. He was a very small, rather ugly man, with hollowed cheeks. He wore spectacles and the corners of his mouth were down-turned. Such hair as could be seen under his short peaked cap with its single star and narrow leather peak-strap was shaven almost to his sallow skin. His curved scabbarded sword hung from a thick waist belt and he wore grey-green shapeless breeches and short-sleeved shirt. His arms were folded. His expression was exactly that of a bad-tempered schoolmaster weighing up a crowd of children who, apart from being an irritation, did not interest him in the least. He contrasted strongly with O'Hana who was round faced and squat with pushed out lips, protruding teeth and a flattened nose.

"I want to speak to your officer," Moore said.

There was a further exchange in Japanese.

"Officer say speak!" called down O'Hana.

"I would like to come up and speak to the officer," Moore said firmly.

He knew that nothing would persuade the officer to come down into the hold.

In spite of several requests not one Japanese had done so since the *Dai Nichi* had sailed from Singapore. The question of their doing so now with all the loss of face that would entail simply did not arise. Also, he suspected, they were fearful of being stricken as severely as their prisoners by the dysentery which had already killed some of their own men. "May I see your officer on deck?" Moore ended.

"No!" said O'Hana without consultation. "All men not sick come up now!"

Moore realised that O'Hana was in a quandary. Japanese troops, he had learnt, stood in awe of another soldier even so little outranking them as by a single stripe, and a private, as was O'Hana, faced with an officer, would be trembling in his boots. He had received an order and it was expected of him that he would see that order was carried out — even if it wasn't possible. Or at least he would work it out that way. Had they been facing each other, Moore had not the least doubt O'Hana would by now have sought to solve the problem by setting about him physically. In fact, short of sending soldiers down or shooting a few of the prisoners by way of encouragement (admittedly a definite possibility), it was difficult to see how O'Hana could solve the problem. Meanwhile the officer was losing face.

"What is this all about, anyway?" demanded Moore with all the bluster he could summon up. "Why you wake sick men? Why can't it wait till morning?"

"We look!" shouted O'Hana.

"You look? What do you mean *we look*?"

"Search. We search," said O'Hana, finding the word. And then, underlining it triumphantly: "*Sosaku!*"

Moore's heart turned to stone. They had been searched twice already. Once before leaving Java; once through a long hot day on the quayside at Singapore. But Japanese searches were always carried out without imagination. They looked in the obvious places, through kitbags, pockets, attache cases. It never seemed to occur to them that skilfully contrived double compartments could exist, that maps could be sewn inside a Dutch wife, that tins could have their lids removed then be soldered back in place so cleverly that it would have needed an expert to tell they had been tampered with. In the camp in Java there had been quite a few revolvers and enough equipment to make several radios; one of those revolvers and sufficient radio equipment had been allocated to their draft and, as it so happened, the latter was hidden in the hollow bamboo poles which had been used to carry coolie-wise the small quantity of supplies they had brought aboard with them. These were even now in the back of his own hold. But it was not these items which worried Moore; if they had eluded two groups of searchers, they would probably elude a third. What *was* worrying was the carving-knife! It had proved, after all, such a simple operation. The moon having by then set, Scammel, the joiner's mate, and Munday, the riveter, had slipped away from the benjo queue and within ten minutes, not having met a single Japanese, had unlocked the galley, helped themselves to a carving-knife (and a little food and drink), relocked the galley, casually dropped the knife down the coal chute as they passed it and rejoined the benjo queue. Within an hour the knife had been passed through a rust hole in the bulkhead by a stoker. Currently it had joined the map and a compass in Moore's Dutch wife.

In a careful search it would be found and the consequences would be horrendous. Not only would precautions be taken to ensure it could never be replaced but almost certainly frightful reprisals would follow. The act of its having been stolen on the ship would infuriate the Japanese and it would be believed to have been taken as a weapon. He would certainly be shot (if not publicly beheaded) as would Yates and a few others who lay near to him — it being the normal Japanese practice to assume neighbours of a would-be escaping prisoner or troublemaker to be in collusion and therefore meriting an equal punishment. Nor need it end there. One discovery might enthuse a more considered search. The torches and the now completed battering-ram would be discovered and quite possibly the broken-up radio and the revolver in another hold.

It did not bear contemplation.

"What do you want to search us for?" he stalled. "You've searched us twice already."

"You steal things! You very bad men!"

"Steal things?" Moore bluffed. "What things?"

"You steal things to make torches! You steal . . . you steal . . . battering-ram!" It came out triumphantly. A newly discovered word, correctly delivered. O'Hana's mouth opened, displaying his huge protruding teeth all edged in gold like pictures in a frame. He was cock-a-hoop.

Huge relief and terrible disgust filled Moore's mind. They did not know of the carving-knife; not yet. But they knew of the torches; and they knew of the battering-ram. And there was only one way they could have known.

"Who told you we have these things?" he called.

O'Hana raised a jubilant hand. "We know!" he cried.

"Nippon man knows everything!"

"But who?"

"You take pipes and screw together! You put them . . . *asoko*! There!" He pointed to the bulkhead between the hold and the fuel bunkers, where indeed the battering-ram now lay, covered with a thin layer of bauxite. "You steal para . . . para . . ."

Moore helped him. An idea was beginning to burgeon.

"Paraffin?" he said.

"*Hai*!" yelled O'Hana triumphantly. "Pa-ra-fin! You steal pa-ra-fin and you hide it there!" And again he pointed — to the area used by the men who were too weak to climb up to the benjo.

There was no help for it.

"Yes," said Moore. "We stole these things. I stole these things. In case the ship was sunk and we could not get out."

"The ship not sink!" stormed O'Hana. "Nippon *genki*! Nippon strong! America *yowai*! Weak!" And, as an illogical afterthought: "If ship sink you go up ladder." He ran his hand, as it were, up the iron-runged ladder. "No need battering-ram."

"You guarantee the hatch-covers will not be put over us?"

This baffled O'Hana.

"Ladder! Up ladder!" he shouted.

"Japanese soldiers won't stop us? You ask officer," Moore insisted.

There was a third conference. Through the whole of it the expression on the officer's face did not alter one iota. He simply stared at O'Hana with his sad mouth turned down and a vague sneer beneath his nose. Even when he spoke, spitting out the words like a faulty-machine gun, strings of words followed by brief pauses, then more words, even then his arms stayed folded and only his lower lip moved up and down.

O'Hana waited until certain the officer was finished. He then saluted and the officer returned the salute briefly and then turned and withdrew.

O'Hana came back to the edge.

"Officer say we are your fathers and your mothers. If ship sink you okay. We look after you. Officer say you have stolen Nippon things and ten men must be shot. You choose. Next time one hundred men!"

"Worboys!" Moore called.

"Yes, Sir?"

"Have the battering-ram, the torches

and the paraffin brought here!"

"Yes, Sir."

"Jim . . ."

"It's all right, Freddie," Moore said urgently. "They obviously know exactly where they are. Please leave this to me." He spoke to O'Hana. "I am having the things we stole collected," he said, very slowly and clearly. "I will have them brought up on deck. Then I want to see your Commanding Officer. Do you understand? Your Commanding Officer. Your Ichiban! I will not choose ten men. I will do for ten. I am Commanding Officer here. I see your Commanding Officer and he must shoot me. Tell him!"

O'Hana hesitated. Moore wondered what he was thinking. Most interpreters were men who had learnt their English abroad and been recalled to their homeland when war seemed a likely possibility. O'Hana was probably no exception. Here was no university graduate but a man accustomed to taking orders who, judging by his accent, had held down a menial job in either Canada or the States.

"I said tell your Commanding Officer!"

Moore shouted. "And be quick about it. I am coming up the ladder. I will wait on deck with the things I have stolen."

And, ignoring the protests beginning to be voiced around him, the somewhat bewildered expression on O'Hana's face and the line of soldiers with their rifles, Moore began to scale the ladder . . .

14

MOORE was not shot; he was not even beaten up. And for all that it was the small hours of the morning, he scarcely had to wait — Fujimoto had clearly expected something of this nature. He was received precisely as he had been when stating his requirements for Glenister's funeral and now, more than ever, Moore suspected that an interpreter was required only to place a distance between them. Throughout almost the entire brief interview, Fujimoto listened to O'Hana's translation with the same aristocratic impassivity; but there was, Moore was sure, as he offered himself as a sacrifice for the ten men to be shot, a faint, quickly disguised reaction — a slight raising of the head, a sudden brief searching in the dark, brown eyes. Moore held the look, nor did he find it difficult to do so. He was not afraid, but angry. A quiet, cold fury towards the man who had betrayed them blotted out all other emotion.

When he had finished, Fujimoto spoke and O'Hana translated: "There will be no food or water for a day."

"There are men dying because there is not enough water!" Moore cried, swiftly, anticipating immediate dismissal.

O'Hana did not speak.

"Tell him what I said!" Moore snapped at him.

O'Hana translated — with great reluctance.

For the first time Fujimoto looked away from Moore as he spoke to the interpreter.

"You may choose," O'Hana translated.

"Between what?"

"Between no food and water or ten men."

Moore knew better than pursue it farther. "Very well. No food or water," he said. "I would like to ask one question."

O'Hana translated; Fujimoto nodded brief approval.

"I would like to know the name of the man who told you we had stolen these things."

Fujimoto did not seem to listen carefully to the translation and then proved Moore's judgement accurate.

"What would you do to the man if you knew his name, Commander Moore?" he said, in almost perfect English.

"I would kill him," Moore said simply.

Fujimoto looked at him for a long time.

"I do not know his name," he said at length. "I know he speaks some Japanese."

★ ★ ★

Brimmacombe, Stacey, Anderson and many of the men, apprehensively awaiting Moore's news were told little — he needed the few hours before dawn to consider the awful decisions he had now to make.

"I have had an interview with the Japanese Commanding Officer," he told them. "No men will be shot. There will be an alternative punishment of which I will give you details in the morning. As must be quite obvious to you all, we have amongst us at least one

301

man who has told the Japanese where our battering-ram and the paraffin we needed to make torches were hidden. You may have your own suspicions as to who that man, or those men, may be. But it is not your responsibility to act on those suspicions, which may, in any case, be ill-founded." And when a man started to shout something from a dark part of the hold: "Will that man be silent, please! Understand this. We are by no means out of the wood as you all know full well without my going into details. They can easily decide to reinstate the original punishment if we do, or say, the wrong thing. Which means that about one in every twenty of us will be executed. Remember that. One in twenty. Therefore, whatever your suspicions, whatever even your proof, you will do nothing. One thing more. Since there is at least one traitor in this hold, until further instructions are given, all men who wish to go to the benjo will collect in tens on the platform, as we did originally under the Japanese, and follow each other up when approval is given down here. You will be met at the top by one of the senior N.C.Os. and escorted to the benjo. You will return in the same manner. There will be no exceptions. Under no circumstances will you talk to any Japanese. Any man who breaks this order will be regarded as a traitor and will be dealt with accordingly. Do I make myself clear?"

There were murmurs of confirmation which, as they began to swell, Moore swiftly quenched by the raising of a hand.

"There will be no appeal," he told them. "Be clear on that. Now do your best to get some sleep. Please do not debate this business now."

Moore nodded to Brimmacombe who crossed to join him in the centre of the platform.

"Freddie," he said quietly. "This has to be played very carefully and I've got a lot of thinking to do. We can't talk here and under the circumstances we can't go up on deck together in the middle of the night. In fact for the moment the less conspicuous I make myself the better. Will you and Andrew work out some sort of roster with Worboys and the other senior N.C.O.s and make sure my instructions are carried out to the letter. So far as . . . " he lowered his voice even more . . . "Stacey and Sutcliffe are concerned, see they don't contact any Japs. Not that I think they'll try. But if they . . . "

"They won't," said Brimmacombe. "I'll be right behind them."

"Thank you." And after pausing to glance around the hold, watching the men settling down, he went on: "As soon as it's light I shall go up to the benjo. You and Andrew follow me up."

"Right," said Brimmacombe.

"That's all then, Freddie — for the moment. Goodnight."

And Moore turned and made his way to join Yates on his groundsheet.

★ ★ ★

In the grey of dawn, Moore recounted his interview with Fujimoto.

"He would say nothing else?" said Brimmacombe.

"Nothing."

"You think he knew the name of the

bastard who split on us?"

"Of course."

"Why wouldn't he tell you then?"

"My dear Freddie," Moore said, "the man organises a Fred Karno Circus to happen in the middle of the night and waits up, fully dressed, to learn the result of it. Why then? Why not wait until a civilized hour?"

"Lord knows."

"Does he? It wouldn't surprise me if the Japs didn't even baffle him!"

"You seem to have handled him very well, Sir," said Anderson.

Moore looked at the young second lieutenant. "Only because he respected my offering to take the place of the ten men who were otherwise to be shot. That fitted in with his idea of honour."

"Do you think, Sir, if you hadn't offered, he *would* have had ten men shot?"

"Unquestionably. There would have been too much loss of face for that to be gone back on. Leave it, Andrew. We have something much more important to talk about — what we are going to do about the man who shopped us?"

"You warned him," Brimmacombe said.

"Warned who?"

"Stacey."

Moore stared at the sea which had become as still as taut silk. It was grey in the early morning light, grey under a grey sky. All colour seemed gone. Even the green of the land was greyish. There were no shadows anywhere. Moore did not like the look of the sea so still, but he was glad there was no brightness to it. His eyes ached from sleeplessness. He turned from the sea to stare at the benjo queue across the open hatch. At this time of the day, only a little after dawn, it had always been shorter than it would later become as those of lesser need who wanted to breathe the morning air before the tubs of food were lowered came up. Only today there would be no food. And there would be no water. He stared at the queerly misty sky which offered no rain.

"We don't know it was Stacey," he said.

"But he's the only one who speaks Japanese," argued Anderson.

How dreadful this is, thought Moore;

and how much worse it's going to be. Here's another boy. He's no different from the rest of them except that he had a good education and they gave him a commission. A likable, decent youngster brought up, no doubt, by sensible, loving parents who helped instil in him principles of behaviour he's proving he can stay with. But no one taught him responsibility. You can't be taught responsibility; you just pick it up as you go along.

"Fujimoto did not say he spoke Japanese, Andrew," he pointed out. "He said he spoke some Japanese."

"Sutcliffe?" said Brimmacombe.

"Sutcliffe or Stacey," Moore said. "Or, just possibly, someone who has some Japanese that we don't know about. But that's unlikely." Kerrison was returning a batch down to the hold. Moore stopped him. "Sergeant!"

"Yes, Sir."

"Will you ask Flying Officer Stacey to come up here, please."

"Yes, Sir."

"Strange, isn't it?" commented Moore as Kerrison started to lower himself over the hatch coaming, "how they let us wander about doing what we like. We might have been ordered to stand up here and watch ten men being executed; instead we're up here about to decide which man we execute. *Abekobe*, isn't it?" He smiled wanly. "You see I speak Japanese as well."

"What does that mean, Sir?" said Anderson. He was very pale.

"*Abekobe*? Topsyturvy, Andrew. Upside down. It's a good word, isn't it?"

Brimmacombe realised how tired Moore was, how strained. His cheeks were hollow, somehow made even hollower by the nascent beard. His eyes were sunken, staring. He was iller than he made himself out to be. Dysentery and responsibility together were hard taskmasters.

"Sir?" said Anderson. "Do we have to go that far?"

"I'm afraid we do."

"Just because we've got a carving-knife?"

"Just because of that."

"Couldn't we put it back?"

"And risk getting caught doing so? Knowing what that would mean? And go

308

through the Pescadores Channel knowing perfectly well that if we are torpedoed — and there's a very good chance we will be — we'll be battened down and tarpaulins stretched across the top?"

"But now that we don't have our battering-ram . . . "

"With tarpaulins on, they won't bother with wedges. So long as we can cut the tarpaulins — and with that carving-knife we can — we'll knock off those hatch covers somehow. Even without torches."

"You don't think that a warning . . . "

Moore read what was in his mind. "That a warning might do the trick?" He shook his head. "It's not my business, Andrew, to play with possibilities. It's my business to do what I can to protect two hundred and fifty . . . no, maybe a thousand men, from the risk of being left to drown or suffocate as those men on the *Lisbon Maru* were left to drown or suffocate. And it's not just my business, it's yours as well. We're not in the position of making choices any more. Only decisions. If we make the wrong decision, kill the wrong man, then that will be a terrible thing which will be on our consciences all our lives. But that's where it will end. But if we fail to do what in our hearts we know we have to do and as a result of that failure we condemn, or even risk condemning, not just one man, but hundreds to an unfair death, then we shall have utterly betrayed the oaths we have taken and the trust that was placed in us." He looked for a long time at the unhappy young man who stood with lowered head before him, hating what he was doing, knowing what he was doing: destroying innocence. And then he made an end to it:

"I'm sorry, Andrew," he said, "but the Americans have a phrase for it. The buck stops here."

★ ★ ★

When Stacey came, Moore said: "I have asked you to join us so that we can get this matter settled."

"What matter?" Stacey blustered, striking his pose, hands clasped behind him pulling his shoulders back.

"Come off it," said Brimmacombe.

"Yes," said Moore wearily. "Let's not

310

waste time. It looks suspicious all four of us being together up here. We could be sent down any minute. You know perfectly well, Stacey, why I've sent for you. Someone told the Japanese where that battering-ram and that paraffin were. And that someone was either you or Sutcliffe."

"Why?" demanded Stacey. "They *all* knew . . . "

"Where the battering-ram was, yes. Not where the paraffin was. It was only two nights ago Worboys moved it to the cesspit area — on my instructions. Until you insisted all officers should know, the only other person who knew where that paraffin was, was Captain Brimmacombe. But the Japanese knew."

"Guesswork," said Stacey. For all his efforts to hold his pose, the fear was manifest.

"I haven't time to argue this," said Moore, yet unhurriedly. "The Japanese knew exactly where that paraffin was. Someone had told them. That someone spoke Japanese. I have that on the authority of the Japanese Commanding Officer. The only man I know who both knew where that paraffin was and who speaks Japanese is you . . . "

"Sutcliffe knew!" Stacey blurted out. "I told him." And, hastily: "In fact it was he who asked me to find out from you where it had been moved to! Sutcliffe is quite good in Japanese now. And he saw Fujimoto. That's when he must have told him. When he got the cigarettes. I didn't speak to the Japanese . . . "

"But you did," said Moore. "They beat you up."

"Sutcliffe saw them! He saw Fujimoto! He was given cigarettes . . . I didn't see Fujimoto! I just got beaten up . . . Do you think they'd beat up someone who was helping them? Why should I tell them anyway?" Stacey's pose had quite collapsed; his face was ashen, his hands shaking.

"Why should Sutcliffe?"

"He admires them! He thinks they're going to win! He gets food! And cigarettes!" Stacey was saying anything. The sentences followed each other in jerky succession, each delivered as the new thought crossed his mind. "He doesn't care for any of us! He's a

312

strange man! No one knows anything about him! Jim! It wasn't me! You've got to believe me! I wouldn't do a thing like that! I wouldn't . . . " He broke off. There were tears in his eyes, pleading on his piggy face.

But Moore was stone.

"Either you or Sutcliffe told the Japanese," he said. "And if it was Sutcliffe, then you are as much responsible because it was you who told him where the paraffin had been moved to."

"But I didn't realise . . . Jim! You can't . . . "

"Shut up," said Moore quietly. "And come here." He moved to the edge of the hold. Stacey followed, trembling. Brimmacombe and Anderson watched in silence from a little distance, wondering what was to happen. "Look at those men," Moore said. "Either through treachery or stupidity you have put their lives at an even greater risk than they are already."

"Yes, I see that . . . " Stacey began eagerly.

"Shut up," said Moore again. "Now listen. And carefully. You will go back into the hold while we decide what to do. You will not say one word of this to Sutcliffe. You will tell him that I have had this meeting to let the other officers know what our new punishment is to be. That instead of continuing on to Japan we are to be put ashore to work in the stone mines. We will be replaced by other prisoners and it'll probably be about forty-eight hours before the switch can be organised. Are you clear on that?"

"Yes, Jim." He started to repeat it, but was curtly cut short.

"A further punishment is that we are to have no food or water for the next twenty-four hours. You may tell Sutcliffe that as well. And nothing more! Be sure of this, Stacey, if you say anything else — anything — then you will not live long enough to miss being short of food or water."

Stacey swallowed. His head moved like a chicken's as he tried to find moisture in his mouth.

"Jim," he said. "Jim, I . . . " He threw out a hand to grasp Moore's arm. "Listen," he began. "Please listen . . . "

314

Moore threw the hand off. "Don't put your hands on me," he snapped. "You make me sick. Now get down into that hold and if you have any ambition to meet again any of these people whose names you drop so frequently, you will do exactly what I've told you to."

★ ★ ★

"That isn't true, is it?" said Brimmacombe. "That we're going to the stone mines?"

"No," said Moore. "Just an extra precaution. If Sutcliffe thinks we're going to be decanted, he'll be that much less likely to try to tell someone we've got that carving knife."

"You think it *was* Sutcliffe, Sir?" Anderson said. Moore nodded. "But why? What did he hope to get out of it? And surely he'd have realised the Japs would do something about it?"

Through the balance of the night, levering himself from one sore hip on to the other, trying to find some reasonable position on the bauxite, Moore had asked himself such questions. Why? What does the man gain? A few cigarettes? When

315

he has a store already? When he doesn't smoke? But cigarettes were currency and men like Sutcliffe fixed no limits. To his like the first fifty thousand pounds was merely a stepping-stone to the first one hundred thousand; the first million to the second. It was a disease — a disease which had them grabbing anything, however small, on which a profit could be made. Life was barter; if you had something of value, you cashed in on it. If others were hurt along the way, that was just too bad, irrelevant. The summons to Fujimoto had no doubt been accidental. But once face to face with him, with the Commanding Officer, Sutcliffe would have felt at home. A curious thought when most men would have avoided such an encounter. But Sutcliffe would have welcomed it. He'd have been back at the boardroom table. Back facing the Chairman knowing he had information the Chairman lacked. Believing that through passing on that information he could establish a relationship to his own advantage. That was the weakness of men like Sutcliffe — the blind spot. They judged everyone by themselves.

Having no honour, they did not believe in honour's existence. In their book everything had its price; and every person had his price. Not for an instant would it have occurred to Sutcliffe hat Fujimoto would have effectively named him.

Moore's thoughts had shifted to Fujimoto. *Bushido*, he thought — 'The Way of the Warrior.' No Westerner could properly grasp the workings of the mind of a man like Fujimoto, the curious blend of affections which allowed a man to see others die in fearful agony and not raise a finger to assist them and yet find his own honour stained by contact with that most dishonourable man of all, the traitor. It would not have occurred to Sutcliffe that Fujimoto would have made his treachery so public. How senseless to kill the goose that lays the golden eggs! Sutcliffe would have imagined discovery of the battering-ram and paraffin would have been made under the camouflage of some routine search; would possibly even have suggested this during their conversation. "I do not know his name," Fujimoto had said. "Only that he speaks some Japanese." By that limited statement, by making such a drama of the search, by granting an interview to himself Fujimoto had assuaged his honour whilst at the same time recovering, as he thought, all the equipment which might, should the worst occur, enable his prisoners to survive. For Moore was under no illusions; Fujimoto would have had his orders — the same orders his opposite number on the *Lisbon Maru* had acted upon. If the *Dai Nichi* was attacked, the prisoners were to be battened down. Fujimoto would not find it dishonourable to allow a thousand prisoners-of-war to drown or suffocate who might otherwise be saved; he would be merely behaving in the way a warrior should — merely doing what he was ordered as a warrior to do.

Moore repeated Anderson's questions: "What did he hope to get out of it? Kudos, cigarettes, protection. Didn't he realise the Japs would do something about it? Yes. But he thought they'd do it slyly. As he would have done it if in charge. He thought they'd cover him. You see, Andrew, he made the same mistake we and America made.

He thought it possible, on the basis of logic, to forecast what the Japanese would do."

Anderson was half convinced. "Yes," he said hesitantly. "I see." And after a moment: "And you're absolutely sure it *was* him?"

Moore shook his head. "Not absolutely sure. It just possibly could have been Stacey."

"So what do we do, Sir — if we're not absolutely sure?"

"We make sure, Andrew."

"How?"

"They both have to pay the penalty."

The young man's eyes opened wide in horror. "You mean . . . " he said. And he waited, hardly daring to say the word. "You mean, Sir, kill them both?"

Moore nodded. "I'm afraid there's no alternative."

"Oh, God," said Anderson.

"Freddie?" Moore said levelly. "Do you agree with me or not?"

"I agree," said Brimmacombe.

"You're sure? Don't let me persuade you."

"Brimmacombe put both hands to his

hips; huge hams of hands for all the deprivation.

"Certain," he said.

"Then," Moore said in a kindly tone to Anderson, "you don't need to give an opinion. The voting would at least be two to one in favour."

"We . . . we haven't asked Dixon. If Dixon were well . . . " He didn't finish it.

"Dixon is going to die," said Moore. "You know that. A few men seem to find the way of shaking it off even without drugs to help them. But Dixon isn't one of them. Dixon is going to die. I give him two days at the maximum."

There was a long silence between the three men. In that silence other sounds were sharp and clear: the call of sea birds, the sounds of the next ten men coming up, low voices from the hospital, the siren of a distant ship, the chattering of Japanese close by, even the hooting of a car.

"I suppose you're right," said Anderson, making up his mind. "But only because I can't think of an alternative . . . " "And then the question: "How, Sir?"

"There's only one way," said Brimma-combe. "They must be strangled."

"Strangled!"

"Silently."

"You've been trained to do it?" Moore asked surprised.

"Yes."

"I thought you'd never seen action."

"I haven't. But I was trained for action." He laughed ironically. "I was trained as a commando. Did you ever hear of Operation 'Workshop'?" Moore shook his head. "No," said Brimmacombe. "You wouldn't have. But as you were at Gibraltar at the time, if it had happened you might have been involved in it."

Another misjudgment, Moore thought. Commando trained. No wonder he wanted to take the *Dai Nichi* over. But he only said: "It had better be Sutcliffe first. Tonight. There won't be any problem there. Fujimoto's expecting it. Anyway what's another corpse here or there so far as they're concerned? They never look at them."

"And Stacey?" said Brimmacombe.

"When we sail," said Moore. "The first night at sea."

15

DURING the two days the *Dai Nichi* was anchored off Takao some minor repairs were carried out and supplies of food and water brought aboard. More prisoners died, some in the hospital, some in the holds, and their bodies were wrapped in sacking. One of the sewn up sacks contained Sutcliffe's corpse.

At first sight the problems of secretly executing a man in an illuminated hold crammed with men had seemed almost insuperable — it might well be that the majority were already convinced of the identity of the traitor (and in fact many had made this plain) but the last thing Moore wished to have made public was the identity of his executioner. Moreover, whatever Sutcliffe's private thoughts might be they would surely include the apprehension that something of this nature was being planned. He must therefore be killed swiftly, silently, unexpectedly and secretly; Brimmacombe, who had been taught how to creep up behind a sentry and with one hand across his throat and one behind his neck, stifle the life out him in moments, could meet the first two of these requirements — the third called for superb timing and the last would have to be Moore's responsibility.

The main difficulty was the light, the naked bulb hanging on its scuffed flex, hard, cold and at Sutcliffe's level, penetrating. Yet it was this very light which offered the solution. If the light could be cut off at the instant Brimmacombe was positioned to carry out the execution, all the other conditions could be met. And so it was organised.

The electrical supply to the hold had been in the habit of breaking down; both in Singapore and off Saigon there had been periods when for unexplained reasons the light in their hold had failed. It was obvious both from this and from the quality of the flex, that the lighting had been provided on a hurried, makeshift basis — if light were normally provided it would have been by conduit and had the *Dai Nichi* not been a turn-of-the-century ship, no doubt it would have been. Therefore, Moore reasoned, the supply was taken as a branch off some main cable and, checking, he soon found the source: an amateurish mess of wires and electrician's tape running across the deck between the two forward hatches with the main run heading for the foremost hold and a junction taken from this to their own. All that was required to plunge their hold into darkness was a good strong two-handed yank on their lead while the main cable was firmly anchored by his foot.

The problem of timing, however, remained — for from the top deck, Sutcliffe's location could not be seen, being masked by the lower deck overhang. Regretfully, Moore called upon the services of Anderson. He might have relied on Worboys, whom he trusted implicitly, but he decided against spreading involvement further. Approached, Anderson reluctantly agreed. He had, as indeed had most of the men in the hold, even including Brimmacombe, accepted Moore as an inspiring Commanding

Officer and in his own case there were by now elements of hero-worship. Even so, the instincts of an essentially fair and gentle man rebelled against the cold-blooded killing of another who had shared (in some respects not without distinction) the horrors of the past three weeks. What seemed to make the business even more unpalatable was having to organise the execution in such precise, almost pernickety, detail.

"It somehow wouldn't seem so bad, Sir," he had said, "if all we had to do was put a revolver to his head and blow his brains out."

"We don't," Moore answered with a rare coldness to discourage any weakening, "have a revolver. And if we weren't on this bloody prison ship, it would be a firing squad for Sutcliffe and that, I can promise you, needs a great deal more dotting of i's and crossing of t's than this does."

By trial and error it was discovered both that Moore, standing in the correct place to dismember the connection, would be able to see Anderson's head when he was four rungs up the ladder and that

Anderson looking up from a position near the ladder's base could see Moore's head and shoulders if he stood in the correct place near the hospital; from thereon it was merely a question of waiting. Shortly after midnight Moore went to the benjo and thence to the hospital; Anderson signalled to the watching Brimmacombe who at once rose from his own space, and, making his way carefully between the encumbering bodies which lay between himself and his victim, stumbled enough to pour water from his bottle over Sutcliffe who jumped to his feet. Moore made the few key paces to the electrical junction while Brimmacombe, covering his movement by apologies, stationed himself correctly. Anderson mounted four rungs of the ladder, Moore yanked out the connection and Brimmacombe strangled Sutcliffe. While he was doing so, Anderson dropped to the platform and howled with mock pain. His yell coinciding with the sudden darkness caused instinctive cries from several wakeful prisoners and commotion amongst a number of the Japanese above; in turn sleeping prisoners startled into wakefulness, forgetting they were still in port, assumed the ship had been attacked. In the ensuing turmoil, which because of the blackness was little removed from panic, it was a simple matter for Brimmacombe, once satisfied Sutcliffe was dead, to slide his feet away and let him lither back on to his groundsheet and then, kneeling beside him, re-arrange his head upon his kitbag. Anderson meanwhile shouted for calm, Moore came quickly down the ladder and, illuminated by torchlight from the decks above, reassured the prisoners and order was restored.

Within an hour the electrical junction had been repaired. The seaman, who was used to carrying out such bodgings in a ship of such antiquity, was more angry at being hauled from his bunk than suspicious of sabotage; it was not the first time some clumsy passenger had caught his foot in a trailing wire. The Japanese, aware of the shortcomings of the vessel which was returning them to their homeland, lay back in their slots; the prisoners settled once again to the misery of another night. And Sutcliffe lay dead, unnoticed, and was found thus in the morning. He was one of three men who died in the hold that night who were all within the same half-hour sewn up in sacking, hauled up by the pulley system and laid in a line ready to be added to those from other holds who had also died and were to be taken ashore by lighter for disposal ashore.

★ ★ ★

"What was so strange," said Moore to Brimmacombe, "was that you wouldn't have known there was any difference between them. A stable-hand, a regular serviceman and a man who would have made the headlines."

"You really believe that?" said Brimmacombe.

Moore nodded: "Sutcliffe had just those qualities men need to reach the top. Single-mindedness, intelligence, ruthlessness, self-control and a kind of charm. When I looked at that middle sack, I realised I had put to death a man who, had he survived the war, might have done very important things."

"*We* put to death . . . ."

"No, Freddie. It is not the hangman who condemns the murderer."

They were back on deck. A thin wisp of smoke from *Dai Nichi*'s funnel indicated they would be sailing that day. Otherwise it was all the same — the loitering Japanese, the benjo queue, the remaining sick men on the hatch covers, the endless files of men ascending and descending from the hold. The only thing different from the previous day was the weather, which was curiously overcast like a cloudless summer sky obscured by smoke. It was very hot, very still and the sun seemed to have lost its glare but not its ferocity.

"What do you think Sutcliffe would have done?" said Brimmacombe.

Moore shrugged. He was dressed as smartly as he was able to manage in best whites; but the whites were stained and dingy. His peaked cap was at a jaunty angle — but he did not look jaunty. His eyes were sunken, his cheeks were hollow, there were lines of pain at the corners of his mouth.

His beard was unimpressive. But he

had done his best — it was possible there would be a funeral service. Anything was possible. It was still not impossible they might all be landed on Formosa. No one could forecast what the Japanese might do.

"I imagine," he answered, "he'd have gone into whatever was the most profitable thing the war threw up. He'd have been working it out. Shortages. Bound to be a lot of those. Might have gone in for commodities. Or property. They say most millionaires make their money out of property."

"You think he'd have made himself a millionaire?"

"Oh, yes," said Moore. "Unquestionably."

"And yet no one on the boat knows anything about him."

"Yes, it's queer, Freddie, isn't it? Well, we'll find out one day — assuming we survive."

Brimmacombe cocked his head at the first depressing remark he had heard from Moore. "You'll be making a report?" he said.

"Of course."

"You'd like some written corroboration

from Andrew and me?"

"Yes, please."

"I'll get on with it right away."

"Yes," said Moore. "I think that would be as well."

"How are you, Jim?" Brimmacome asked.

"Don't worry. I shall do. But I'm going to be spending most of my time in the queue unless things improve. There's just one thing. About Sutcliffe."

"What's that, Jim?"

"He'd have got to the top. No question. But only by using others as stepping-stones. We may, between us, have destroyed a quite remarkable man but the one thing certain is that we've saved an awful lot of others from despair."

* * *

Brimmacombe watched Moore join the benjo queue. Would he do? he wondered. The man had dysentery. Many men had dysentery, probably the majority. Some could not resist it while others seemed to possess the chemistry if not to throw it off, at least to contain it. But they were

331

mostly young men, in their prime, while Moore was approaching forty — after Toms, the oldest in the hold. If Moore should die, then command would fall to him. It was something which at the beginning he would have been glad to assume but now, he admitted, he was not so sure about. Moore's example would be difficult to follow and there would only be Anderson, young, raw, inexperienced, to help him. Dixon was dying. It was odd how willingly Dixon seemed to have succumbed. One would have imagined that a Battle of Britain hero would have fought as hard as any. He remembered, with regret, his early strictures — how clearly, he thought, Moore had seen it: "They made him a Flight Lieutenant for what he could do in his Spitfire; not what he could do in a prison ship." The only consolation was that his dying was, relatively speaking, a peaceful affair. Some died so horribly, screaming their last few hours away, knowing they were going and sobbing aloud their desire to live.

Then there was Stacey. Supposing, Brimmacombe asked himself, Moore were suddenly to deteriorate — could I, with only an uncertain Anderson to back me, go through with it? Do I have that courage? The man should die; Moore's reasoning was sound. Either he, not Sutcliffe, had betrayed — the hold; or if it had been Sutcliffe, then he had done so on information obtained by bribery from Stacey. For bribes came in many forms — it had not necessarily been cigarettes which had corrupted Stacey: the consideration had been perhaps more subtle.

He got no further with these deliberations for, turning away from watching Moore edging his way slowly towards the benjo, he saw, to his astonishment, the man who had been occupying his thoughts accompanying the interpreter, O'Hana, towards the midships superstructure.

"Stacey!" he called unthinkingly. "Where the hell d'you think you're going?"

Stacey stopped in his tracks as if hit in the back. He turned. There was a strange expression on his face; it was as if he had been drugged. His eyes met Brimmacombe's but in them there was no recognition.

"I said," bawled Brimmacombe, "where d'you think you're going?"

Stacey shook his head as if to clear it, then spoke: "I don't know," he said in a dull, flat tone. "I've been sent for."

O'Hana took a hand.

"Speedo! Speedo!"

Brimmacombe ignored him. "Who's sent for you?" he demanded.

"I don't know," said Stacey, then added listlessly: "Fujimoto, I suppose."

O'Hana struck him fiercely across the face. "Colonel Fujimoto!" he screeched.

"Yes," said Stacey, hand up to his cheek. "I'm sorry. Colonel Fujimoto." And he turned away, following an angry, muttering O'Hana and was lost from view as he entered the midships structure. He was only to be seen once more: in a launch which was apparently sent especially to collect him. He stood at the stern in his accustomed pose, hands clasped behind his back, his peaked cap at an angle, looking up at his three fellow officers watching his departure. He stood for a long time staring up at them but he made no signal.

16

ON November 14th, 1942, in a sudden flurry of activity, the *Dai Nichi Maru* weighed anchor and, as part of a substantial convoy, set off for Japan taking, as Moore had forecast, a route northwards between the west coast of Formosa and the Pescadores Islands. Her destination had been discovered to be the port of Shimonoseki at the western end of the Inland Sea which divides the Japanese main island of Honshu from its southern neighbour, Kyushu — Shimonoseki being, as it happens, about midway between Nagasaki and Hiroshima. The distance to be covered was nine hundred and forty-eight nautical miles and Moore had calculated that, if all went well, in five day's time the ordeal would be over.

All did not go well. Within a few hours of quitting Formosa the *Dai Nichi* developed some fault the nature of which was never to be discovered by the prisoners — perhaps she had engine trouble, perhaps a blocked oil-feed, perhaps a bearing had gone. For several hours she lay hove-to while the balance of the convoy steamed on and was soon lost from sight. Meanwhile the weather was steadily deteriorating and the sea roughening. When movement was restored it was at a slower pace, perhaps four knots. There was no hope of catching up the convoy or, more to the point, of avoiding the typhoon sweeping up the China coast which, presumably, had been the cause of the abrupt departure from Takao. Hour by hour the sky darkened, the rain fell more heavily, the wind increased, the sea grew worse. Finally, opposite an island of the Pescadores Group, the engines were stopped, the anchor was dropped and the *Dai Nichi*, taking advantage of the little shelter the island gave, prepared to ride out the storm.

★ ★ ★

Yates held on grimly to the bulwark rail staring at a scene more desolate than any he could recall. Ahead was a long and quite deserted bay against which fearful breakers conjured from a grey and sullen sea crashed endlessly. There was not a sign of life but on a bluff of hill, shrouded by vapour, was a solitary radio mast which somehow seemed to emphasize abandonment to nature. The rain poured down relentlessly, driven by the gale which whined and shrieked through the *Dai Nichi*'s rigging. Her decks, glistening grey, heaved and pitched, the water on them, unable to escape fast enough through the scuppers, racing madly, now in this direction, now in that. Waves, interrupted in their shoreward path, smashed angrily against her flanks, twisting her, bucking her, rolling her, straining her against her anchor, throwing up geysers of bitter drenching spray. Above, troops of black clouds turned the light sepulchral.

Yates was barefoot now: the linen straps had long since torn away from his clogs and nothing he had been able to fashion since had proved effective. So now he climbed the iron ladder, and went down the iron ladder, three times daily in feet which were rust-ingrained and painful. Between the toes the skin was a cracked and bleeding mess of tinia; the nails were broken, ingrowing at the corners, lodged with filth. His crutch was raw with some undefined complaint and the skin of his testicles peeled daily. Strange smartings hurt his eyes, filling them with water so that everything was blurred. In the seams of his torn and soiled shorts lice had made their home and came to feed upon his body whenever it grew warm.

Yet he had no trace of dysentery. Three times a day he picked his way in the penumbra of the hold amongst the stench, the filth and the dying men, calling for volunteers — pleading, cajoling, shaming, commanding men to come up with him; and, finally successful, he stood by the benjos, superintending the operation, sticking his head into each lavatory in turn to ensure it was fully cleared, enduring the appalling reek and the evil sight of bloodied excreta and the foulness of it all. Yet he had no dysentery.

It was not of such things he thought

as he stood holding on to the *Dai Nichi*'s rail. The benjo cleaning had become a part of life — he neither dreaded, nor welcomed, its onset; he did not see himself heroic nor even resolute. What he did realise was that he had become a person. Through all his life he had seen himself as an object which, almost accidentally, existed in a world peopled by others who had direction and purpose.

It had never occurred to him that he could initiate anything; he was a mere follower doing his best to fit in unobtrusively.

Self-effacing more than shy, he had asked little more than to be left alone in peace. Waverley Hotel had, in fact, quite suited him, for a little boy who behaves himself is, in such an establishment, barely noticed.

But because his life had always been run in this minor key he had never been able to stand away clearly and look only at himself; he had lived a life with his back against a wall, viewing the world in front defensively. At school his defence had been self-effacement — and this had not always worked; at home, (insofar as Waverley Hotel could be regarded as home), he had known no way of dealing with a stepfather who had assumed a role into which only a son of undeniable capacity could have fitted with distinction.

And then there was this other thing — this shameful dissimilarity which set him apart from normal men and women, which inhibited him from sharing Commander Moore's Dutch wife, from allowing their bodies to touch. He had woken some nights to find himself pressed up against his Commanding Officer and the temptation to stay like this, to feel the warmth and sureness of Moore's body against his own, even to plead for an arm to be put around him, had been all but overwhelming. And when he had hastily moved away, jammed his head on the hard, uncomfortable wickerwork which was his pillow and created a physical space between them, the utter loneliness of his life had saddened him. His abnormality was a closely guarded secret, kept, he suspected, largely because of the little interest he had aroused in others, and penetrated, so far as he believed, only by his stepfather. 'Cissy,' Legette had often called him, even publicly. But Yates understood. 'Cissy,' was the word he used — but only as a euphemism for something more accurately descriptive.

Were it not for this vicious corruption which he harboured, it is astonishingly probable that Yates would have found a greater contentment in his voyage on the *Dai Nichi Maru* than he had ever known before. Even as it was, through the daylight hours, when he and Moore were largely about their separate occupations, he was conscious of a sense of freedom, a sense of being able to make decisions which was entirely new. For the first time in his life he was well thought of, even praised, and men expressed surprise that he would do what they could not bring themselves to do.

And so he stood, in the pouring rain, in the howling wind, dressed in sodden khaki shirt and shorts, barefoot, bareheaded, gazing at a vista of inexpressible bleakness, accepting his lot phlegmatically, quite without despair.

In the hold life was slipping away from Dixon. Too weak now to use a utensil, he lay quite still, fouling himself. He was in little pain but was troubled by a raging thirst. He could see that it was raining and his befuddled consciousness indicated there was some connection between his discomfort and the weather. For the rest he concentrated on the sky. Through the portion of the open hatch in his line of vision he could see the derrick mast swaying backwards and forwards interrupting the dark, black, endlessly shifting clouds. What was strange about the clouds was that they moved both ways, sideways as well as forwards. He had never seen clouds do that before. There had been clouds like these before . . . somewhere. But the clouds had not been moving forwards and sideways at the same time. It was a mystery. If only that thing wouldn't keep interrupting — wouldn't keep getting in the way . . .

Worboys brought him a drink. The tarpaulin catchment had been erected.

Dixon drank avidly, licking his flaking lips with pleasure. A little was spilt over his face and neck as the ship gave an unexpectedly heavy roll. But Dixon didn't notice. His thirst was for the moment assuaged. He could give all his attention to the clouds . . .

* * *

Farr was dying miserably, in frightful pain. The pain came in waves, a gnawing pain, as if, somehow, one of the rats had got inside his bowels. Then it would subside. When the paroxysm took him, Farr screamed — when it left him he waited in anguish for its returning and contemplated death.

Farr did not want to die. In the more peaceful intervals he would keep repeating this: that he didn't want to die. He wore only a shirt — there was no point in wearing more. His flanks were fouled and he no longer lay on a groundsheet but on a blanket. When the urge came upon him, Hodges would lift his wasted body, easily, and slip a utensil underneath, then trudge

343

with it to the cesspit area and return. Sometimes it took too long for him to return and then Lenny would stand in for him. For the rest of the time they played cards interminably: Hodges and Lenny — against Mac and Nobby.

* * *

The worst place of all was in the hospital. Such men there as still possessed the capacity for rational thought now saw the hold as homely, warm and comforting. For the first time cold was added to their suffering. They envied the men below their security and companionship. The fear of death by drowning no longer occurred to them. They lay on the hard hatch covers, wrapped in sodden blankets, listening to the shrieking wind, staring at the straining tarpaulins, wondering how long it would be before they were ripped and torn away. From time to time a cascade of spray would salt their faces but soon the rain would wash the salt away. They writhed with pain and shivered with the cold. They no longer thought, as before they had thought, of home, of freedom, of love and tenderness, of food and jollity. Their entire concentration was now given to less felicitous subjects: to their helplessness, their torment and to their bodies which they found disgusting.

★ ★ ★

After a number of hours the anchor was raised and the *Dai Nichi* set off slowly northwards. This was not because the weather showed improvement but because it was clearly worsening and it was obvious the ship was in danger of dragging her anchor and being driven on to the rocky beach.

Such was the visibility that within a matter of minutes, for all the slowness of her progress, the *Dai Nichi* was out of sight of land and the world shrunk to an awful wilderness of wild windswept water in which one small, old, tired ship struggled to survive. Huge waves, their crests over-balancing, torn off in gigantic shreds by the howling gale, bore down and smashed the *Dai Nichi*'s sides forcing rivulets of water through her plates. She shook and staggered, bowing and rearing to the onslaught. At times her foreparts dug so deep into the sea as to raise her stern clear of the water and then her propeller thrashed with a terrible, grinding vibration which seemed to threaten to tear her hull apart while huge cataracts smashed down, engulfing her.

It was unimaginable that the peak of malevolence had not been reached, yet hour by hour, as the typhoon tracked northwards slowly overtaking them, the weather worsened. The wind increased in force, the waves grew higher, the tumult grew — the ship fought on, inching her way, rolling, yawing, rearing, crashing down. The noise within the hold was awe-inspiring and the fear of submarines quite replaced by doubt as to how long her rust-thinned plates could hold against such savage battering. The only comfort was the engine pulse and the slow grind of propeller shaft . . . Until, suddenly, this was stilled.

The stillness came as a terrible shock. It was as if the ship had been deserted by its crew — as if, the prisoners felt, they had finally been abandoned. Now the motion changed. Soon beam on to the sea, no longer fighting it, the *Dai Nichi* lay at its mercy, wallowing, settling into the attitude of least resistance. The bucking, rearing, yawing changed to a sickening rise and fall accompanied by a savage uneven rolling with the *Dai Nichi* heavy in ballast slow to incline but recovering savagely. The sounds also changed. While the ship had been at anchor or making way, the huge waves had smashed against her hull and her bows had crashed down against tons of angry rising water and the sea had crashed upon her deck and hissed and slithered along its length; there had been no rhythm to the thudding and the banging and the seethe of water. Now there was a different symphony — a strange swishing sound which seemed to come from underneath and a sucking and a squelching as if each wave was reluctant to quit its prey, but paused momentarily hoping to drag her down into its black green depths. And as well as the sucking and the squelching, the racking stress caused scraping and creaking sounds as if each girder had been loosened at its joints and was trying to break free and each plate had thrown its rivets and was rubbing up against its fellow. Irregularly punctuating these different sounds was the lunatic behaviour of the fuel in the adjacent bunker. As the *Dai Nichi* canted over slowly the coal slithered with an extraordinary hissing, tumbling, grumbling roar; but when the fierce recovery occurred it was catapulted clear across to bang and clatter frantically against the hull on the windward side. Before, against the bedlam, men had raised their voices to carry on a conversation, now, except in the momentary madness of the coal shift, they could talk in normal tones; before, apart from the engine pulse and the grind of the propeller shaft, the sources of sound had been limited to the immediate area of the hold, but now tapping of metal on metal from, presumably, the engine room, was curiously clear. And, against all this background, there was a ghostlike and irregularly repeated twanging, which at first baffled interpretation but turned

348

out to be a mandolin which, hung high on some projection, thrummed its strings on every roll.

On earlier occasions when the sea had been rough, there had been problems in preventing gear from shifting. This was now magnified and it was almost as much as a man could do to keep his own position on the slimy bauxite which, most curiously, had enough innate cohesion to retain its slope. With each vicious roll there was a clatter of metal objects escaping from their owners, curses as kitbags roly-polyed down the hill, abuse, apology and insult. Nothing would keep in its place. The men arranged and re-arranged themselves, dug their heels into the bauxite, clung to each other through the worst gyrations. Above their heads the bulb, now lit, swung and circled violently, sending vast shadows chasing idiotically anywhere. Taken together the banging and the hissing and the twanging, the slithering and the sliding and the rolling, and the disturbing shadows, now here, now there, now gone, created an atmosphere as close to Bedlam as any man might imagine in his most fevered nightmares.

★ ★ ★

At the time the engines were stilled, Brimmacombe happened to be with Moore.

"They've shut the engines off!" he cried, alarmed.

"Yes."

"Can she ride out a sea like this? Without engine power?"

"The ship can ride it out — provided we don't get a cargo shift. Whether the men can is another matter."

"Have you ever been in a storm like this before?"

"No. And if I had been I'd have been better equipped to cope with it."

"Would you have shut off the engines?"

"Yes, I think I would."

"But surely they don't cut off the engines in a naval ship?"

"No, Freddie, they don't. But this isn't a navy ship. This is a broken-down old tub the best part of fifty years old which probably hasn't been properly serviced

350

since the Japs bought it and has been most likely done to death ever since. You heard that screw coming out of the water?"

"Yes."

"Well, what you have to do when that happens is to slam the throttle shut or you risk tearing the mainshaft to pieces. I don't suppose the controls on this old girl are quite as responsive as they are on a destroyer."

"No, I don't . . . God, that was a lurch!" cried Brimmacombe, breaking off and grabbing at Moore to stop himself tipping over. "Sorry, Jim!"

"Not to worry."

"If it goes on like this . . . Christ! . . . What in God's name was that?"

Moore waited until he could again be heard. "That was the coal shifting in the bunker."

"Sounded like a bloody bombardment! Can the plates take it?"

"They'll take it. It's only lumps of coal."

"How long's this going to go *on* for God's sake?"

"Days, maybe."

"I thought typhoons were . . . you know. Come and gone."

"We're not into it properly yet."

"Say something cheerful."

"All right. We're on the worst side of it. In the dangerous semi-circle."

"How d'you know?"

"From the direction of the wind."

"From the . . . Hallo! Here we go again!"

Brimmacombe waited for the new assault upon his ears to lessen.

"God, Stacey was lucky!" he said enviously, when it had.

"Got off in the nick of time." And after a moment, quietly: "Did we kill the wrong man, Jim?"

"We did what we had to do."

"That isn't an answer."

"It is, Freddie."

"Well, it's not a good answer."

"You mean it isn't the answer you want me to give." There was a long silence between them, through which they listened to the various sounds. At the end of another shift of coal, Moore said: "There are a number of possible answers. The worst one is that we *did*

352

kill the wrong man. The thing against that is that they didn't come looking for a carving-knife. Another answer is that Stacey's going is pure coincidence; that they want him as an interpreter — that's quite a reasonable possibility. An officer in a prison camp who speaks English and good Japanese is a pretty useful chap to have around . . . " He broke off. "What the hell's that twanging?"

"God knows," said Brimmacombe. "Go on. You're cheering me up."

"Well, stretching it, I suppose he's got connections." Moore shook his head. "No. If it had been that, it would have happened in Japan."

"If it had been what?"

"If someone had been pulling strings. Arranging a swap. Could happen. Not very likely but if we're to judge by the names he dropped, he certainly knew a lot of people."

"Maybe he asked to be taken off. Guessed what was going to happen . . . But then they'd have come looking for that carving-knife . . . " Brimmacombe smiled wryly. "All a bit of a waste of time, Jim, wasn't it? Pinching that knife.

If we used it, all we'd do would be fill the place with sea!"

"It's still a long way to Japan."

"How long would we last in this lot; if we did get off?"

"We wouldn't last five minutes. But if it's any comfort, neither would any of our friends."

★ ★ ★

"He's gone," said Hodges.

"Poor bleeder," said Nobby.

Hodges shook his head. "Lucky sod, you mean," he said. But his eyes glistened with tears. Suddenly he was angry. "Who owns that bloody thing!" he shouted.

His shout silenced all conversation within a considerable radius. He staggered to his feet just as the Dai Nichi rolled.

He swayed like a drunken man but somehow contrived to keep his balance.

"Who owns that bloody banjo!" he yelled.

"I do," replied a distant voice.

"Then stop it making that bloody row!"

"I can't reach it. Not while it's rolling."

"Have we got to listen to that bloody thing twanging all the way to fucking Japan?"

"Look," the voice called back. "If you want to . . . "

But all the spirit suddenly left Hodges.

"Oh, Christ!" he said. And flopped down on the bauxite.

He stared at the corpse of the man he had known ever since his early days in the army. "What are we going to do with him?" he asked.

"There's nowt we can do . . . not till this gives over," Lenny said.

"Bastards!" Hodges said. "Bloody bastards!" And he looked up to where the Japanese were. There were none to be seen; they had all withdrawn into their slots. "You bloody bastards!" he shouted up at them. "Do you hear me? Bloody bastards!"

"Easy, Bill," said Lenny. "Easy." He put a comforting arm on Hodges' shoulder.

"Oh my God," said Hodges in sudden misery. And he burst into tears. Lenny

355

stared at him. He had never thought to see a man like Hodges cry. Between them a man lay dead.

Beside him Mac was vomiting. In the background a mandolin twanged. Behind the bulkhead the coal had begun a new commotion.

17

FOR two days the *Dai Nichi* wallowed in the storm and by the end of them the conditions of the prisoners were beyond belief. Although temporarily permitted to use the stairways from the lower deck (which were easier being sloping instead of vertical), only the fittest and the most determined dared use the benjos and risk being swept overboard, and by now there was almost nothing in the hold which was not soiled by blood, mucus, excreta or vomit. The stench was unspeakable; the air was foul. The bulb, replaced more than once, unceasingly cast its sweeping shadows but its light never could penetrate the furthest depths. Men lay dead and dying. With the temperature at last fallen, men died unnoticed, wrapped in blankets — assumed asleep. When they died, the lice quit their cooling flesh and sought new hosts. There was no way by which the dead could be removed and no place within the hold to shift them to — they were merely moved a trifle for the better convenience of those around them. In the case of Farr, his corpse served as table for the desperate bridge which Lenny Brooks insisted they continue — this was not indifference, not even apathy: it was simply the practical thing to do. The rats nosed around the dead and there were unpleasant ripping sounds but there was nothing which could be done about it. There was sobbing and shrieking from men in pain and jabbering from men who were delirious. But the hiccuping was the worst, for hiccuping meant death was near. There was more than dysentery: there was malaria, fevers, raging toothaches, kidney problems — all manner of complaints. There were men with tropical ulcers, open wounds and broken bones. But there was no doctor, no bandages, no medicine.

Life of a kind went on. The huge bucket of food was lowered twice daily (only now from the lower deck) and swung ferociously before it reached the platform where a party braced against it, keeping it from sliding off, the men who still had appetite helped themselves to any quantity they wanted. The food was still the same: weevil-ridden rice and the pink fishy-flavoured soup which sometimes had a few slices of dried potato lurking at the bottom. For all the torrents pouring from the sky, water was strictly rationed to half a pint per man per day, for, with the ship now firmly battened down, Worboys' tarpaulin catchment had been dismantled. Yet for all its stench, its airlessness, its horror, there was a strange cosiness about the hold. Men dressed in shirts and shorts did not care to exchange it for the howling, bitter wind; the driven rain, the swirling snow. They did not want to look at the battlefield which was the sea. Yet what there was to see was so remarkable that those who ventured up recounted it at length to their less spartan companions. The waves were towering tall and the *Dai Nichi* lay amongst them, used by them as they chose. Her rolling added to the theatrical effect, exaggerating their height still further. One moment she appeared to be poised on the pinnacle of a gigantic crest, on the edge of a black-green slippery slope of awesome depth down which surely she must slither to her doom — and then, amazingly, in a twinkling almost, the slope had vanished and been replaced by a giant wave, seemingly a hundred feet in height, its crest seething with white foam and spray which had nowhere else to go but crash down vertically. These made the horizon — the waves; they were too high to see beyond and in any case the torrential rain and the driven spray dramatically reduced the visibility. It was as if the world had been swept clear of everything but a small grey boat in a wild tempestuous sea under the lowering clouds.

★ ★ ★

The surviving members of the so-called *hospital* had been brought down — a macabre, nightmare business involving wrapping each like a parcel in roped tarpaulin and lowering them, swaying dangerously like pendulums, into waiting, upraised arms below, and although the overall numbers had been reduced by death, because of the roped-off area the hold was no less crammed. Those who could read or play cards were vastly in the minority and (except for men too ill to be concerned with anything but their own discomfort) existence resolved itself into stunned hours of lying on the bauxite which were only broken by the twice daily meal, the water ration and the performing of bodily functions. With only the most stubborn of exceptions, such occupations as washing, shaving and keeping kit in order were abandoned. Tobacco was exhausted. Small luxuries were a memory.

And yet morale stayed high. This was the most extraordinary thing about that voyage. Faced with death all around them, the majority assumed they would survive and with an incredible patience accepted their situation. The officers and N.C.O.s no longer had any significant part to play — Toms had abandoned all ideas of concerts; the future possibility of being a cook had not been considered by Rudge for many days; Kerrison had vanished somewhere into the gloom; Anderson, astonishingly recovered from both dysentery and sea-sickness, rebuilt his health through sleep; Moore, iller still, grimly determined to get through, now strictly limited his activities. Of more than two hundred men there were now just two who stood out brilliantly: an officer and an N.C.O. — Brimmacombe, tirelessly making his rounds, always encouraging, never glum; Worboys, organising the little there was left to organise: the food, the water, the recording of the dead. Even Yates had lost his purpose; had it been possible to sluice the benjos there would have been no volunteers.

He was however amongst the few who continued to use them at the slightest temporary easing of the storm and whenever he was absent, Moore worried, imagining him swept overboard. Head back on his Dutch wife, he passed much of the time wondering about the lad who had earned his admiration and yet of whom he knew so little. They talked, quietly, of many things: of Moore's home life, his wife, his children, village, hobbies, experiences. Now there was nothing which Moore was not willing to share. But Yates held back. The mystery of how he had come to own these queer possessions — the pair of pyjamas which he never wore, the pith helmet, the wicker basket, the books — was not explained. Nor, for a time, would he budge on that even greater mystery, his refusal to share the Dutch wife, his insistence on using the wicker basket as a pillow. But in this Moore sensed suppression rather than evasion and perceived a growing urge in Yates for the penitent's comfort of the confessional box. He waited patiently — and at last his patience was rewarded.

It was during the second night of the storm. Moore had been sleeping fitfully and woke to find, as he had not infrequently found before, the boy's body against his own. This did not trouble him; on the contrary he found it as comforting as if it had been Charlie. But Yates awoke suddenly and at once shifted himself away.

"Why do you do that, Yates?" Moore asked quietly.

"Do what, Sir?"

"Shift away from me as if I had the plague or something."

There was no immediate answer. But

the reply when it came shocked Moore with its challenging misery.

"Because I'm a bloody pansy!"

There was another long silence before Moore said: "And what makes you believe you are?"

"You think I don't know . . . Sir?" It was not the kind of pause which Sutcliffe had employed — the pause which insults. It was a pause of sheer forgetfulness. For that brief moment, Yates had forgotten where he was. In that brief moment something even worse than what was happening to him in this hold had filled his mind.

"I'm not at all sure you do," Moore responded. "You certainly don't give me that impression."

"Well I am!" Yates spoke like a spoilt child determined to have his way. "I have been ever since school."

Since school, thought Moore. "Is that where you discovered you were a pansy, Yates?" he asked. "At school?"

"Yes." A curious mixture of reluctance and relief was in the reply.

"Did they know at school?"

"It wasn't like that at all."

"What *was* it like then?" Moore insisted. "Tell me, Yates." And, after a moment, almost as if it were an afterthought: "there'll never be another chance like this, you know."

It struck home. The man who had nursed a secret which had poisoned his whole boyhood seized the opportunity.

It was not a pretty story.

★ ★ ★

"My stepfather sent me to this school," Yates began. "St Winifred's . . . You wouldn't think that an *army* man would send his stepson to a school with a name like that, would you, Sir? Particularly run by a woman! But it was cheap you see. He couldn't run to the kind of boarding school you probably sent your own son to."

"Preparatory school."

"That's right. That's what he used to say at Waverley. 'My son's gone to prep school — it's the best thing you know. Toughen them up when they are young and then they don't have problems.'"

"How old were you? When you were sent there?"

"Six."

"Six!" said Moore. "That was young."

★ ★ ★

The house was Victorian. You came in through a gate off a main road, along a narrow path hemmed in by laurels into the hall. On the right was Mrs Latham's office, on the left a room beyond Yates's remembering, but beyond that, still fresh in his mind, what had once been an important conservatory and had now been converted into a classroom. At the back was a kitchen area where, in the evenings, the younger boys were sometimes allowed and a kindly woman read them *Black Beauty* while they toasted dry bread before an open fire which was very hot and created a lot of ash; and with the fork being too short they were always dropping the bread they were toasting into it and the bread they ate was grey and tasted salty. There were two floors of bedrooms — the first with a bedroom at the front in which Mrs

366

Latham slept and which abutted another at the back. Then the stairs mounted another flight to another two or three bedrooms in one of which Yates slept for the first of his terms at St Winifred's. That was all of the house Yates could remember. Outside there was a shed, or perhaps it had been a barn, which had been converted into a classroom. So there was St Winifred's: three or four dormitories for the boys and a couple of classrooms.

But there was plenty of land including a field which, being called 'Seven Acre Field', was probably of that size. This and the kitchen had been the best part of St Winifred's to six-year-old Philip Yates. There were oaks in the field and horses and the smell of dung which had all been magical after Waverley and the hot, hard Highbury pavements. Even more magical than the field had been its boundary which had been a quietly flowing river where he had lain by the hour peering into it from its bank, lying on his stomach, dangling a worm tied to a piece of cotton — not to catch the fish, but to watch them putting their mouths around the worm and to lose himself into a life beneath the water which was nothing to do with stepfathers who insisted that experience was more important than a home, into a separate world which seemed all freedom. And across the river (out of bounds) was a thick mysterious wood, a jungle embowered with sweet smelling honeysuckle where huge butterflies which no one else but Yates had seen and which had never been seen anywhere else flitted by and the days were always joyous and unforgettable.

Yates paused. He had told his story this far with great conviction and Moore was by it taken out of the everlastingly rolling hold with its irritating, twanging mandolin, its vile odours, its filth and horror into a younger, sunlit world, watching an innocent little boy who had never had the kind of opportunities he had had himself, gaily chasing butterflies, smelling new flowers, hearing new bird-song, communing with fish in a cool, fresh, gently flowing stream. How magical that must have seemed — how truly a Shangri-la. If only, thought Moore, that could have been the sum of it; if only the story could have ended there, how different a person might the youngster beside him have become.

"Go on," he said. "What happened?"

What happened was that for some reason Yates was moved from the bedroom on the top floor into the one on the first floor, the room which backed Mrs Latham's. In this dormitory there were five beds — four occupied by small boys like Yates, the fifth by a much older boy whose name was Morris Sams. Sams slept in the corner by the window, farthest from Mrs Latham, and there was another bed between his and Yates's and two across the room.

The first time it happened, Yates had been suddenly awakened by Morris Sams climbing into his single bed, whispering to him to be quiet and to pull his pyjamas down. The question of refusing did not arise. Morris Sams was a giant. Morris Sams was all encompassing, greater than the masters, greater than Mrs Latham. Morris Sams was a big boy. When the pyjama trousers were down, Morris Sams was telling him to lie on his front and pull his bum apart and then there was this searing pain, that went in and out until some strange thing happened and Morris Sams was panting and whispering that he should tell no one and was gone, gone from the bed, softly back to his corner, leaving only pain and mystery behind.

That was the first time. After that the sounds were recognisable, for Morris Sams was catholic in his tastes and there were three other small boys to choose amongst. Yates never knew when he heard the coverlets thrown back who it would be tonight. Sometimes, when it was his turn, he would hear the creaking of Mrs Latham's bed and her voice calling out what was that noise in there — and when that happened Morris Sams would freeze on top of him: huge, heavy, a great weight blotting out the world and part of him still stuck in him. And always, when this happened, Morris Sams would wait, whispering to him to call out nothing was happening Mrs Latham and then lie quiet — and after a while, Morris Sams would pull himself out and go back to his own bed and for several nights there would be quiet in the dormitory.

Then, one day, someone in the conservatory asked one of the two masters how babies were born and another small boy called out I know, Sir, Morris Sams did it to me last night. And Morris Sams was taken off somewhere and something happened because he came back and his eyes were red and angry. But his parents were paying fees and so he didn't leave the school but moved to another dormitory. And the other boys there said it went on just the same.

"You never told anyone of this before, Yates?" Moore asked.

"No, Sir."

What a terrible thing, thought Moore, a little boy, growing up, nursing such a secret through the years. But even so, it hadn't been Yates's fault. He couldn't have stopped it happening. Any more than the other three little boys, or the boys in the other dormitory, could have stopped it happening. He said as much.

"Yes, Sir," agreed Yates. "But you see, you haven't got the point." Suddenly it was very easy — suddenly he wanted to tell everything about it. "The thing that matters, Sir," he went on, "was that I enjoyed Sams doing it to me. When I heard the creak of his bed, I used to feel my heart beating in anticipation. And when he went to one of the other boys, I was jealous. And lonely. All by myself in my bed while another boy was having it done to him. There was something extraordinarily intimate in it — the warmth of his body, the weight of him, the whispering, the way the rest of the world seemed blotted out."

★ ★ ★

Moore had assumed the role of Commanding Officer — for three weeks he had concentrated on that role. He felt that, on the whole, he had discharged his responsibilities capably. Now, with his own dysentery far advanced and with the conditions made utterly hopeless by the raging storm, he had come to accept there was no more for him to do — that now his responsibilities could be limited to his own survival. It wasn't so. Before his responsibility had been a general one — now it was particular. Many more would die before the *Dai Nichi* docked — and many afterwards from the sickness they carried ashore. But Yates was a survivor. He had escaped in a launch from Singapore and lived to be taken prisoner while all the others had perished; he had taken on the most revolting and dangerous job the *Dai Nichi* had to offer, and executing it with determination and distinction, come through unscathed. He would live and he deserved to live. But he must not live to carry for the rest of his life a cross even more killing than the one he had so willingly accepted here. He is, thought Moore, but one man out of two hundred. He is the one man I really know. Had I slept next to another, then perhaps I would have known that man equally well — perhaps discovered some other awful hang-up. Perhaps Yates is merely representative of these service youngsters all around enduring this frightful voyage with such astonishing restraint and resolution. But I cannot know them all and he is the one I know — and he has proved himself. And such strength as I have remaining should properly be used to extricate him, if I can, from the mortification to which he has condemned himself. If he is homosexual, then he must learn to accept his homosexuality as a peculiarity of temperament, or whatever the psychologists would call it; if he is not, if he has merely convinced himself, then, if I can rid him of this delusion, at least that will be one gain to set against the losses of this dreadful journey.

* * *

"You should have talked about this before," Moore said. "Told it to someone."

"Who?"

How much could be said so swiftly, Moore thought sadly — the whole world dismissed in a syllable.

"Not your mother?"

"Oh, no."

Moore guessed that Yates had loved his mother. But that she was lost to him — that Legette was in the way.

"Your stepfather then?"

"He didn't need to be told."

"What's that supposed to mean!" Moore was angry.

374

"He just knew."

"How could he know!?"

"He just did. He used to call me Cissy."

Moore was really angry now. He could see this so-called Captain Legette. "Tall, slim, good-looking. Very dark." Rightly or wrongly, Moore had a picture — a picture he did not like. He should be here, he thought. My God, he should he here! The *Dai Nichi* would cut him down to size!

"What of it?" Moore demanded. "He was merely being unpleasant. To call somebody 'Cissy' doesn't mean what you seem to think it does."

"I looked it up."

"Looked *what* up?"

"Sissy. In the dictionary. It means an effeminate man or boy."

"You can look up anything in a *medical* dictionary and find you've got it!"

"Yes, Sir. But that's what I am."

"Tell me," said Moore. "Has anything like what you told me happened at school, happened since?"

"Not exactly."

"And what does *that* mean?"

"Well there was this man at Waverley. He used to invite me to his room. When I was on holidays. He used to give me sweets . . . "

"And?"

"Well . . . well he liked to . . . to play with it."

"And you let him?"

"Yes, Sir."

"For the sweets?"

"Well . . . I don't think so. He had a gas fire. And a gas ring he used to boil a kettle on. He used to make me tea. And he had a wireless. You know, the kind that had a crystal. He used to let me play with his wireless."

"And in return you let him play with you. And you quite enjoyed his playing with you." And when Yates didn't answer: "Come on, come on! Admit it! No sense in holding anything back now. You quite enjoyed him playing with you."

"Yes. I did."

"And you think that's odd? That you enjoyed him playing with you?"

"Well, it *is* odd, isn't it?"

"No, it damn well isn't!" Moore had

actually forgotten where he was. For the first time since leaving Singapore. The only thing he had not forgotten was to keep his voice down — but then that had become a habit anyway. It was a habit with them all by now. To accommodate their voices according to the noises round them.

"Listen to me," Moore said. "When you left this school, you went to another boarding school?"

"No, Sir. I stayed at St Winifred's all the time."

"That was the only education that you had. A school like that!?"

"Yes, Sir."

"All right. If you had gone to another boarding school — if you'd gone to a Public School like I did. And Captain Brimmacombe did. And Lieutenant Anderson did. If you had, you'd have seen a lot of boys enjoying being played with. You know what 'endemic' means?"

"Yes, Sir."

"Well being played with, as you call it, and enjoying being played with, is endemic at boarding-schools. But it doesn't mean that Public Schools are crammed with homosexuals — although they have them. Naturally. It's a substitution, Yates. That's all. A substitution. It's how we're made, by God. If we're touched in the right way, in the right place, we respond. It doesn't have to be a girl who does the touching. Have you ever had a girl?"

"No, Sir."

"Kissed a girl?"

"No, Sir."

"Touched a girl?"

"No, Sir."

"Danced with a girl?"

"I didn't know any girls, Sir."

"You never went anywhere where there were girls? Parties? Sat next to one in a car?"

"No, Sir. And I've never been in a car. Except a taxi sometimes."

"But you must have seen girls. Sat next to them on buses. Opposite them in trains."

"Yes."

"Didn't you look at them? At their bodies? At the way they were shaped?"

"Yes, Sir."

378

"Didn't that . . . didn't that stir you?"

"Well, yes, Sir, but.."

"But nothing!" Moore said. And he didn't mind if the next man *could* hear him. This was too important.

"Listen to me," he said. "I don't give a damn what happened to you at St Winifred's. I don't give a damn your stepfather called you 'Cissy' — although by God, I wish he were here to say it again in front of me. I don't give a damn that a commercial traveller mucked you about and you enjoyed him doing it. Firstly you are anything but a sissy. You're probably the bravest man on this whole damn ship! You're certainly the gutsiest! Secondly you are certainly not a homosexual."

"Then why did I enjoy . . . ."

"What Morris Sams did to you? Because you were lonely. Because you had no one in the world to give you love. Because Sams was a human contact — the first real human contact you'd ever had. Don't you understand, Yates? Until Sams sodomized you — let's use the word and have it in the open. Until Sams sodomized you, you didn't have

379

existence. You were just a bit of flotsam in a damn big uncaring world filled with a lot of selfish people who knew exactly where they were going — or at least you thought they did. Sams gave you an identity. And by God you grabbed hold of it! How you grabbed hold of it! Six! And how old are you now? Twenty! For fourteen years! I'm a sissy, you shouted! — Only you didn't know what it even meant — I'm a sissy! It solved all your problems. Let you off the hook every time. Because you couldn't cope with people — and how could you be expected to with that sort of apology for an upbringing you had? — you reached out for your one excuse: that you were peculiar. Different. A misfit. And every time anything happened, or anybody said anything which remotely touched on your being what you had decided that you were, you grabbed hold of that as well and added it to the store." He sat up. "Do you have any cigarettes left?"

"A few, Sir."

"Good. Well, I've got a call to make. And while I'm gone, I want you to think over very carefully what I've said. And then when I come back, I'd very much like to share a cigarette with you. And after that I want you to tell me exactly how a man who spends two days wading through a Sumatran mangrove swamp ends up owning a pair of pyjamas, a couple of books, a wicker suitcase and tins of Kensitas and Players cigarettes! And how he still has cigarettes after three weeks of the hell we've had to live with!"

18

ALTHOUGH dysentery until its latter stages does not have any noticeable effect on the power of thought, it is an enervating disease. For several days, Moore had been fighting the temptation to let things slide and the advent of the typhoon had given him the excuse his mind and body craved. He had been prepared to lie as comfortably as the conditions allowed and chat interminably with Yates until the storm had blown itself out and allowed them to complete the comparatively short passage through the East China Sea to Japan. By a tremendous effort of will, he followed the example of a handful of fitter men and somehow hauled himself up the ladder and stairways to the benjo. But each succeeding trip, fighting his way across the deck, judging each savage roll, each brief pause in the gale, had sapped his failing strength. He was conscious he had about reached the limits of both his mental and physical stamina. The concentration he had been obliged to give to Yates's problems together with the emotional effect of contemplating the wasted, twisted youth of a boy for whom he had, by now, so much affection and respect, took the little which was left. Had he not felt that he must leave the boy alone to consider what he had said, he would probably have decided the time had come to accept that benjo-visiting was finally beyond him. As it was each rung of the iron ladder, each step across the lower deck, the terrible weight of the bulkhead door, each tread of the stairways, was an ordeal, and forcing open the iron door at the end of the narrow passageway on the starboard side under the bridge superstructure against the wind, utterly exhausting. Weak, shaking, half-bemused, he had to clutch at the nearest rail-stanchion to avoid being blown overboard by the sheer force of the gale.

For a full two minutes he stood recovering, one arm firmly locked around the metal upright, glaring at the awful scene. It was night but bursts of lightning, seeming to echo amongst the caves and strata of the storm-rent clouds, patchily lit the raging sea in a spectral glow. Moore had ridden gales at night before but this was a different experience. The sea was truly mountainous, as bad as any he had seen in days when he had had a good ship under him. And then he had been part of the struggle, occupied and above all, fit. Now he was a discarded bit of sick rubbish of less account than had been the youngest able seaman under his command.

The abrupt exposure to a gale of such titanic power, the sudden piercing cold, the shock of such gigantic seas, the bedlam of sound, all flung together at Moore at such a critical moment further disturbed his mind, and, holding on with all his strength to the stanchion, he was taken by a queer delusion the wind was a personal enemy which had decided to concentrate its entire force against a man who had once treated its power with less than due respect. The rain lashed down in torrents, the spray came in great drenching clouts which hit him with astounding strength;

the bulwark against which he leant so desperately kept dipping down into a massive chasm as if to bury itself beneath the snarling, uprearing monster of the next foam-capped wave which towered above him, only at the final moment, with the sea seething at the deck's very edge, to ride up in a huge cartwheel as if trying to shake him off and send him hurtling across the slanted, streaming deck to crash against its fellow on the other side. From one such crest, at this angle, with a broad explosion of lightning coinciding with a sudden cessation of the wind, as if it were preparing itself for a yet harder blow, he caught a brief glimpse of a larger scene — a wild ocean of cataclysmic power: all the waters of the world once held in place by a gigantic dam, suddenly released and tearing dementedly towards eternity. And as quickly, the lightning faded, turning all to blackness, and the wind, its strength recovered, catching him unprepared, tore him from the stanchion and he found himself hurled first against the base of the derrick mast, striking his hip and head with sickening blows, and then, as he staggered to recover, his feet slipped away from him and he fell forwards, twisting as he fell, upon the nearby batch of winches and cannoned off them to sprawl on the deck between them and the hatch coaming. Half stunned he lay helpless as a great lurch picked him up and sent him slithering down the slope, gathering speed, planing on a bed of water, gasping for breath. He struck projections, a pipe he rode up and over, a cleat which caught him fiercely in the stomach and then the slither ceased abruptly as he fetched up against the bulwark on the opposite side. But no sooner did he gain a brief respite than the ship, rolling the other way, hurled him back again. This time he did not find the opening between hatch and winches but was thrown across it, his head against the winch motor housing, his feet against the base of the derrick mast — but only momentarily! For at once a great sluice of water floated him from his resting-place entangling him somehow with a derrick pendant. And so his mad career continued. Back and forth he went, hurled against object after object, bruising his limbs, his ribs, his face, a piece of flotsam retained aboard only by the bulwarks, now invisible in the awful blackness, now illuminated by a lightning flash. Vainly he tried to grasp at one or other of the mysterious impediments which cut and bruised and slashed him: the cleats too small, the winch drums too fat, the bitts too slippery. But at last, almost accidentally, his clawing, reaching hands, finding a derrick pendant, slid down the rope to fasten on a pulley block. Now he lay on his stomach, his chest held up, his legs stretched out behind him, half stunned, confused, bemused, and vaguely aware he had no business to have come up alone at night. Now the hold had lost its horror, now it was a haven of peace and sanity — a safe retreat, a warm inviting shelter. He forgot the rats, the stench, the corruption, the dead and dying men. Here in a wild and hellish blackness punctuated only by the eerie lightning glows, tugged by the wind, drenched by the rain and spray, he was an irrelevance, of no more account that a broken spar cast into an empty ocean. You bloody fool! he told himself.

And then he shouted it: "You bloody, bloody fool!" And the wind laughed at him and tore the words from his mouth, and the rain lashed his recumbent body, and the deck treated him like a man tied to a see-saw, and his arms began to ache from the effort of holding on and the pain in his chest became excruciating. This won't do, Moore, he told himself; this won't do at all. Either let go and let the next lurch make an end to it or work it out. Work it out! Plan! . . . Plan? The word seemed strange. A half-remembered problem of insuperable difficulty. Yet through the fog, remnants of resolution still remained. Where was he? What was this thing? This curious thing? He felt it over with his fingertips. Ah, yes! A pulley block! But which? With difficulty he turned his head over his left shoulder and in a renewed flash of lightning saw to his faint surprise a ghostly figure, lurching a zig-zag course, close past him. He croaked out for help but even a full-throated bellow would have failed against the screaming wind. He saw the figure turn at the corner of the derrick base and then the lightning died. Now, he told himself most seriously, I must compose myself. If one man can succeed, it proves it can be done. He tried to visualise the geography of the ship. The stairway must be there! Then the benjo *there!*. Which is easier? It was as if either way offered safety. The benjo must be nearer. Then it must be the benjo. That seemed intelligent.

He pulled himself to a sitting position, clasping the pulley to his chest as if it were a drinking friend, and, for all the agony it caused him, swivelled himself around so that it was to one side of him. He remained thus for a long time, bent sideways, clutching the pulley block, battered by wind and water trying to make a plan, and then, having made one, quite deliberately and without anxiety, when the deck was slanting to port, released himself in a sitting position and swooshed downhill, legs stretched out and feet upturned, arms raised, palms flat — and was brought to a halt by the bulwark. He had not calculated the risk involved except in the vaguest way. His illness, the storm's battering, the effect of his fall, the bitter cold and long exposure, the agony of moving, had together produced an alienation not unlike that brought on by alcohol or fever. Had he chosen the wrong time to let go he might have broken his ankles or been tipped into the sea. As it was, the tilt reversed, slowing his progress, and he barely bumped his feet. Quickly he got to them and grabbed the bulwark rail, gravity trying to wrench him from it and start the mad gymnastics once again. As soon as the pressure lessened, as the ship began to level, he released the rail and, literally, ran towards the benjos.

They were still there. Stoutly built and raised up sufficiently to clear the bulwarks, their walls were high enough to escape the worst pummelling of the sea. Until he reached them, it had not occurred to Moore to wonder if they would be there, but now, seeing them when the lightning struck: square, forthright, accepting the frightful wind, the rolling of the ship — he was impressed. At least, he thought, the blighters can build benjos! He clawed his way along the step, his hands above his head hanging on to the beam above the urine trough until he reached the first compartment. He waited for the wind to slacken, then pulling it open, somehow got inside. The wind at once slammed its door shut against him. In the darkness, crouched over the invisible channel, he did what he had come to do, his hands pressed against either side of the wooden walls for support. The benjo rolled as the ship rolled and Moore rolled with it. In this compartment, not above three feet square, protected from the wind, it was, relatively speaking, warm and reassuring. And while the gale had not removed the sweet cloying smell, at least darkness brought invisibility. Moore leaned back with an extraordinary feeling of relief, even comfort, braced himself against the rolling — and gave himself up to thought.

Someone should write a book about benjos, he told himself. Important places, benjos. No, not important, vital! And places of refuge too! Private places. Places in which a man could think. Like it or not benjos were very high in one's priorities! And a very important subject of conversation! For example that man, Yates. He was all to do with benjos. Yet, come to think on it, they never talked about them. Now that was very odd! Yes, very odd. What did they talk about then? Pyjamas! How perfectly ridiculous. Could do with pyjamas here! It was cold. Not as cold as outside the benjo. But, all the same, cold. But you couldn't have everything. You had to make choices. For example, between cold and privacy. This, he told himself, is the one place, the only place, on the whole damn ship one could *get* a bit of privacy! Where one could think without having a damn mandolin twanging in one's ear! Yates! Rum sort of fellow, Yates. But decent. Pity the fellow didn't . . . How about that? Wonder how Charlie would take to it? And Angie? And Ros? Bit late in life to be adopted . . .

He mused on it, hearing the ocean rise and fall through the slots in the floor, often wetted by its spray, listening to the howling wind. He was very cold. His teeth were chattering; his head and stomach ached, and whenever he moved his chest hurt fearfully and all the time he had to breathe carefully to avoid the pain. But he felt secure. And private. And really rather comfortable. After all, he told himself, to have something to rest one's back against was quite a bonus nowadays. And so he went on and, gradually, his rambling thoughts became even more disconnected and wandered off in strange directions and quite soon he fell asleep.

★ ★ ★

A man who has held views about himself for the greater part of his life changes them slowly and unwillingly and for two good reasons. Firstly, however ill those views may have been, they have become guide-lines which, if discarded, will leave him floundering without direction; secondly, he cannot easily convince himself that the old view he is endeavouring to discard is false and he is subconsciously aware that to stifle an unpleasant truth in favour of a seductive fallacy is a very dangerous thing to do.

Yates remained unconvinced. The best that could be said of the effect of Moore's arguments was that they had admitted a fresh, if highly questionable, stream of thought through what had been an unbreachable barrier. There had been no doubt; now, however faint it might be, there was doubt — and that doubt would nag at the self-criticism with which Yates had grimly and mechanically scourged himself.

The more immediately telling effect was that Yates was infused with a feeling of burning gratitude towards a man he had regarded as being on a totally different plane of life. True they had shared a groundsheet and even cigarettes; true they had talked in a way which was rare between a Commanding Officer and an other rank; true Moore had confided quite intimate details of his private life. But while all this had been going on Yates had assumed that if Moore had known the real truth about himself there would have been no sharing and that the moment he discovered it, the sharing would stop. The realisation this wasn't so shed an entirely new light upon the way he viewed himself. Already stiffened by the compliments of the men around him and having, through his benjo cleaning, discovered purpose, this new progression (for this was how Yates saw it) enormously increased both confidence and resolution. I am not as I thought I was, he could tell himself; I have a place in the scheme of things. He was of a sudden imbued with impatience — anxious for the voyage to end and his stint as prisoner of war to be over so that he could make up for the wasted years and grasp at life's opportunities. It followed that he was now more concerned about the dangers of the voyage than he had been before and, as one of the few who still took the risk of using benjo rather than cesspit, he was aware that for all the awfulness of the hold, a positive calm prevailed down here compared with what was going on aloft. With his head now buzzing with questions to do with the possibility of survival, he could hardly wait for the return of the one man with enough experience of the sea to answer them.

It was fortunate for Moore — but for the impatience he had bred, he would have died.

* * *

Yates had the same obstacles to overcome as had Moore: the swaying ladder which sought to throw him backwards as he climbed, the heavy bulkhead door, the narrow stairways, sloping but steep, the final top deck exit, the violent gale, the drenching rain and spray, the frightful pitching. But Yates was hardly more than half Moore's age and he was fit. His mind was clear and he was able to judge the wise moment to leave one point of support to take advantage of the angle of the ship and grasp another. By such means he crabbed and fought his way towards the benjos, head down to the wind, soaked through to the skin, jabbing his bare feet against the cleats, his shins against the forgotten water pipe. Finding Moore asleep in a compartment and remembering something he had read in the story of a shipwreck, he was convinced that unless he were somehow wakened and kept awake until he could be taken down into the hold, he would be dead by morning. But he also realised that even if he could wake Moore and somehow persuade him to try to fight his way back across the deck, the chances of success were negligible.

For a time he was overcome by a feeling of desperation while the utter loneliness of his situation quite appalled him: to be shut up soaked to the skin through the balance of the night in a stinking compartment which pitched and jarred with every thunderous wave which shook the ship was unimaginable; to attempt to drag an insensible man through the pitch darkness of the maelstrom awaiting them outside the relative calm of this awful shelter would be suicidal. He tried to beat Moore about the face and to bawl him into wakefulness but the cramped quarters and the storm's ferocious din defeated all his efforts. He felt panic welling up inside him. Schemes as wild as the elements battling about him chased through his mind, tumbling over each other, each one dismissed by another equally absurd before it could even be thought through. Above all he was obsessed by the conviction that if he left Moore alone while he sought assistance, then he would surely die before it could be fetched.

Then, casting hopelessly around, he

remembered the small compartment at the derrick base where he left his benjo-cleaning gear. No more than a commonsense utilization of a necessary strengthening to the derrick it had been, presumably, some sort of additional bosun's store which, perhaps because the crew had imagined it might be looted by soldiers or prisoners, had been emptied of everything of value and now contained only a few useless bits and pieces, torn tarpaulin, old brushes, mops and such like. Midway across the deck it was not really all that far away, maybe twenty-five yards or so. If somehow he could get Moore to it, get him inside — it was never locked — and keep him awake, then, in the morning he could leave him long enough to summon help to get him down again.

But how to get him there? Extricating Moore from the compartment would be, in itself, a tremendous undertaking but even if he could achieve it a single sea, sweeping inboard, could whisk him away. Even if he timed that right he lacked, he knew, the physical strength to carry or haul such a burden and raise it over

the store coaming on his own. He toyed
with the thought of seeking help but his
obsessive belief that to leave Moore was
to have him die negated this. How could
it be done? How, how, how? he asked
himself. It was impossible. And yet, he
argued, insensible men had been saved
from foundering ships. Yes, but that
was by equipment, by breeches buoy.
He had no cradle. Rope. Yes, he had
rope. Ample rope. The rope tied to
the buckets. Smaller pieces in the store.
But what use was that? Without a sling,
without a pulley? There were pulleys of
course. Plenty of them. Pulleys at the
derrick heels, pulleys at the pendant
feet and halfway up. Yates did not
give names to all these pulleys — he
did not know their names. He did not
really understand their purpose. But so
much time supervising the benjo cleaning
had engraved their position on his mind.
There was, he calculated, tarpaulin in the
store. And there were ropes. If he could
truss Moore like a parcel and run the
other end of a rope through a pulley
block, could he then haul him across?
He shook his head. No, there was too

much water. He might achieve all that only to be left with a drowned man on his hands. If it could be done it could only be done with Moore's co-operation. He must walk, or at least be upright. It was then it came to Yates. The derrick arms! While out of use they were dropped to the horizontal and ran fore and aft at a height of about six feet continuously from their end housings through to their heels which were bolted to the store walls. If a loop of rope were passed over the nearer of them and passed under Moore's armpits and another rope was fixed around a belt of folded tarpaulin placed around Moore's waist and run through a pulley then couldn't he haul him across with the confidence that even the worst of seas couldn't take him overboard? Surely that, at least, was possible.

He gave himself no time to allow doubts to destroy purpose. Temporarily abandoning Moore, he fought his way along the deck, hanging on grimly to the benjo structure and then the bulwark rail until he was opposite the derrick base. Cascades of water drenched him, his bare feet were numbed with cold, the gale whipped his face. He clung grimly to the rail awaiting a lull and when it came hastened the few paces to where he placed the store. The door was on the port side, in fact within only a foot or two of the pulley lock to which Moore had clung. Seizing the iron handle, Yates hauled it down, fought against the wind to open the door, stepped over the coaming, barking his shin cruelly in the process, and, entering the compartment, allowed it to slam shut behind him. The coaming was quite high but, he calculated, not high enough to keep out the not infrequent flooding of the deck when the *Dai Nichi* recovered too slowly from her roll — it would have greatly helped to use the lightning's fitful brilliance through an opened door but not at the expense of a foot of water. In pitch blackness, tossed painfully from one iron wall of the metal box to another, he scrabbled for and found a bucket and with fumbling, bleeding fingers, set about untying the knotting at the bucket handle, breaking his nails, petrified at the way the time was passing. The first bucket untied, he set about its fellow only to realise there was no need to do this, that in fact if its rope was to be passed through a pulley, the bucket would serve as a useful stop. And all the time he was thus engaged mysterious articles came at him from the darkness striking his arms, knees, ankles, chest and head as if a poltergeist were loose.

With the ropes prepared he began his search for a piece of tarpaulin sufficiently small to serve his purpose. It was a maddening, time-consuming business feeling along invisible edges, which he soon abandoned. Leaving the shelter, tying the door back to a second guy pendant pulley block, he struggled vainly to thread the end of the bucket rope through its nearby fellow but this proved impossible without a knife to sever the rope already occupying it. In desperation he searched around, hanging on grimly to the nearest hand-hold. A sudden flash of lightning bathed the deck in brilliant intensity showing him a cleat. He waited for the deck to level then swiftly slipped the end through, pulling it hard until the bucket clanged up against it and then he passed it round the handle and through the loop, making a knot. Abandoning this rope he took the other and, passing it over the derrick arm, pulled on it until the two ends were about equal and then tied the lengths together into a knot thus forming a loop which could slide easily along the arm with two long hanging lengths for tying around Moore's body. He searched for and found his first rope and now, holding a pair of ends in one hand, and one end in the other, ignoring the risk involved, ran the twenty-five or so paces to the benjo. He was already weary beyond words and for all his efforts his limbs were stiffening with cold.

He found Moore gibbering nonsense.

"Sir!" he shouted, delighted, imagining Moore had wakened.

But Moore merely went on gibbering, quietly, so that it was impossible for Yates to make out a word of what he was saying, and it was only because of a temporary lull in the clamour of the gale that he had heard him speak at all.

"Sir!" he bellowed. "Wake up! Wake up! For God's sake! Please! Please wake up!"

But there was no response. In any case the brief lull in the storm was as quickly replaced by a sudden appalling shriek as if the wind had abated only in order to regroup. In absolute tumult it howled around the wooden structure in which Moore slept. The door, opened by Yates, smashed back against its jamb — the fact it was there at all spoke well for the unknown carpenters who had built the benjos. Rain poured down, almost it seemed in a solid sheet. The night, except for the lightning bursts, was as black as pitch. The whole madness of the universe was concentrated on a wooden box.

Realising that at least for the moment there was nothing he could do to win Moore's co-operation, Yates set about threading the rope around his waist. Even this, the simplest of the things he had to do, was fraught with difficulty. Moore was slumped back in a corner, a channel of ordure bisected the compartment which rocked fearfully with every roll, the door was smashing dangerously to and fro. With immense difficulty he levered himself into the compartment and lying across Moore felt his way to thread the single-ended rope about his waist, with the utmost toil managing to effect a knot which, while it left a margin of freedom, formed a circlet close enough not to slip down below his hips. This probing and prodding eventually penetrated Moore's subconsciousness sufficiently to make him start up and mumble. His utterances were too indistinct and the clamour too great for Yates to decipher a single word but, much encouraged, he started to belabour Moore, slapping him around the head, punching and kicking him as best he could in the confined limits of their strange cell, and, whenever the curious gyrations of their now interlocked bodies allowed, bellowing in his ear. He had not the least idea if Moore understood but the movements of his body indicated an objection to this extraordinary performance. Yates withdrew, putting a bare foot directly in the horrid channel as he did so, aware of this only by the rasping of its rough-cut, splintering edge along his ankle. Now, pulling back on the rope, he literally hauled Moore to a sitting position, aided by *Dai Nichi*'s sudden roll to starboard which sent Yates sprawling backwards sliding until he was brought to an abrupt halt by striking the hatch coaming with the crown of his head. Dazed for a moment he lay watching a fork of lightning display a ragged curtain of clouds which seemed so low he could almost have put up a hand to touch them, while all the time, like an inverted bed of nails, the teeming rain lashed down on him. Yet he still held the rope whose wetness had prevented it searing his palms as his hands slipped back along it. He pulled on it, pulled in fact against Moore's body which was wedged in the compartment opening, and it was only when Yates was halfway back across the deck Moore realised what he was doing.

It was a fearful business skewering Moore's legs out and down on to the deck but somehow managed, and this, together with the clouts of stinging spray which continually buffeted the two of them, the cold, the din, the alternating black of night and lightning's brilliance, at last brought Moore back to limited awareness. He sat on the benjo threshold, his legs dangling out while Yates, his back to the door which continually swung and struck him, kept his position like a man semaphoring, one hand grasping the opening's lintel, the other (across Moore's front, preventing him from falling out) its jamb.

In a lightning flash, Moore saw him — a wild figure, thin hair streaming, naked legs and arms and part of his chest where the shirt had torn gleaming wet.

"Good God!" he said. It seemed to sum it up. The whole thing was so impossible.

The sound, whisked by the wind, came as a passing whisper and was gone. "Sir!" Yates shouted. And, leaning forward, directly in Moore's ear. "Sir!"

"All right," said Moore, now astonishingly alert. "Don't *do* that!"

"Getting . . . you . . . to . . . the . . . store!" Yates shouted.

This made no sense. What store? How could he?

"Can't!" Moore shouted simply. "No good! Go back!"

"Rope!" Yates yelled. And when this was not understood — or its understanding not made clear — he yanked on the rope around Moore's waist like an angler striking.

"Oh," said Moore, surprised — although too low to be heard. He put out a hand and felt the rope and Yates felt the tug on it.

"Other . . . end . . . tied!" he shrieked. "Can't . . . go . . . overboard!" He realised he had lost the ends of his sling. "Listen . . . Sir!" he shouted, — but broke off as a vicious roll almost threw Moore backwards, and it was all he could manage both to keep his own place and hang on by the rope to Moore. "Listen!" he yelled again, when things were better. "Store . . . by winches! Getting . . . you . . . there!"

"Impossible," Moore answered comfortably. He had lost all feeling, and all fear. And then, realising this was not a drawing room, he leant forward and croaked it louder: "Impossible!"

"Not!" Yates shouted. "Sling! Made sling! Slide . . . you!"

"Slide?" said Moore disbelievingly.

Yates lip read the word in a lightning flash.

"Slide!" he bellowed. "Along derrick

arm. Along . . . derrick . . . arm! Stay there! Understand, Sir? Stay . . . there! Understand?"

Moore grinned. "Message . . . received . . . and . . . understood," he croaked.

The witticism was lost on Yates. He didn't hear it. Waiting for a renewed burst of lightning, he glared wildly round for his sling. He saw it — the wind or gravity had moved it back all the way to the pulley block.

"There!" he shouted, pointing.

It meant nothing to Moore.

"Getting it!" Yates cried. "Wait! Wait there!"

Moore had no alternative intentions. He watched Yates go, arms waving in an attempt to keep his balance on the slippery, sloping deck. Saw him fall and then it was pitch black again. Moore shook his head. His mind was in a curious state. It was quite clear but incapable of relating; it was a mind suitable to be cast adrift and be at home in wildness such as this. It did not really occur to Moore that he might be saved. He was not even worried if he was saved or not. A strange protection eased the cold and wet which numbed his body and his mind. He was quite prepared to do what Yates instructed just as a man hypnotised will carelessly do what he is told to do, however absurd those actions are.

Yates, meanwhile, had got to his feet and accidentally found his rope when an end lashed his face. He came back with it, using the loop, leaning back as the ship rolled to port and rejoined Moore.

"Damn!" he cursed. He had realised that it was useless putting the end under Moore's arms and tying them behind. The lower loop would simply whip up over Moore's shoulders if he couldn't manage it properly. He thought for a moment. And then a new solution, a better solution came to him. He felt around Moore's stomach.

"What . . . " Moore said. There was more than this but it was the one word Yates picked out.

"Sling!" he shouted. "End! . . . Tying . . . under . . . knot! Here!" He poked Moore in his belly and with no more ado worked one end under the circlet round Moore's waist and tied it to the other in a double knot. But no sooner had he done this than he realised it wouldn't work. The rope would be too long. He'd have to untie the knot and start again. It was a laborious business with the ship rolling, and the wind raging, and the rain torrential, and his fingers numb and torn. But he managed it.

Now he *must* have co-operation.

"Nearer . . . derrick . . . arm!" he shouted in Moore's ear. "Must . . . get . . . nearer! Nearer . . . derrick . . . arm!" And he yanked on the first rope, bewildering Moore who nevertheless made no objection and for the first time stumbled to his feet.

Yates waited, breathlessly — waited for the deck to level.

"Now!" he screamed. And, getting behind Moore shoved him forward. "Go on!" he yelled. "Go on, Sir! For God's sake! Go on!"

Moore reeled like a drunken man but with Yates shoving from behind, tottered across the deck until arrested by the hatch coaming. This, two or three feet high, gave some support and holding the sling tight with one hand and his other arm around Moore's waist, Yates managed to keep him there through another roll, and the moment that ended and the ship started to recover, thrust one end of the sling rope under the waist rope and tied his knot. Now his shoulders sagged momentarily in sheer relief. The storm could not win Moore now. All but hung by a stout rope to the derrick arm, nothing could take him overboard.

He put his body hard against Moore's and his arms about him, holding him against the roll — or rather benefiting from the fact that Moore could no longer do more than sway a yard or two hung rather like a punch bag with legs.

"Listen!" he shouted in his ear. "Going . . . pull . . . you . . . store! You . . . walk! That helps!" And releasing Moore he started off backwards, paying out the other rope until there was several feet of it. "Now!" he yelled, unheard into the wild night. And he pulled.

It was a curious business. Moore was literally pulled along the deck, like a sack half hung on a rod. To some extent he helped. Not consciously. But it was easier and less painful moving his feet

412

to keep pace with his body. Halfway along an extra gigantic wave struck the *Dai Nichi* and, surging through a gap where part of her bulwarks had been torn away, seethed foaming around them both, momentarily waist high, sucking their legs like the current on a dangerous beach as it surlily withdrew. Now roles were reversed. Only by hanging grimly to the rope tied around Moore's middle did Yates retain his contact. But the dangerous moments passed and Yates half hauled, half assisted, got Moore to the end of the derrick arm.

Now there was one more hateful task: to unfix the sling. Yates took his precautions. Taking the loose part of the waist rope, he wound it round and round the nearby pair of bitts until the length between them and Moore was almost taut. Now he was free to use both hands, both to look after himself and undo the knots. This took him perhaps five minutes. Moore, meanwhile, was held taut by ropes which guyed him in two directions. But he was secure. Cursing, weary beyond words, almost incapable of thinking, yearning for a knife which would cut the tie in a single slash, Yates fought the knot while Moore now relapsed into a sort of coma, swayed, buffeted by the gale, water, salt and fresh, streaming over him, in a night of spectral madness filled with furious sound and coruscating light.

But it was done.

★ ★ ★

The coaming was no obstacle. Yates merely tipped Moore over it like a sack pushed by its upper part over a low brick wall. He unwound the waist rope from the bitts but he made no attempt at untying it. He was too spent to undertake a task to which necessity did not drive him. There would be time enough with dawn. The door would not shut properly with a rope between it and the frame but if he could find something to tie the handle to, it could be pulled close enough to keep out most of the wind and water. He groped and found a bracket.

★ ★ ★

414

Thus they spent the balance of the night, in darkness sometimes absolute, sometimes queerly broken by the flicker of lightning through the thin slit between door and jamb, rolling to and fro, kept company by brooms and buckets — two men blind and shivering in the madhouse of an iron box, flung about like dice in a shaker, battered by invisible objects hurled at them from all directions, one desperate, the other ill, wandering in his mind, unable to control his bowels or to consider doing so. Yet, even so, Yates managed to wrap Moore in old tarpaulins both for warmth and for protection and to tie a piece of rope around the bundle. Having done this, he lay on top of him, embracing him for the warmth and protection his body offered. And he talked to him, shouted at him, sang to him, sometimes even kicked and pummelled him. The rolling helped. The buckets, the brooms, the mysterious, unknown objects which belaboured them helped. The gale's madness helped. Moore was kept awake sufficiently.

* * *

When, at last, shreds of a gloomy dawn filtered through the cracks between ill-fitting door and frame bringing the end of that fearful night, for the first time Yates left Moore. He fought his way across the seething deck yard by yard, from handhold to handhold, glaring with hatred at the gloomy silhouettes of the rusting funnel, the sealed-up ventilators, the dementedly swaying derrick mast, the yapping pendants, the rattling pulley blocks. At the frightful, raging, hateful sea. Drenched and stung by cataracts of spray deafened by the malevolent, shrieking wind, shuddering with cold, blear-eyed with weariness, he hauled open the iron door against the wind which sought even at the end to defeat his purpose and the comparative peace and warmth of the protected world below amazed him. He stumbled down the iron stairways, staggering with exhaustion and the cursed, uneven rolling, twisted off the lower deck on to the hated ladder and descended barefooted, rusted rung by rusted rung, shouting for Brimmacombe and Worboys . . .

19

FOR two days Moore lay comatose, tended lovingly by Yates who had stripped him of his sodden clothes, gently dried his wasted body and dressed him in the pyjamas which had lain for so long an unexplained mystery in the cane attache case. This done, Yates had persuaded others to provide clothing and blankets so that, as far as the word could have meaning in such a place, Moore was made comfortable. Hour by hour, Yates guarded him with dedicated vigilance. When the *Dai Nichi* lurched excessively, he lay across him to stop him sliding; in the quieter, more regular rolling periods, he bathed his face, gave him water, combed his hair and beard. Ever watchful of his dysentery, he was seldom late with a utensil and afterwards always cleansed him. In doing these things, his feelings were akin to those of a son tending a loved father laid helpless by a stroke. Moore's condition was perhaps not worse than that of many others in the hold but Yates had shut his eyes to all else around him.

★ ★ ★

Moore's emergence from the tormented world of hallucinations and incoherent gabbling coincided with the abatement of the storm. Perhaps the pulsing of the engines and the grinding of the propeller shaft were sounds which better than any others could pierce the fog of jumbled thoughts and lunatic imaginings. With hatch covers at last removed, he could see the loosened derrick head, swaying between its guys, silhouetted against a gloomy sky. He was puzzled by this and by the absence of things he had been aware of through his stupor — the twanging of the mandolin, the insane clatter of the coal hurling itself to and fro behind the bulkhead, the huge rise and fall of the ship on towering waves. It was disturbing. He tried to sit up but a voice said "No, Sir," and a hand pressed down on his shoulder. He was annoyed at being told what to do and yet relieved

418

that apparently no effort was required of him. He made some remark, closed his eyes and promptly went off to sleep.

★ ★ ★

Later still, when his mind had cleared, Moore accepted he had played his final part as Commanding Officer. His risks were quite apparent: if the dysentery didn't kill him, there was an excellent chance pneumonia would instead. There remained about four days of sailing ahead of them before they reached Japan where, possibly, he would be given medicines and treatment. In the meantime the danger of attack by submarines had been restored and no man in his state could climb thirty rungs of the iron ladder (once again defined as the only exit) nor expect others to haul him up. He was unworried — the idea of dying had so lost its sting that he gave it little thought beyond the rueful reflection that after all the trouble others had been to on his behalf it was his business to stay alive.

Like most men who have come through a period of unconsciousness he was little interested in the world outside his immediate surroundings; the trials he, in company with many others, had endured had so penetrated his psyche that the other world, the world of peacetime, wife, children, home, were too far distant to be bothered with. There would be time enough for them one day, maybe. For the present there were his own discomforts, a sense of idiocy at being dressed in a pair of pyjamas from which the seat had been removed, of repugnance at his body, of relief that nothing further was expected of him but to lie and chat, and of puzzlement as to how he had both survived and been got down again.

He addressed Yates on this and at first received only evasive answers and, lacking the energy to pursue the matter, let it slide. Equally things which had perplexed him before, such as the story behind the mutilated pyjamas he was wearing, hardly seemed worthy of bothering with. He was content enough with the small talk offered. He had no interest in any others in the hold — an attitude which was not uncommon. Fear consumes energy at a ferocious rate and after a time the body gives up the struggle. The storm had been a climax to four weeks of horror and physical strain and with the general feeling that, one way or the other, the ordeal was near its end, lethargy had become the ruling temper. Moore was not the only one being carefully tended by a friend but solicitude now hardly extended beyond the man on either side.

★ ★ ★

The time came when Yates could no longer satisfy Moore with his evasions.

"Now tell me how you got me down!" he demanded — for he now had only the vaguest recollections of what had happened.

That Moore should make the assumption he owed his life to Yates demonstrated the peculiar bond which had been forged between these two quite different men: the one approaching middle age with behind him successful civilian and wartime careers based on the advantages of gentle upbringing and privileged education; the other barely out of his teens (and young for his age at that) shabbily schooled, corrupted, undervalued, living his formative years under the shadow of a fearful misapprehension — two men who could scarcely have been more differently drilled to face an identical ordeal.

This thought was paramount in Moore's mind as he listened to Yates's halting, almost apologetic, explanation. The point was not so much that Yates had displayed courage, initiative and endurance of outstanding order but that Moore was only too well aware that he would, at Singapore, have looked elsewhere for such an example. Yates had stood on their heads all the stock notions he had so loyally followed through his life. And if when a *real* test came, the principles by which one had always made judgements were shown irrelevant, on what basis was one to carry on?

What of his own performance? He had prided himself that, at least, he had acted capably — but was not the reality that he had done no more than slavishly follow a set of guide lines good enough for a two-and-a-half-striper on the bridge of a destroyer but with absolutely no relevance in the hold of a Japanese prisoner-of-war ship? He had arbitrarily put himself in charge of more than two hundred and fifty men of whom he knew absolutely nothing and presumed the qualifications and experience to instruct them how they should behave. He had tried to apply the rules of Public School and barrack square to a situation as totally removed from either as boardroom procedure from ghetto polity. He had purblindly judged his selected deputies by the standards of club and wardroom. What on earth were club and wardroom to do with Number Two Hold of the *Dai Nichi Maru*?

And his deputies had done more or less the same sort of thing: judged each other and the mass of men around them from standpoints which were only relevant to the ways of life by which they had lived and to which they hoped, one day, to return. Stacey had judged by snobbishness, Brimmacombe by the philosophy of the rugger pitch, young Anderson by the principles of his class. By what colossal conceit had they, outnumbered fifty to one, presumed the right to lay down the rules and regulations of behaviour here? The claim was that it was for the benefit of the majority — was not the reality that it was an arrogant, and, as events had proved, quite ludicrous, attempt to perpetuate so far as possible their superiority and accustomed way of life? And what was the reality now that the chips were really down? Now that four weeks of unimaginable suffering and degradation had stripped the veneers away? Where was the discipline epitomized by his own four ridiculous A to D Squads?

The truth of the matter was that there was now no discipline except self-discipline. A quiescence had fallen on the hold. Men performed those functions which their bodies dictated, ate if they had appetite, drank whenever there was water, emptied their bowels and bladders. For the rest they scarcely moved. They did not need to be told how to behave — they *knew*. Each acted according to his own inner motivation. Yates was merely an example of such motivation. What did he know of what Smith, Brown and Jones were doing for Tom, Dick and

Harry in the dark, distant corners? What would he ever know? What would anyone ever know? There would be no citations, no medals, issued for the men who had spent more than a month travelling, in shirts and shorts, from the tropics of Java to the winter of Japan two decks down on a bed of wet bauxite ore. At best they would be a statistic — at worst unheard of. How curious it would be if a second *Cossack* did a second *Altmark*! They would all be off-loaded and feather-bedded and their experience used to illustrate the bestiality of our enemies, the Japanese. It would make great reading! And in that reading the real importance of the experience would be stifled. That men forced to endure the most gruesome of conditions do not need to be instructed but find within themselves (if, that is, these qualities are in themselves to find) the strength, the commonsense, the endurance and the self-discipline to survive.

He looked up, through the shaft down which Yates, with Worboys and Brimmacombe, had somehow managed to bring him, watching the derrick head continuously swaying against the leaden patch of sky. Where were the Japanese? There were none in sight. Of course there were none in sight — they had adjusted too. What of the Japanese? What of the Japanese if there *were* a second *Cossack* doing a second *Altmark*? Their shrift would be very short indeed. But, someone might say in mitigation, they had their deaths as well. As many? a voice, harsh with preconceived judgment, would demand. No, true, not as many. They had started fitter, were of a race inured to travelling rough, had better food . . . Better food! How that would be picked up. Better food! And probably medicines! And *they* didn't have a bed of sopping ore to sleep on! How true. They had the comfort of their chests of drawers and twice as many, if identical, benjos! (And, after all, they were the victors.) Whichever way you looked at it, you came back to the same thing — that judgements were made from current personal standpoints, and until there were Platonic universal rights and wrongs, it would be ever thus.

Then Sutcliffe? The second *Cossack*'s

Commanding Officer would judge the killing of Sutcliffe an entirely proper action on grounds of self-preservation and military justice. Stacey's case might, conceivably, have raised a doubt or two, but probably not. Yet Sutcliffe had achieved more than any other man in the hold — because of him ten men had been taken ashore and given a slight chance to live. And Stacey, saved by the bell, might well, through his knowledge of Japanese, mitigate the sufferings of prisoners on Formosa far more than he, Moore, had on the *Dai Nichi* or might in any future prison camp.

Yet, even granting this, he did not feel guilt at having Sutcliffe killed — at the time he had been convinced there was no alternative and, anyway, in the context of lying with numbers of dead men scattered around awaiting burial when the sea grew calmer, and numbers of others likely to die before they docked, the killing of one more hardly seemed a matter of prime importance. His guilt was of a different nature. Yates had lived his youth in the strait-jacket of a mistaken belief he was homosexual — his own strait-jacket, he decided, had been quite as stultifying. He had seen life like a man with tunnel-vision and had been in the process of trying to direct his own children down that same long tunnel along which one progressed knowing little of the world through which the tunnel bored. Nursery, Public School, family boardroom, Royal Navy — that said it all. He had never *known* a Yates; he might have employed a Yates: to wash his car, to dig his garden, to cut his hair. But he had never known one.

★ ★ ★

"What will you do when the war is over, Yates?" he asked.

"Don't really know, Sir."

"Haven't you thought about it?"

"Not really. Got to get this lot over first."

"You should use the time."

"Don't imagine there'll be a lot, Sir. I mean, they'll have us working, won't they? Stands to reason. In your case it might be different. Being an officer. Lots of officers who were prisoners in the last war took all sorts of examinations. I read about it somewhere."

"That's right," Moore agreed. "Many got themselves qualified as lawyers and so on. But that wasn't what I was meaning. You must have learnt a lot in the last four weeks. I certainly have."

"Yes, I've learnt a lot all right, Sir. But I can't see what use it'll be in civvy street."

Reflecting that the remark was very close to his own recent thoughts Moore said: "What you mean, is that you think things will be the same for you. That all that's happened down here won't have significance?"

"Shouldn't think so, Sir. I mean, I might be a bit more careful about wasting things. But even that's not likely to last for long."

Moore smiled wryly. "That's a rather depressing philosophy. You're saying that experience changes nothing. I'd like to think that what we've had to put up with at least will have some value. And I believe it will. I certainly don't believe that anyone who survives this trip is going to end up the same man. I think he's going to know far more about human nature than most people and certainly far more about himself."

"But will people believe him, Sir?"

Moore thought about it. It was a very good question. Yates went on: "You see, as I see it, Sir, it'll all be a bit of a nine-days' wonder. The war, I mean. We'll go back, those of us who get through, and we'll start telling them all that happened and they'll all be very polite — for a bit. But really what they'll want to do is tell us what happened to *them* — and then get back to ordinary things. I don't think it'll change things. I mean they don't, do they, Sir? Wars. What about the last one? The war to end all wars they said. And how long did it last, not having another one? Twenty-one years. I mean that lot . . . " He jerked a thumb towards the Japanese. "We'll go back and say a lot of things about the way they treated us and I expect we'll be believed. But they'll still go on copying the things we make. And it'll all be cheap and nasty as Jap things always are, but we'll buy them just the same. Because they won't cost so much. I mean in the long run people put themselves first, don't they, Sir?"

"You haven't."

"Cleaning some benjos out? I do that because doing it I don't feel I'm nothing."

"You mean that's why you started doing it. That's not why you go on doing it."

Yates nodded. "That's true, Sir. And you're a lot to do with that. And I'm grateful. Not that I think you're right. About what you said, I mean. But the thing is I don't feel so bad about it as I did. Would you like a cigarette, Sir?"

"No thanks, Yates. I imagine it'd taste like the wrath of God. You have one though."

"That's all right." Yates paused. "Last thing you asked me before you went up on top was how I'd still got cigarettes. They give them to me. Keep topping my stock up, so to speak. And you asked me some other questions . . . "

"I don't want those questions answered," Moore said quickly.

"You remember," Yates said, "I told you about how I got away from Singapore?"

"Please," said Moore. "I don't want to

know. And I'm very tired. Anyway . . . "

"Just hang on, Sir. Just for a minute. Can you?"

Moore nodded. He was tired. Yet he sensed he was improving. That his temperature was falling.

"I'll hang on," he said. "But I don't want to know how you got those things . . . "

"I killed a man, Sir. On that launch. Or rather we did. Me and this other fellow. It seemed the sensible thing to do. Him being a Staff Officer and knowing all about me. And there *was* some water on the raft. That was a lie, saying there wasn't. We worked it out, how long it would last. And it wasn't very long. Before we got rid of him we took all the money he had and split it."

"Why do you insist on telling me?" Moore said.

"Because I've been alone all my life, Sir. Until now. When we get to Japan, they'll split us up. You'll go off to some officers' camp most likely. I'll be alone again then. I wouldn't be able to tell it to anyone else." He saw the spasm on

432

Moore's face. "Sorry, Sir." He reached for the utensil.

* * *

Afterwards, Moore said to him: "You didn't kill the other man, did you?"

"No, Sir."

"Did you think he was likely to die? When you left him?"

"Most likely, Sir."

"Did you take his share of the money?"

"No, Sir."

"Why not? When you knew he was most likely going to die?"

"Didn't seem right, Sir."

"Curious, isn't it?" Moore said. And after a moment or two. "You killed a man on that raft; I killed one on this ship."

"Yes, Sir. I guessed that. I expect a lot did."

"And?"

Yates shrugged his spare shoulders. "I suppose it was what you thought you had to do."

"He talked the Japs into sending ten of the men in the hospital ashore. They'd all have died if he hadn't. Every one."

"You knew that at the time, Sir?"

"Yes."

"Must have been difficult. Deciding."

"It didn't seem difficult."

"Would you have him killed now, Sir?"

"No."

Yates got to his feet. Nothing that he had done or said quite impressed Moore so much as this decision of his not to comment.

"Better get back to the benjos, Sir," he said. "Reckon it's just about calm enough to start cleaning them out again."

★ ★ ★

Moore shifted a little to watch Yates setting off on his endless quest for volunteers — in doing so he felt, through the padding of the Dutch wife, the carving-knife which the Geordie and the joiner's mate had risked their lives to steal. Well, there was still quite some way to go. He heard Yates calling out:

"Sanitary fatigue! Volunteers please!"

Moore watched him picking his way

around the gloomy hold, weaving an awkward path among the living and the dead. "Sanitary fatigue! Three volunteers please!"

It took Yates quite some time to get his volunteers — perhaps ten minutes. But in the end he got them as he always did. Moore watched him leading the way, hand over hand, up the iron ladder. He watched long enough until all four men had pulled themselves up and over the hatchway coaming. Only then did he close his eyes, ready to sleep. He rather thought that he would make Japan if it took no longer than four days. If he was right, if he did make it to Japan, he knew exactly what he had to do . . .

20

WHEN the sea had quietened sufficiently the dead were taken up from the holds and thrown overboard, watched by a single guard smoking a cigarette. Meanwhile the *Dai Nichi* ploughed on alone, unprotected, slow — a sitting target for any American submarine. But there was no attack. Day succeeded day with the same unchanging routine: a permanent benjo queue supplied by continual streams of men up and down the iron ladders; the same meal of weeviled-rice and pink fish-flavoured soup twice daily; the water ration; the daily burials at sea. The weather, keeping company, was unchanging too — sunless, bleak.

It was cold now with a chill wind from the north and occasional snow which drifted prettily down through the reopened hatches. The prisoners coming up on deck were, according to their possessions, differently clad. Some wore trousers, true only khaki drill but very enviable. Others struggled up one-handed, holding a thin blanket round their shoulders; others again braved it in shirts and shorts because they had nothing else. Some wore forage caps and some pith helmets; some had boots and some had only clogs. As they inched along the queue the men stamped their feet so that there was a continual ringing sound to add to the shuffing of the sea and the faint moan of wind through rigging. And they blew their hands to kill the numbness or slipped across to the steam pipes, which in the colder weather steamed at leaky joints, and put their hands around them and then tried to transfer the borrowed warmth to their thin cheeks. A few resumed collection of mugs of hot water in which to cleanse their bodies. The hold had its accustomed sounds: the rats, the slap of waves, the creak of rusty joints, the grind of the propeller, the pulsing of the engines, the clang of shovel on coal muted by the bulkhead, the cries of the unfortunate, the quick-syllabled chatter of the Japanese above, the subdued occasional conversation of the inmates, the snoring, sneezing, farting. The squalor now was almost beyond description with everything tainted with blood, bauxite, mucus and excrement. The reek of faeces, decaying rats and men, unwashed feet and bodies, rust, bauxite, sodden clothing, created an odour so offensive as to be almost tangible. In a word *Dai Nichi*'s holds had reached the depth of ultimate degradation. Each was a veritable Sheol. Day followed day; night followed night. But the end came at last.

* * *

The first sight of Japan was a horizon showing cranes, derricks and ships seen through driving rain and sleet and that evening the *Dai Nichi Maru* crawled through the straits between the towns of Moji and Shimonoseki at the mouth of the Inland Sea. It was a dismal sight. The towns were sombre, colourless, congested beyond belief. Prisoners were not prevented from being on deck and with faint surprise they noted the unenthusiasm on the faces of the

438

victorious Japanese lining the rails, viewing their homeland — after the wealth, the warmth, the colour of Java and Singapore, their country held little promise.

Through the following two days, during which the Japanese disembarked, the prisoners remained on board, collecting together their few possessions, disposing of final casualties. On November 26th, 1942, they prepared to go ashore. It was then Moore told his fellow officers of his decision.

* * *

"Are you sure you're doing the right thing, Sir?" said Anderson.

"You're out of your mind," said Brimmacombe.

"Think it over again, Sir," said Anderson.

"I've done all my thinking, Andrew," Moore replied. "It's the right thing for me."

He had shaved off his beard and, having removed the insignia of rank from his shirt, had then exchanged it for something more nondescript and of lesser quality. His cheeks were sunken and his chin very pointed, his eyes had a harsh staring look and the brows were pulled down over them. His dysentery had stabilised and he had shaken off the fever; he was very weak but able to fend for himself. His condition was about average for the hold.

"I've never heard anything so dotty!" said Brimmacombe. "In the first place I don't see how you can get away with it with all of us knowing who you are and in the second I'm blowed if I can see why you want to. Anyway!" he spoke triumphantly, "you've got a duty to your family!"

"By which," said Moore, with a faint smile, "you mean you think I've a better chance of surviving as an officer than as an other rank?"

"I should bloody well hope so," said Brimmacombe — then wished he hadn't. "I mean," he went on hastily, "you're ill, Jim. Bloody ill. Yes, and before you say it, so are a hell of a lot of the others. But you've done all you can for them. Now it has to be every man for himself."

"I know what you mean, Freddie,"

Moore said kindly. "And you're a decent scout. And what you're saying is right for you. But it isn't for me."

"But what *about* your family?"

"You really see a connection?" Moore shook his head. "If I survive the war — and that's just the luck of the draw for all of us whatever kind of camp we're in — I shall go back to my wife. The fact I've masqueraded as an other rank won't make any difference so far as she's concerned."

"It may to your children."

"It's going to be a different world, Freddie, through which we'll go blundering on, seeing our lives out through it. But all the time we'll be dropping behind. Because it'll be moving too fast for us to cope with. Because there will be new values we won't understand. Our children will cope because they'll be the one's creating this new world and these new values. If they look on us kindly, they'll see us as a lot of boring old has-beens who *will* keep talking about an experience which has little relevance to the lives they will be leading. If they talk unkindly it'll be to heap the blame for all their ills upon us. They're another generation, Freddie, and because of the way wars like this one speed things up, by God there's going to be one hell of a generation gap!"

"You didn't think like this at Singapore."

"In Singapore, I was still cocooned by the threads of my upbringing. The *Dai Nichi* rotted those threads away. The trouble is that my children are old enough to remember me as I was which is how they'll classify me. And that will be right because fathers have no business changing their children's horses in midstream. If I tried to become a different father to them, they just would not believe it. They'd see me as a silly old buffer trying to cash in on something to which I had no right whatsoever."

"Then I don't see the point . . . "

"Look, Freddie," Moore said. "I'm not suggesting I'm going to go back to England to set the place about its ears. I shall probably slip back into the old routine, and gladly, like you and Andrew here, and poor old Stacey if he gets through. Be the same heavy father who thinks he knows it all and doesn't in his children's eyes know very much at all. But there's still *me*, the inner me, you know. I want to use this opportunity to learn about the people who make the majority of the country I'm going to live in and in the process, hopefully, learn about myself. And maybe, Freddie, through that process be of more use to the world I live in than I've been so far."

"It's Yates, isn't it, Sir?" said Anderson. "Because of what he did for you. For all of us."

"Yes," said Moore. "Yates has a lot to do with it."

"But . . . " Anderson didn't quite know how to put it. "But," he blurted out, "it won't work, sir. It can't possibly. I mean . . . all right, a few weeks in a ship's hold, but . . . It has to be better in a camp. And, Yates . . . well, he won't have anything to offer you."

"What makes you so sure of that?" Moore asked quietly — and half explained. "I'm not going to tell you of that young man's upbringing. But it was frightful. So frightful that it got in the way of everything else. He never developed. He's got no . . . *character*. That's what you're hinting at. And of course you've got good grounds. But you know, Andrew, lots of plants which are stunted because they've had the wrong environment develop perfectly well once they're given a proper chance. I want to try to help Yates have that chance. In fact I owe it to him. Not just because he saved my life, but because of the way he did it. But that isn't the whole of it. I'm also doing this because it's what I want to do, ought to do and feel I *must* do." His tone changed, became almost light-hearted. "Well, Freddie," he said, "dotty or not, can I rely on you not to let me down?"

"I bloody well ought to — for your own good!"

"But leaving that to my own judgement?"

"You know what it is," Brimmacombe said to Anderson. "He's doing a Lawrence of Arabia on us."

"You know," said Moore, "you're not so far out at that. Thank you, Freddie. And we'll have that steak and Guinness in Dublin one day. And you, Andrew?"

"Yes, of course, Sir. But I'm sorry if you won't be with us."

"Well, of course I may. No one can forecast what the Japs will do."

"What about Worboys, Sir? And Toms? And the others?"

Funny about Worboys, Moore thought. At the beginning we discussed everything; and I haven't spoken to him in days.

"I'll speak to them only if I have to," he answered. "There isn't any point in spreading it around. If we all end up in the same camp, then I may *have* to do some more thinking. But if they split us up . . . Well, we'll see. If you end up with any of them and not with me, no need to pass it on. All right?"

"You're mad!" said Brimmacombe. "But there's my hand on it."

Dear old Freddie, Moore thought, smiling inwardly. Still thinking in rugger terms.

★ ★ ★

He did not tell Yates immediately but when they disembarked he accepted the loan of his blanket to drape around

445

his shoulders, borrowed his pith helmet and allowed himself to be supported; in such a posture he was inconspicuous. The prisoners marshalled untidily on the quayside presented a pathetic sight, hundreds of men dressed in tropical rags, emaciated, unshaven, grey. They were grouped in four batches according to their holds but the batches were reasonably close. To change to another batch was the simplest thing.

There were benjos along the quayside. "Help me to a benjo, will you?" Moore said to Yates. And to a guard. "*Benjo kudasai?*" And patting his stomach. "*Hara itai!*" The guard nodded. The ship was not yet emptied of all its human cargo and men with dysentery were streaming to benjos all the time.

They went into the benjo which was almost a replica of those on board the ship.

"Listen, and don't argue," Moore said. "I am Leading Seaman Jimmy Moore. Do you understand?"

"Sir . . . " began Yates amazed.

"Not, Sir. Jimmy! And what's your Christian name?"

"Dennis . . . "

He broke off. They were passing water into a trough. A woman had come in. She nodded: "*Konnichi-wa.*" She wore checked blue pantaloons, rather Turkish in style. She turned with her back towards the trough, undid the tie to the pantaloons, dropped them, leaned forward and passed water noisily. She pulled up the pantaloons, tied them, said something unintelligible and left.

"Well," said Moore. "We're in a different country, Dennis."

★ ★ ★

When they left the benjo they crossed diagonally to the group mustered from the third hold. An interpreter was trying to get some order into things. He shoved them unceremoniously into a line. "Right face!" he kept shouting in a very American accent. "Right face!" A man was coming along the line with a sort of trolley. On it were numerous little boxes made out of plaited palm leaves. He handed these out towards the first men he reached who did not understand.

447

"Food!" yapped the interpreter. "Take it! And right face!" Men started to open the boxes. "Don't open! Later!" yelled the interpreter. "Keep right face!"

Moore covertly inspected the men in his group. There was no one whom he recognized. Certainly neither Pete nor Charles was amongst them. He wondered about them vaguely. If they had been left behind in Singapore or transferred in Formosa; or if they had died.

The man had nearly finished supplying the group with their boxes which were apparently called '*Bentos*'. The interpreter was hurrying him along. Evidently he felt under pressure. Moore sensed that as soon as the last *bento* had been given they would be moving off. His instinct was correct.

"Right face!" the interpreter called. "March off by the left!"

They straggled off, a double column of ragged men laden down with the most extraordinary collection of luggage, each clutching a bento, some in forage caps and slacks, some in pith helmets and khaki drill shorts. Some, obviously of the Formosa intake, in American gear.

It was a crisp bright day but very cold. As they turned away from the quayside, Moore noticed a group of upwards of twenty men standing apart from the rest. Anderson and Brimmacombe were in the group; and so was Pete. But not Charles. As they rounded a corner the *Dai Nichi Maru* was lost from sight.

They continued on, hurried by the interpreter and extra guards who herded them through the streets of Moji. There was no time to take in what they saw. A ferry whisked them across the straits, taking them away from the island of Kyushu on to the island of Honshu. Disembarked they were hurried into a tunnel which led in turn to an endless series of wooden-walled corridors which connected up to the various quayside wharves and ferry services. At each intersection and crossing, crowds of Japanese were standing quietly watching. One old man was holding a large photograph of his uniformed son up in front of him, not for the prisoners to look at but for the soldiers who also thronged these corridors to recognize. And then there was another. And women were doing the same. Other women walked alongside holding white scarves asking passers-by to complete a stitch and, when it was done for them, bowed and accosted someone else. Everything was haste. It was very cold. Some of the men with dysentery simply passed their stools as they scampered along. There was no waiting. The interpreter and the guards kept yelling. The passages were interminable. The weaker prisoners, which included Moore, were half-helped, half-dragged, along by their friends. There was no talking. It was too exhausting, too much of a rush. The sound of feet clattering on the wooden floors, drummed in the ears. It all ended on a railway platform.

★ ★ ★

Yates stood beside Moore, an arm through his supporting him. It was now bitterly cold. A Siberian wind whistled along the platform. Yates helped Moore to a benjo and afterwards found a space for him on a bench. He opened his *bento* for him. It was nine-tenths filled with rice and the other tenth with small pieces of seaweed, orange, daikon and the like. The rice was ice-cold and pure white. A pair of wooden chopsticks was included. A different interpreter came along. He had a notebook and a pencil. He was taking names. When he reached Moore and Yates he said to Yates "You! Name?" "Dennis Yates", Yates said. "De . . . ni . . . su Eh . . . tsu" the interpreter repeated and drew queer symbols on his book. "You! Name?" he said to Moore. "James Moore," Moore said. The interpreter found this a little easier. "Jay . . . mi . . . su Mo . . . ra," he wrote. And moved on.

Epilogue

THE survivors of the *Dai Nichi*'s voyage were, as indicated, split into smaller groups and sent to different camps in Japan. Two of these groups, each originally of one hundred men, were located near the Inland Sea, one at Onomiti and the other (my own) on Innoshima Island. We worked in dockyards; the one on Innoshima, known as Habu, is currently owned by Hitachi as is possibly the one near Onomiti. A third group of one hundred and fifty men were sent to Hokkaido where, I believe, they worked in a coal mine.

Of the total complement of these three camps (three hundred and fifty men) no fewer than sixty-six died horribly in the first few weeks from the sickness contracted on the voyage. I have no record of the numbers of those who died at sea but it was substantial. Adding both groups together there is little doubt but at least one-third of the thousand or so prisoners who boarded the *Dai Nichi* at Singapore did not survive. Few of these deaths need have occurred.

Other titles in the
Ulverscroft Large Print Series:

TO FIGHT THE WILD
Rod Ansell and Rachel Percy

Lost in uncharted Australian bush, Rod Ansell survived by hunting and trapping wild animals, improvising shelter and using all the bushman's skills he knew.

COROMANDEL
Pat Barr

India in the 1830s is a hot, uncomfortable place, where the East India Company still rules. Amelia and her new husband find themselves caught up in the animosities which seethe between the old order and the new.

THE SMALL PARTY
Lillian Beckwith

A frightening journey to safety begins for Ruth and her small party as their island is caught up in the dangers of armed insurrection.

THE WILDERNESS WALK
Sheila Bishop

Stifling unpleasant memories of a misbegotten romance in Cleave with Lord Francis Aubrey, Lavinia goes on holiday there with her sister. The two women are thrust into a romantic intrigue involving none other than Lord Francis.

THE RELUCTANT GUEST
Rosalind Brett

Ann Calvert went to spend a month on a South African farm with Theo Borland and his sister. They both proved to be different from her first idea of them, and there was Storr Peterson — the most disturbing man she had ever met.

ONE ENCHANTED SUMMER
Anne Tedlock Brooks

A tale of mystery and romance and a girl who found both during one enchanted summer.

CLOUD OVER MALVERTON
Nancy Buckingham

Dulcie soon realises that something is seriously wrong at Malverton, and when violence strikes she is horrified to find herself under suspicion of murder.

AFTER THOUGHTS
Max Bygraves

The Cockney entertainer tells stories of his East End childhood, of his RAF days, and his post-war showbusiness successes and friendships with fellow comedians.

MOONLIGHT
AND MARCH ROSES
D. Y. Cameron

Lynn's search to trace a missing girl takes her to Spain, where she meets Clive Hendon. While untangling the situation, she untangles her emotions and decides on her own future.

NURSE ALICE IN LOVE
Theresa Charles

Accepting the post of nurse to little Fernie Sherrod, Alice Everton could not guess at the romance, suspense and danger which lay ahead at the Sherrod's isolated estate.

POIROT INVESTIGATES
Agatha Christie

Two things bind these eleven stories together — the brilliance and uncanny skill of the diminutive Belgian detective, and the stupidity of his Watson-like partner, Captain Hastings.

LET LOOSE THE TIGERS
Josephine Cox

Queenie promised to find the long-lost son of the frail, elderly murderess, Hannah Jason. But her enquiries threatened to unlock the cage where crucial secrets had long been held captive.

THE TWILIGHT MAN
Frank Gruber

Jim Rand lives alone in the California desert awaiting death. Into his hermit existence comes a teenage girl who blows both his past and his brief future wide open.

DOG IN THE DARK
Gerald Hammond

Jim Cunningham breeds and trains gun dogs, and his antagonism towards the devotees of show spaniels earns him many enemies. So when one of them is found murdered, the police are on his doorstep within hours.

THE RED KNIGHT
Geoffrey Moxon

When he finds himself a pawn on the chessboard of international espionage with his family in constant danger, Guy Trent becomes embroiled in moves and countermoves which may mean life or death for Western scientists.

TIGER TIGER
Frank Ryan

A young man involved in drugs is found murdered. This is the first event which will draw Detective Inspector Sandy Woodings into a whirlpool of murder and deceit.

CAROLINE MINUSCULE
Andrew Taylor

Caroline Minuscule, a medieval script, is the first clue to the whereabouts of a cache of diamonds. The search becomes a deadly kind of fairy story in which several murders have an other-worldly quality.

LONG CHAIN OF DEATH
Sarah Wolf

During the Second World War four American teenagers from the same town join the Army together. Forty-two years later, the son of one of the soldiers realises that someone is systematically wiping out the families of the four men.

THE LISTERDALE MYSTERY
Agatha Christie

Twelve short stories ranging from the light-hearted to the macabre, diverse mysteries ingeniously and plausibly contrived and convincingly unravelled.

TO BE LOVED
Lynne Collins

Andrew married the woman he had always loved despite the knowledge that Sarah married him for reasons of her own. So much heartache could have been avoided if only he had known how vital it was to be loved.

ACCUSED NURSE
Jane Converse

Paula found herself accused of a crime which could cost her her job, her nurse's reputation, and even the man she loved, unless the truth came to light.

CHATEAU OF FLOWERS
Margaret Rome

Alain, Comte de Treville needed a wife to look after him, and Fleur went into marriage on a business basis only, hoping that eventually he would come to trust and care for her.

CRISS-CROSS
Alan Scholefield

As her ex-husband had succeeded in kidnapping their young daughter once, Jane was determined to take her safely back to England. But all too soon Jane is caught up in a new web of intrigue.

DEAD BY MORNING
Dorothy Simpson

Leo Martindale's body was discovered outside the gates of his ancestral home. Is it, as Inspector Thanet begins to suspect, murder?

A GREAT DELIVERANCE
Elizabeth George

Into the web of old houses and secrets of Keldale Valley comes Scotland Yard Inspector Thomas Lynley and his assistant to solve a particularly savage murder.

'E' IS FOR EVIDENCE
Sue Grafton

Kinsey Millhone was bogged down on a warehouse fire claim. It came as something of a shock when she was accused of being on the take. She'd been set up. Now she had a new client — herself.

A FAMILY OUTING IN AFRICA
Charles Hampton and Janie Hampton

A tale of a young family's journey through Central Africa by bus, train, river boat, lorry, wooden bicycle and foot.

THE PLEASURES OF AGE
Robert Morley

The author, British stage and screen star, now eighty, is enjoying the pleasures of age. He has drawn on his experiences to write this witty, entertaining and informative book.

THE VINEGAR SEED
Maureen Peters

The first book in a trilogy which follows the exploits of two sisters who leave Ireland in 1861 to seek their fortune in England.

A VERY PAROCHIAL MURDER
John Wainwright

A mugging in the genteel seaside town turned to murder when the victim died. Then the body of a young tearaway is washed ashore and Detective Inspector Lyle is determined that a second killing will not go unpunished.

DEATH ON A
HOT SUMMER NIGHT
Anne Infante

Micky Douglas is either accident-prone or someone is trying to kill him. He finds himself caught in a desperate race to save his ex-wife and others from a ruthless gang.

HOLD DOWN A SHADOW
Geoffrey Jenkins

Maluti Rider, with the help of four of the world's most wanted men, is determined to destroy the Katse Dam and release a killer flood.

THAT NICE MISS SMITH
Nigel Morland

A reconstruction and reassessment of the trial in 1857 of Madeleine Smith, who was acquitted by a verdict of Not Proven of poisoning her lover, Emile L'Angelier.